Death Of A Wild Swimmer

ALSO BY PETER BOLAND

THE CHARITY SHOP DETECTIVE AGENCY MYSTERIES

Book 1: The Charity Shop Detective Agency
Book 2: The Beach Hut Murders
Book 3: Death At The Dog Show
Book 4: The Vanilla Killer
Book 5: Death Of A Wild Swimmer

Death of a WILD SWIMMER

PETER BOLAND

The Charity Shop Detective Agency Mysteries
Book 5

JOFFE BOOKS

Joffe Books, London
www.joffebooks.com

First published in Great Britain in 2025

This book is a work of fiction. Names, characters, businesses, organisations, places and events are either the product of the author's imagination or are used fictitiously. Any resemblance to actual persons, living or dead, events or locales is entirely coincidental.
The spelling used is British English except where fidelity to the author's rendering of accent or dialect supersedes this.

Cover art by Nick Castle

ISBN: 978-1-80573-061-3

PROLOGUE

A thick, cloying aroma overwhelms my senses from the moment the car door opens. I hop out and raise my head, catching sniffs of the odour as it rides the onshore breeze. It's strange and unfamiliar, and really shouldn't be here. It usurps the usual redolence of the beach — the spice of sea salt, the thick welts of seaweed and the vast mineral deposit of sand. The heady tang ensnares me, and I'm unable to resist its intoxicating gravity. Instinctively, I'm pulled towards it, running from the car park across the beach, curious to see what's generating this ungodly stench.

The natural give of the sand cushions my every stride, but it also slows me down. I need to find more purchase if I want to quicken my pace. So instead of heading directly in a straight line towards the source of the smell, I divert to where the sea slides up onto the land, making that delicious rasping slurp, then recedes to leave a firm, slick plain, as pristine as freshly laid concrete. I ignore the icy water sloshing against my legs as my strides lengthen with increasing urgency. The odour intensifies. I'm getting close.

My eyes, which, I'll admit, aren't as good as my nose, detect something dead ahead, and I mean that in its most literal sense — up ahead something is dead. I'm not shocked by this. Pummelled by prevailing winds and currents, this stretch of beach is known for snagging corpses when the sea's done with them. On my runs I've encountered dead seagulls like fallen angels, shrunken jellyfish and cuttlebones strewn like pizza toppings. But nothing this big before or with such a distinctive smell of death.

At first, I think it's a large log washed up on the shore, caused by one of the recent storms. But this doesn't smell like a rotting log, doesn't look like one either, unless it's been bleached white by all that time floating in brine. As I get closer, it becomes clear that this is no tree. It's a person. A naked one, apart from a pair of swimming trunks. My running stalls, and I slow to a trot, then to a creep as I reach the body. I do several measured and cautious circuits, noticing the poor chap is lying on his front, face plunged into the sand as if he's searching for something. Wondering just how he came to be here, I begin deciphering the encyclopaedia of smells emanating from him. But then my owner goes and spoils it all, catching me up and breathlessly yelling.

"Benji! Benji! Leave! Leave!"

Like a robot unable to break its programming, I've been well trained and obey his commands. Reluctantly, I back away, but the glut of odours is still driving me wild. It takes all my effort to do as I'm told, standing there obediently like the good boy I am, panting with my sweaty tongue lolling out the side of my mouth. But I can't help thinking why human beings always want to stop our fun. They never want us going near anything interesting.

A new odour reaches my ever-twitching nose. The air instantly becomes saturated with it. Now, this one I have encountered before, many a time. It's a blend of smells — two, to be precise: fear and panic coming off my owner in waves. He's frantically gabbling into his phone, words stumbling over one another as he attempts to inform the police that he's found a dead body. Well, technically, I found it, but I won't hold that against him. I never hold anything against him.

CHAPTER 1

January, the month that never seems to end, finally breathed its last and gave up its dreary stranglehold over the fledgling year. The calendar equivalent of dragging one's feet, Fiona was glad to see the back of it. An unbidden sigh of relief escaped from deep within her chest, as the shop said hello to a new Monday morning and a freshly minted month. Okay, February wasn't much of an improvement on its older, longer sibling, and the pair of them shared a rivalry over who could be the dullest, grottiest month, but she'd take February over January any time.

At least February had Valentine's Day, the first proper event of the calendar, unless you were really fastidious and pointed out that it was actually New Year's. (Although you'd be forgiven for thinking it was Easter, judging by how quickly the supermarkets swapped Christmas decorations for Easter eggs.)

The ladies adored the most romantic day of the year. Not that they were intimately involved with anyone, but that didn't matter — any excuse to decorate the shop and transform it into a blissful scarlet haven. They didn't have that many Valentine's decorations, if they were honest. The financial year's budget for anything decorative was naturally blown at Christmas. However, that didn't stop them from having a good go at making their own and seeking out any suitably coloured donations that could be dusted off and repurposed to make a splendid romantic window display.

Gazing down at the rail in front of her, selecting red garments for the mannequins to wear, Fiona pushed her salt-and-pepper hair out of her eyes for the umpteenth time. It had grown into a mane and had lost that swept-back look she favoured — a style that was easy to manage on a daily basis, which basically involved running a comb through it after she woke up. But its current length prohibited such low maintenance. The farthest she normally allowed it to reach was down to the nape of her neck. But now it was getting dangerously close to the tops of her shoulders and would require the addition of various gooey substances to hold it in place. She puffed another stray hair away from her eyes. She knew she should make an appointment with her hairdresser, but really couldn't face it.

Her mind wasn't functioning properly at the moment. Vague and distracted — just a bit of brain fog, she kept telling herself. Her focus and motivation had shrivelled to the point where decision-making had become an impossibility, not just for making hair appointments but for everything. She couldn't even decide what clothes to pick from the rail in front of her, although she'd been at it all morning.

Enviously, she gazed at Daisy, whose effort hadn't wavered once since they'd started. Her colleague sat at the table surrounded by craft paraphernalia, various glues and cutting instruments and glittery things, plus a stack of red sugar paper. With the steady hands of a Harley Street surgeon, she chicaned her scissors around the paper, producing perfectly shaped chains of hearts, and even the odd cherub she'd sketched. Concentrating hard, the tip of her tongue pointed upwards and never once left the corner of her mouth.

Partial Sue, on the other hand, pinballed erratically around the shop, without any plan or thought to what she was doing, grabbing items in a supermarket sweep to arrange in the window.

Fiona pulled her baggy cardigan around her, as if she had a chill. "I'm so glad January's over."

"Me too." Partial Sue had moved on to the DVDs, cruising along the shelves, pulling out romcoms, presumably to create a small cinematic display.

Daisy ceased snipping and raised her curly head. "I quite like January and February."

"What?" the other two ladies replied, the shock halting them from their respective tasks.

"Well, someone has to be kind to them," Daisy replied. "We're a charity shop that helps unwanted dogs, and I think January and February are the unwanted dogs of the year. No one likes them. I feel sorry for them. They need a bit of affection, that's all."

"I'm partial to dogs," Partial Sue replied. "But I'm not partial to January or February. I'd even go as far to say that we should get rid of them. Strike them from the calendar. Go straight to March or, better still, April. Start the year at Easter. That would be much better."

"That's how it used to be before we adopted the Gregorian calendar," Fiona said. "March used to be the first month of the year."

"But then March and April become the months nobody likes," Daisy replied.

"I'm not sure how it works." Fiona desperately wished they could fast-forward to spring, when everything exploded back into life and popped with colour. "But I'd do anything to leave this depressing time of year behind."

"Or we do what the Wicker Man's done," Partial Sue suggested. "Go away for January and February."

Their retail neighbour sold second-hand wicker furniture — not that often, truth be told. Hardly ever, in fact. Leading them to wonder how he made any money. Trevor, to give him his proper name, was currently in Perth, seeing his relatives, or "rellies", as they said down under. He'd given the ladies the keys to his shop and left a note on the window to tell prospective buyers to call in at Dogs Need Nice Homes. As expected, the ladies hadn't been troubled once since he'd left, which was part of the reason they'd agreed to his proposal.

Daisy continued sticking up for the calendar's least favourite double act. "I think you're both being mean. It's not their fault someone stuck them right at the start of the year. They've been given the worst time slot ever."

"Ah." Partial Sue's diminutive frame quivered, as a rebuttal popped into her head. "But only if you're in the northern hemisphere. If you're in Australia, like the Wicker Man, it's the other way around. January and February are boiling. Beach weather."

"So are you saying you'd like January and February if you were in Australia?" Daisy asked.

This stumped Partial Sue for a second. "What I'm saying is, it's all relative. Depends on your perspective."

Fiona's current perspective wasn't a good one. If she was being honest, since Christmas had ended, happiness had eluded her and nothing made her smile, not properly anyway. Oh, she could pull off polite smiles by the dozen, but joyful, heartfelt grins had been hard to come by. This was to be expected, of course. The most wonderful time of the year was followed by the most awful, when everyone felt their spirits tumble. However, this wasn't the usual seasonal downer that began to fade once you started getting on with the distractions of everyday life, which mostly involved answering annoying emails and collecting parcels from neighbours even though you'd been in at the time.

No, this was something different. Deeper and more persistent, she felt a presence that she hadn't sensed for a long time. Like a mournful dirge, it played far off in the distance at the periphery of her mind. Barely perceptible at the moment, she caught snatches of it here and there, little more than fragments of a tuneless lament. Nevertheless, the lament was one she knew well. The *It* had returned.

To clarify, the *It* was the name she had given to the depression that had plagued her since retiring. She had named her affliction because, somehow, assigning it an identity made it easier to deal with. Thinking of her despair as a person or an object kept it contained, gave it limitations, whereas calling it depression made it too wide and vague and pervasive, like smoke whose stench could creep and spread far and wide, through the minutest of cracks. She'd managed to keep it at bay for the past year or two, and there had been a point where she'd banished it completely.

This made it sound as if a mighty battle had raged, and Fiona had emerged triumphant and victorious. In reality, it had been far more subtle and simple than this. She'd come to the realisation that having her friends around her was all she needed to keep the *It* in check. Daisy and Sue were the *It*'s kryptonite. They were her unstoppable force and the shop an impenetrable fortress of friendship, even though they had no idea of the struggle going on in her head. She had never dared tell them, not wanting to burden them with her problems. It would've been wise to seek professional help, but she couldn't stomach the idea of revealing her most intimate thoughts to a stranger. Besides, the mere presence of her friends had been enough to ward off all attacks. After a while the *It* had given up and left her alone, but Fiona had never become complacent. She knew the *It* hadn't been erased and was merely lying dormant, perhaps regrouping and biding its time.

Why this debilitating presence had chosen now to make a reappearance, she couldn't tell. Most likely, the *It* knew the period after Christmas was when Fiona would be at her lowest and weakest. Gaining the smallest of footholds, the *It* had grown incrementally stronger by the day, but had maintained a safe distance. She knew there would come a point when it would mount an attack and attempt to assail her defences. How she would defeat it this time, she had no idea.

"Fiona, are you okay?" Daisy asked.

She'd been staring gormlessly into space. "I'm fine. Just usual Monday morning blues."

"Well, you know what's good for that." Partial Sue began gathering up the cups. "Tea, anyone?"

Fiona and Daisy were about to answer when the doorbell chimed. They turned to regard a generously proportioned woman standing in the doorway. Of a similar age to the ladies, she was swathed in a large parka, its fur-lined hood creating a halo around her head. A bulging shopping bag hung by her side. She forced out a smile, the kind that wasn't sure if it wanted to be there or not. "I have some donations. Er, here. Er, in this bag."

"Well, you're in the right place," Partial Sue replied. "We like donations, big or small."

The woman took an uncertain step forward and spoke conspiratorially. "Erm, I also have something else."

The ladies looked at her expectantly. Her eyes did a circuit of the shop, gazing at items on display, everywhere except in the ladies' direction. "Is this where you solve murders?"

They nodded.

"The Charity Shop Detective Agency," Daisy proudly announced. "At your service."

The woman hesitated for a beat. "I have a murder. Well, I think it's a murder. Actually, I'm not sure. You know what, it's probably me just being silly. Don't worry. Forget I was ever here." She turned on her heel and headed back out of the door.

CHAPTER 2

Still clutching her cups, Partial Sue pinged forward, as if she'd glitched from one place to another, closing the distance before their visitor had a chance to shut the door behind her. "Please, why don't you come in?"

The woman halted her exit and turned around. "I don't want to be a nuisance or waste your time."

"Not at all," Daisy reassured her. "Look, I'm making heart chains for Valentine's, see?" She stood up and unfurled one, holding it outstretched in front of her, just in case the woman didn't believe her.

"It's probably nothing." The woman's self-confidence dwindled by the second.

"Why don't you let us be the judge of that?" Fiona said.

Partial Sue gently guided her back into the shop. "I'm just about to make tea, would you like one? And we have cake."

Far too tempting an offer to refuse on a grey Monday morning, the woman's face lit up. "Well, I can never say no to tea and cake."

She was clearly their type of person.

"Who can? It's physically impossible." Daisy began clearing her craft paraphernalia off the table. Partial Sue showed the woman to a seat while Fiona introduced everyone, including Simon Le Bon, her scruffy terrier, who, for some reason, remained snoozing in his bed by the till.

"Pleased to meet you all." The woman finally smiled, plumping her rosy cheeks speckled with broken capillaries. "I'm Beth Trenchard." Her small, bright eyes crinkled as she grinned fleetingly. She suddenly reverted back to being serious. "I'm afraid I have a confession to make."

Fiona worried that Beth was about to confess to the murder that may or may not have happened.

Beth held her shopping bag aloft. "These donations aren't up to much. Just a few ratty old jumpers I found under the bed. I felt awkward coming here today, so I stuffed them into a bag to use as an excuse."

"Please don't feel awkward," Fiona reassured her.

Partial Sue returned with the teapot and four cups. Ever the magpie when it came to donations, she gestured towards the bag. "May I?"

Beth handed it to her. "Be my guest, but I'm not sure they're resaleable."

Partial Sue rifled through the contents. "I dunno. These woolly jumpers look okay to me."

"Really?"

"We give some of our more careworn jumpers to this lovely lady who takes them away and unpicks them, then crochets them into bright and chunky throws for the shop. They fly out the door like hot cakes. These would be perfect for her."

Beth appeared happier. "Oh, I might buy one myself. I do love a good throw, especially a handmade one."

Partial Sue nipped into the storeroom with the bag, then returned to pour the tea while Daisy sliced up the cake, a Victoria sponge, distributing a piece to everyone. Not standing on ceremony, Beth tucked in immediately, taking small sips of her hot beverage in between. "Oh, that's a nice cup of tea," she remarked. "And the cake's divine. Not too sweet."

"Yes," Daisy agreed. "You never need to overegg cake with sugar — or, er, egg, for that matter."

Fiona wondered how she might gently nudge the small talk back to a conversation about murder, but Beth was ready to approach it head on. "I think someone I know was murdered."

"Have you been to the police?" Fiona asked.

"They're convinced it was death by misadventure," Beth replied. "But I don't believe that and neither do a lot of people I know."

"What makes you think it was murder?" Daisy asked.

"Well, do you remember the body found on Hengistbury Head beach recently?"

The ladies nodded. A grisly start to the New Year — how could they forget? The story had shocked everyone. The local beauty spot was popular with walkers all year round and beachgoers come summer. However, from time to time it could be an unforgiving place to venture into. A sandy hook at the end of the bay, nature would throw everything it had at the pretty headland. Relentless wind and waves hacked away at the soaring cliffs and pebble-strewn beach. It wasn't the first time a dead body had been found there and probably wouldn't be the last.

"His name was Colin Barclay," Beth continued. "He was a member of my wild swimming club."

The ladies offered their heartfelt sympathies. Daisy, who sat closest, reached out a reassuring hand, placing it on top of Beth's. "This must be very hard for you."

Beth's eyes glistened but she held back the tears. "Thank you. It is. We were all in shock. Still are. But most people who knew him are convinced it wasn't an accident."

Condolences out of the way, Partial Sue wasted no time getting down to the grim details. "From what I read in the local news, he — I mean, Colin — got into difficulty swimming alone. Banged his head on some rocks and drowned."

"Yes, that's the gist of it, but it doesn't make sense. You see, I knew Colin well. We all did. He was a member of my club, the Southbourne Wild Things. I'm the founder. That makes it sound very strict and formal — it's not, I assure you. Wild swimming's not about rules. It's about enjoying yourself."

Fiona couldn't see how much enjoyment could be gained from plunging one's body into icy water on a daily basis. It sounded more like medieval torture. Just the thought of it caused her bones to ache and set her teeth on edge. But she'd heard how easily people became addicted to the eccentric pastime. On days when she headed into work insulated by several thick layers, the thermometer barely hovering above zero, a procession of happy souls would be trooping the other way, down to the beach with their towels. But more incredible, as far as Fiona could tell, was that their number appeared to be growing exponentially.

"So Colin fancied a dip alone," Partial Sue speculated. "Had a spot of bother, hit his head and drowned. That doesn't seem too far-fetched to me."

Beth shook her head. "There's a saying in wild swimming: the colder the water, the warmer the friendships. It's about more than swimming. It's about the shared experience, like-minded people — and perhaps a little daft, too — coming together. We may go in the water gasping and groaning but we all come out smiling. You can't beat that. Colin was a bit of a loner before he joined us. A little awkward, I would say, but he found a community. Loved the camaraderie, just as much as the swimming. He wouldn't have gone in alone. He just wouldn't. What would be the point? Plus, there was something weird about his body."

"You saw the body?" Fiona didn't hide her shock.

Beth's eyes glazed over mournfully. Her mouth turned down as she slowly nodded. "Yes, I had to identify him."

CHAPTER 3

"Were you down as his next of kin?" Partial Sue asked.

Beth took a large sip of tea and carefully placed the cup back down on the table before answering. "No, I have no idea who was his next of kin. Colin wasn't married and didn't have any living family, as far as I know. But he was found in his swimming trunks. No ID on him. Police didn't know who he was. They thought he might be a wild swimmer and began contacting groups in the area to see if anyone recognised him. They tried us first, seeing as we're the nearest club to Hengistbury Head. My contact details are on the website. They showed me some pictures first but then I had to go along and formally identify the body."

Daisy shuddered. "That must have been horrible."

Beth sniffed. "It was. Last time I saw him we were in the sea, freezing our bits off but loving every minute of it. Next thing, I'm looking at his dead body with people holding clipboards standing next to me. It felt like it was happening to someone else, not me."

Partial Sue wanted to drill down into the details. "So when exactly was the last time you saw him?"

"The seventh of January. It was a Friday. We had our usual eight o'clock swim at Southbourne at the bottom of the zigzag near the groyne. Afterwards, we got changed and said our goodbyes. That was the last time I saw him alive. Then they found his body on the fifteenth, a week later.

"Any arguments, altercations, disagreements that day?" Partial Sue asked.

Beth baulked at this suggestion. "Gosh, no. Bad feelings don't like cold water, as we like to say. Stops you worrying about all that stuff that doesn't matter."

Whether she knew it or not, Beth was an evangelist, that was for sure. Every mention of wild swimming, her eyes glinted and a string of one-liners tripped off her tongue, selling its wholesome benefits. Normally, Fiona was immune to any sort of sales talk. Being a fairly good salesperson herself, she knew all the tricks. However, in her present mental state, talk of washing away all the bad feelings in her head sounded extremely appealing. She desperately wanted the *It* gone, and wondered if drenching it in icy water would send it packing. The only thing holding her back was the thought of all that freezing water swirling around her body, a body that was inclined to stay warm and cosy, preferably next to an open fire with a hot steaming mug in her hands, rather than having unfathomable cold gnawing at her bones. Fiona shivered spontaneously, her body sensing what she was contemplating.

She suddenly became annoyed with her selfish thinking. She had to remind herself that this wasn't about her personal issues but about the death and possible murder of Colin Barclay. Fiona shooed away the ideas in her head and refocused her mind. There was something she'd been meaning to ask before she'd become distracted. "Beth, earlier you mentioned there was something about Colin's body. If it's not too painful, what did you mean by that?"

Beth swallowed hard. "Well, his whole body was discoloured, pale like porcelain, but his head was brownish. And he had scratch marks."

"Scratch marks?" Daisy asked.

"Yes, he had these long, thin, red scratches on the outside of his arms, running from the top of his neck, down his shoulders, to his wrists."

"Did he have them anywhere else?" Fiona asked.

Beth nodded. "I couldn't see the rest of him as he was covered up, but I was told he did."

"How strange," Partial Sue commented. "Did you ask the coroner what they were?"

"I didn't, I'm afraid. I was in shock."

"Did they look uniform or random?" Partial Sue asked.

"Oh, definitely random, like long country lanes."

"And his head was a different colour from his body, you say?" Fiona asked.

Beth nodded. "That's right. I mean, his whole body had become pale — due to being in the water, I suppose — but his face was darker, and everything was swollen, of course."

"Did you see the head wound?" Partial Sue asked.

Beth shook her head. "I didn't, so I'm assuming it was at the back."

The colour drained from Daisy's face, so Fiona decided to change the direction of the conversation to a less grisly subject. "You said that Colin had been a bit of a loner before he joined. What was he like? How did he get on with the others in your club, any problems there?"

Beth smiled, as she gleefully settled back into her favourite topic. "Cold water is a great leveller. Doesn't matter whether you're a prince or a pauper, when those shoulders go under, the cold is the same for everyone. That's where the camaraderie is born. Nearest thing to a Blitz spirit, I imagine, uniting us in a cold-water brother and sisterhood. No one's better than anyone else, especially when you're in there as God intended — apart from your swimming cossies," she chuckled.

Beth had avoided answering her question, Fiona noted. Or was she just letting her enthusiasm run away with her? Either way, Fiona was beginning to warm to the idea of cold-water submersion with a bunch of others who were silly enough to be out there. Nevertheless, she needed answers. "So how did Colin get along with everyone else in the club?"

Beth sighed, her shoulders slumping. "He was a bit Marmite, I'm afraid. He reminded me of my late older brother. He had an awkward way about him. Never very good with people, but he was kind and would help anyone who needed it. Colin was the same. One time when we were swimming, I mentioned my gutters were all leaking. I didn't have the money to get them repaired. Afterward he came straight round with his ladder and fixed them."

"He sounds like a nice man, so why didn't everyone like him?" Daisy asked.

Beth hesitated, clearly wondering if she should speak ill of the dead. She rubbed her eyes. "He used to be a sports teacher and had a habit of telling people what to do. Volunteering advice when it wasn't asked for, or even necessary, which grated on a few people. Micromanaging, I guess you'd call it."

"What is there to manage in wild swimming?" Partial Sue asked. "I'd have thought it was all pretty straightforward. You turn up, swim, then get out again."

"Well, that's exactly it. Wild swimming is a simple pleasure. It's about freedom and being in nature. There are no changing rooms and lockers, or stench of chlorine, and certainly no posters telling you what you can and can't do."

Fiona remembered those posters well from the last time she was in a public baths, which must have been decades ago. A series of seedy cartoon scenarios outlining the rules. She'd forgotten all of them, apart from two: "no petting", showing a couple getting amorous, and "no bombing", which most kids ignored. The only other thing she remembered from public swimming pools was there would always be a disembodied plaster floating around somewhere. Probably the reason she hadn't been to one for ages.

Beth continued. "It's the joy of doing something naughty and a bit silly. Having said that, you have to be careful, and we all look out for one another, especially if someone is struggling with the cold or having trouble warming up. But Colin was one of those blokes who thought he had to take charge. Organise everyone. I think when he joined it did spoil some of the joy of just turning up and going for a dip."

"But I thought you said bad feelings don't like cold water," Partial Sue pointed out.

"Generally, yes," Beth replied. "I'm probably overexaggerating things. Let's just say it took the edge off it a bit. People got used to him after a while and just ignored him. Got on with their swimming."

"So Colin had no friends outside the club?" Fiona asked.

"Not that I know of. We were his only friendship group."

"And he had no family either?"

Beth shook her head. "I think we were the closest he had to a family. Wild swimming forges unbreakable friendships, as I always say."

Fiona didn't know how her two colleagues felt about the situation, and of course she'd need to gather more evidence, but she had a fairly obvious theory forming in her head. In murder cases, first suspects were always spouses, and if the murder victim was unmarried then the spotlight would fall on their immediate family. Colin had no family apart from his swimming club. And, like a large extended family, there were a few siblings who didn't get along with him. He'd put their noses out of joint with his mansplaining, spoiling their enjoyment. Perhaps someone in the Southbourne Wild Things had had enough. They'd killed Colin Barclay and made it look like an accident.

CHAPTER 4

A bright red, dishevelled pile teetered on the carpet. The Valentine's decorations were now neglected and in a sorry state, as the year's most romantic day had been eclipsed by a far more compelling proposition. Crime always came first, and the ladies unanimously agreed to take on the case right away, much to the delight of Beth. To be fair, they took on every case that came their way, as they were committed to helping anyone who needed it or wanted answers, but this one was particularly intriguing. A dead body washed up on a local beach, one that the police had dismissed as an accident, gave them more incentive than most: an opportunity to discover what had really happened and prove the verdict wrong, but, most importantly, to bring to justice the killer, who would be sitting pretty, feet up, smugly thinking that they'd got away with it.

Of course, there was still the chance that the initial verdict had been correct, and this had indeed been a terrible accident. That Colin had been in the wrong place at the wrong time. But that seemed unlikely from what Beth had told them. She bustled happily out of the shop, texting her club the good news, promising that everyone would be extremely cooperative and answer their questions.

Fiona wondered if the killer would be among them. She decided to gently test her theory with the others.

"Are you thinking what I'm thinking?" she asked.

Partial Sue jumped straight in. "Guy with no friends and no family joins a group of wild swimmers and starts telling them what to do. Well, that would annoy the hell out of me. One of them decided to shut him up for good. Made it look like an accident."

Daisy was having none of it. "If he was that annoying, wouldn't you just swim somewhere else or join another club? Committing murder seems a bit over the top."

Partial Sue screwed up her face defensively. "You heard Beth. They're a tight-knit group. 'Wild swimming forges unbreakable friendships,' she said. Why would you want to go somewhere without your besties? Forced out against your will because of some know-it-all. Besides, from what we've just heard, wild swimmers are extremely zealous about their pastime. Personally, I think they're daft, but imagine if her-over-the-road came in here every day and started telling us what to do. Our backs would be up in no time."

Her-over-the-road, Serena Waterford — or the Wicked Witch of Southbourne, as Sophiè Haverford was sometimes known (they had an endless string of derogatory nicknames for their nemesis) — ran the Cats Alliance charity shop opposite. She had a superiority complex as large and ugly as one of those multistorey car parks you can never find your way out of. She also made a habit of dropping in every so often, just to remind the ladies she was better than them in every conceivable way. That was bad enough, but if she were to start doing that on a daily basis, the ladies might not be responsible for their actions.

Daisy conceded the point. "Yuk! Fair enough. That would drive me bonkers."

"Okay," Fiona said. "So, we have a good working theory to pursue, which means questioning the Southbourne Wild Swimmers, but first I'd like to look into the mysterious markings on Colin's body, see what that uncovers."

Daisy, the most proficient of the three with technology, and who knew her way around the internet better than Fiona knew her way around Waitrose, or Partial Sue around the twenty-five-pence shop, whipped out her phone and soon had her nose deep in cyberspace. The others did too, although this was a futile exercise as Daisy always beat them to the answer, and this occasion was no different. "Got it!"

Fiona watched as Daisy's eyes flicked from left to right, reading the contents of her screen as if she were watching a microscopic tennis match. Gradually they slowed down and became heavy lidded, accompanied by a paling of her skin. Her chin trembled and she gave a nervous hiccup.

"Daisy?" Fiona asked.

"I think I need some air." With a shaking hand, she placed her phone face down on the table, got uneasily to her feet and wobbled towards the door.

Fiona went after her, followed by Partial Sue. "Daisy, are you okay?"

"Yes. I'm fine. I read some things that made me a bit squeamish." Another hiccup popped out of her mouth. Gently, they guided her through the front door and sat her down outside on the shop's generous windowsill. A few breaths of cold, dank air appeared to do the trick, bringing the colour back into her cheeks.

"Can we get you anything?" Partial Sue asked. "Cup of tea? Glass of water?"

Daisy waved away the offer. "No, I'll be fine. Just give me a minute, I'll be right as rain. You two go in."

"I don't think that's a good idea," Fiona said. "We'll stay with you, until it passes." So they waited, perched either side of her on the edge of the sill.

Fiona knew the torture of what Daisy was going through, when your mind fixated on something horrible, and no matter how hard you tried not to think about it, your brain kept pinging back to it again and again, like Simon Le Bon when he'd found some ungodly smell he wouldn't leave alone. She knew that the best remedy was distraction, to give Daisy's mind something else to focus on.

Partial Sue had the same idea, although her approach to distraction was to replace the thought with something equally but unintentionally nauseating. "You know, the twenty-five-pence shop is selling recycled toilet paper now."

This snatched Daisy from her stupor quicker than if she'd plunged her whole head into a bucket of smelling salts. "Ergh! Recycled toilet paper! That's disgusting! You mean, you're wiping your bottom with something that's already been . . ." She didn't finish her sentence, hiccupping and grimacing at the thought.

However, it had done the trick. But Fiona thought it would be wise to quickly clarify that the product's green credentials weren't derived from some other unmentionable colour. "When they say 'recycled toilet paper', that's a bit of a messaging slip-up. That doesn't mean it was once toilet paper. It means they've made it out of recycled newspaper and household correspondence."

Daisy gasped, relieved. "Oh, that's better. I get it now."

"It's a great idea," Partial Sue said. "You get to wipe your bottom on what was once the gutter press and overpriced fuel bills. What could be better?"

Daisy laughed. "I can't believe I thought it was actually second-hand toilet paper. How daft of me." Reenergised, she got to her feet. "I'm feeling much better now."

Relieved that Daisy had rallied, they trooped back into the shop. Fiona and Partial Sue retook their seats and began reading what Daisy had found on her phone, an article entitled "Variations in Bodies Found in Water". Just to be on the safe side, Daisy headed into the storeroom to make the tea, using the noise of the boiling kettle to mask any discussion they were having about drowned bodies.

Huddling around the screen, Fiona and Partial Sue eagerly read on. They gleaned that most victims were found face down. However, on some occasions, they would float on their backs for a while, then sink to the bottom. The body would be pulled along by the undertow, acquiring all sorts of strange cuts and grazes — known as "travel marks" — then resurface a while later.

Partial Sue stared at Fiona. "Well, that adds up. If Colin's body had sunk to the seabed, it would've picked up those scratches Beth told us about."

"Yes, but it doesn't really help us establish what happened to him before that. He would've picked up those injuries after he died, regardless of whether he was murdered or it was an accident. And it still doesn't explain why his face was a different shade compared to the rest of his body. Oh, here we go, look at this bit: '*A reddening of the face may be indicative of hypothermia.*'"

"So, maybe he didn't drown in the classic sense," Partial Sue remarked. "He knocked himself out, floated unconscious in the cold water on his back, catching hypothermia, then drowned. His body eventually sank, where it picked up those marks. It all sounds pretty plausible."

Reluctantly, Fiona had to agree. Her eyes scanned ahead, hoping for anything to the contrary. At the end of the article she spotted something telling. "Listen to this: '*Establishing the cause and manner of death for bodies recovered from the water is far more challenging compared to those found on land. Changes and injuries sustained in a liquid environment are far harder to recognise and interpret. They often defy rational analysis. Any pathologist must tread carefully to avoid being too dogmatic with their findings or too hasty to reach a verdict of accidental drowning. Generally speaking, water blurs evidence and is a particularly suitable medium for camouflaging foul play.*'"

"Now there's a cravat if ever I heard one." Daisy appeared, brandishing the teapot and a verbal faux pas, a positive sign she was back to normal and mostly unfazed by talk of drowning.

"It's 'caveat'," Partial Sue corrected. "But yes, you're right. Whoever's written that article is telling us to keep an open mind. Anything could've happened to him."

Fiona nodded. "I agree. It's the perfect environment for covering up a murder. '*Water blurs evidence.*'"

Daisy lifted the teapot and poured them each a cup. "Well, there are plenty of places to bang your head along the beach.

Loads of big wooden groynes sticking out to stop the sand washing down to Milford-on-Sea."

"Don't forget the big ones made of lumps of Purbeck stone," Partial Sue added. "You could get a nasty clunk on the head from one of those. There are signs telling you to keep off, but everyone ignores them. Beth said the club swims near the rock groyne at the bottom of the zigzag. What if Colin decided to dive off it and slipped?"

Fiona shook her head. "From what we've heard, I can't imagine Colin was a rule-breaker, especially if he liked telling people what to do, and it still doesn't explain why he'd be swimming alone."

"I think we already know the answer to that question," Partial Sue said. "I bet he was out with someone from the club, and they knocked his head against the groyne. Left him in the water. Made it look like an accident."

"That's what we need to find out," Fiona replied. "We need to question these wild swimmers one by one. Sift out some suspects."

"Sounds straightforward enough." Partial Sue had her phone out. "We should draw up a schedule, work out a timetable with Beth when we can visit each member, and pick their brains."

"Yes, we could do that," Fiona said. "But if the killer's among them, it would give them a nice heads-up to prepare and get their story straight. I'm thinking of something more spontaneous, unexpected."

Daisy and Partial Sue looked confused.

"You want us to pounce on them in the street, like we're doing a marketing survey?" Daisy suggested.

"Yes, sort of," Fiona replied. "But not in the street. In the sea."

"Oh, no." Eyes full of panic, Partial Sue held both hands up. "I'm not going wild swimming. Not on your Nelly. I am not partial to cold water in the slightest."

"Me neither." Daisy shivered.

"I'll do it," Fiona volunteered.

"Really?" Partial Sue asked. "That's going to be painful."

"Of course. But it might be better with just one of us. Less threatening. If the killer is indeed one of the Southbourne Wild Swimmers, then this would undoubtedly be the best way to get answers. To be part of the club, watching from the inside, observing their behaviour." If she'd thought about this earlier, Fiona could have suggested this to Beth, slipping in undercover. Too late for that now. Beth had already texted everyone at the club that the ladies of the Charity Shop Detective Agency were on the case. However, showing up at the beach unannounced would be a good second choice and would still wrongfoot them. Her unexpected presence could force the culprit to act suspiciously.

Partial Sue and Daisy regarded her with sympathetic eyes, as if she were making a great sacrifice for the cause. But if she were brutally honest, Fiona had an ulterior motive. She wanted to see if plunging her body into bone-chilling water had any effect on the *It*.

Bad feelings don't like cold water, Beth had said. That phrase had stuck in her head, and she wanted to put the claim to the test. To see if all the anecdotal evidence she'd heard was true, that wild swimming was a great antidote to depression. Truth be told, Fiona was getting desperate. The *It* was on the rise, slowly but surely making an unwelcome return, circling the borders of her mind, testing for weak spots. She wanted to banish it for good, and if that meant drenching it in cold water every day for the foreseeable future, then so be it.

CHAPTER 5

The last time Fiona had worn her swimming costume, back in the summer on the beach, it had lost much of its elasticity, billowing out like a spinnaker every time she entered the water. Some of this could be put down to the age of the fabric, but who was she kidding? Her girth, regardless of what she did or didn't eat, appeared to be heading in the wrong direction. Buying a fresh, new cossie that actually fitted properly would give her a much-needed confidence boost, especially if she was about to expose her body in front of a bunch of strangers, then submerge it in an inhospitable English Channel — in February, no less. That idea was challenging enough, but the thought of emerging from the sea with the gusset of her dilapidated costume hanging around her knees — well, she wouldn't want to inflict that on anyone. There was no question. She had to have a new costume for the exercise.

This posed a problem: where do you buy a swimming costume in February? Swimwear was definitely not in season. Of course, she could've gone to one of those vast, hangar-like sports chains on an uninviting retail estate (or retail village, as the nearest one was called, although it bore no resemblance to a village), but she preferred to support local, independent shops. The only place she could think of that would sell swimwear in the depths of winter was the local surf shop. Pushing open the door of Ocean Masters, Fiona got a pleasant whiff of coconut mingled with pungent rubber. She deduced that the former came from the wax for rubbing on surfboards to give them grip, while the latter derived from their stock of wetsuits. Although, on this occasion, said stock appeared severely depleted with large gaps along the length of the rail, with just a few odd sizes hanging forlornly. It was a mirror image on the opposite side of the shop, except with surfboards. The wooden rack that displayed the boards upright in a regimental row stood mostly vacant.

Catching Fiona staring at all the negative space, a thickset man darted out from behind the till. He'd lost his hair, so didn't sport the typical sun-bleached locks of a Californian surfer but instead made up for it with a smartly trimmed right-angled horseshoe moustache. Desperate not to miss out on a sale, he was quick to assuage her worries. "We're waiting for a new delivery if it's a wetsuit or a surfboard you're after."

Fiona felt flattered that he deemed her agile enough to have a go at surfing.

"I can take your measurements for any wetsuit you want," he went on. "It's very important to get a suit that fits properly. Or if there's a particular board you're after, I can order it in."

"Actually, I'm here to buy a swimsuit."

His eyes dropped momentarily, as he realised he wasn't going to sell a big-ticket item today. "Yeah, sure. This way."

Fiona followed him through the shop, awash with pale wood and a display of yellowing vintage surfboards clinging to the walls, some as short and sharp as toothpicks, while others were long and wide enough to use as a gangplank for a cruise liner. These were interspersed with brightly coloured posters of surfers pulling into perfect azure waves, nothing resembling the crumbling, dark waters of Southbourne beach. But they weren't enough to distract her from noticing that other areas of the shop were also bereft of stock. Bare shelves were a clear indication of one thing — a business struggling to pay its bills.

Thankfully, the swimsuits on the rail in front of her were plentiful, but then nobody wanted to buy swimwear at this time of year.

"I'll leave you to browse," the man said. "Feel free to try anything on." He nodded to the shop's one and only changing room clad in thick bamboo.

Fiona ignored the bikinis and went straight for the more modest one-piece costumes. Flicking through a rainbow of colours, she alighted on a rather handsome, understated teal swimsuit. Produced by an Australian surf company, it wasn't cheap but was well made and beautifully finished. She selected her size and tried it on. The costume fitted perfectly. Fiona had a philosophy when it came to buying clothes, a kind of quit-while-you're-ahead mentality — if something suited you, then get it and ignore the rest. The temptation to continue seeking out something better or even cheaper would always, in her experience, send you down a fashion rabbit hole from which you might never emerge.

As she exited the changing room, swimsuit in hand, the man appeared almost out of thin air like the shopkeeper from Mr Benn. "How are you doing?"

Fiona held up the costume. "I'll take it."

"Excellent." The man took it from her, beaming.

She followed him towards the counter.

"So are you off on holiday somewhere nice?" he asked. "Do you need any sun cream? We have some very good ones that are non-toxic."

Keen to capitalise on the swimsuit purchase, he was going all out to upsell. Fiona didn't mind. She would do the same if she were in his position. "Oh, no. Not a holiday. I'm having my first go at wild swimming tomorrow."

This stopped him in his tracks, his eyes widening with possibility. He changed direction and headed over to another part of the shop, near the wetsuits. "Oh. Well, you'll definitely need some neoprene booties and gloves for going in, and a changing robe for when you come out."

Fiona didn't realise she'd need so much equipment for what would be a brief dip in very cold water, and from what she had heard from Beth, Southbourne Wild Swimmers were purists who would frown upon her if she turned up with booties and gloves, spoiling the whole back-to-nature experience. However, the changing robe seemed like a good idea to throw around her shivering body after she came out. She pointed to a smart navy-blue one. "How much is that?"

"They're all a hundred and eighty-five pounds."

Before she had time to protest at such an expense, he plied her with benefits. "It's waterproof and has a fleecy lining, which you'll be thanking me for when you come out of the sea tomorrow. This is what I use when I go surfing. Not that I get the chance that often — I'm always stuck in here — but if you're going wild swimming, it's essential kit." He unhooked it off the rail and added it to her other purchase. "Now, let's pick you out some booties and gloves."

Fiona couldn't justify spending that amount of money on what might be her first and last wild swim. She hoped this would become a regular habit, but if it proved too painful for her ancient bones, then she'd be stuck with a rather expensive dog-walking coat. "I think I'll just take the swimsuit for now."

"I would strongly recommend you take boots, gloves and the changing robe. I can give you ten-per-cent discount. What say we try on some nice five-mil booties and gloves, and you'll probably need some decent goggles too. We've also got flippers and diving gear, if you fancy a wild swim underwater."

She could understand his desperation for sales, especially if he was struggling to pay bills. But now the upselling was turning into hard-selling, foisting items on her that she didn't really need. "I don't intend on putting my face in the water." She smiled at him, although she was on the cusp of becoming annoyed.

"Okay, just the gloves, booties and robe then."

Fiona did her best to remain polite. "Not today, thank you. I can always come back for them later."

Perhaps reading the irritation behind her eyes, he didn't push it any further and returned the changing robe to the rail. "Of course." They headed to the till. "Anything else you need, don't hesitate to call or come back. I'm Roger, by the way. Roger Masters."

"Oh, hence the name of your shop, Ocean Masters. I like it."

"Yes, it's a good fit. Although I wouldn't say I'm a master of the ocean. To be honest, I'm what you call a soul surfer. Just doing it for the buzz."

"That's the best reason for doing anything," Fiona replied. "As long as it's not hard drugs."

Her guffaw took Roger by surprise. Perhaps he didn't credit Fiona with a sense of humour. "I like that. Anything else you need, don't be tempted to buy online. Anything water-related needs to fit properly and you can only do that by trying it on in a shop."

"You'll get no argument from me. I'm Fiona, by the way. I'm a retailer too. Of the charity shop variety." She smiled.

Roger didn't smile back. "Oh, okay." A non-committal response if ever there was one. Maybe he didn't think a charity shop counted as proper retail, or perhaps he thought they were stealing his customers. Fiona couldn't see how. Their stock was far more sedate. Although, from time to time, they had their fair share of surfwear: the odd T-shirt, pair of shorts or shortie wetsuits that kiddies had grown out of, but nothing that would put them in competition with a bona fide surf shop.

Roger managed a parting smile as he finished up her purchase, urging her again to return if she needed additional equipment. Once outside, she was relieved to be free of such an intense sales environment. She hadn't experienced one of those in a long while. However, a few paces down the road, she got a flicker of butterflies in her stomach and a squeal of tinnitus as the reality of what she was about to do sank in. Tomorrow, she'd walk into the sea, with only a teal swimsuit between her and the harsh waters of the English Channel.

Common sense chastised her, pointing a bony, accusing finger at her for her stupidity. Normally, she loathed common sense and knew it was best avoided, even if it was her own. It was usually the basis of ignorant gut reactions and ill-informed opinions, but on this occasion, she had to agree. What was she thinking?

CHAPTER 6

Anticipation and a fair amount of anxiety woke Fiona two hours before her alarm was due to go off. Through sleep-encrusted eyes, she stared at the bright red digits on her clock, which appeared to mock her insomnia: 4.42 a.m., they starkly announced. There was no point attempting any further slumber — she'd just toss and turn, wondering — or, more accurately, worrying — about the morning ahead. Decisively, she snapped back the duvet. Better to get up and start the day than procrastinate, even if the birds weren't awake and the central heating hadn't come on yet.

As she swung her feet out of the covers and straight into her awaiting slippers, Simon Le Bon raised his furry head off the bed, his muzzle smushed on one side where he'd slept on it. With two indignant and questioning eyes, he glared at her for waking him up. She ignored his guilt-tripping and reached for her phone to check today's forecast. She'd been checking it all yesterday evening to get an idea of what she was letting herself in for, and to see if it would improve. Groaning, she saw that it hadn't, and the current forecast wasn't any more inviting. Overcast skies, twenty per cent chance of rain and a predicted air temperature of six degrees Celsius. At least it wasn't windy. Now for the most important statistic — the sea temperature. She flicked onto another site, which cheerfully informed her that it was above average for the time of year. Eleven degrees instead of the usual ten. Would that one degree make any difference for her baptism into the world of wild swimming? She doubted it. Ten or eleven degrees both sounded terrifyingly cold. So much so that the site issued a warning below that anyone thinking of going in the sea shouldn't do so for more than five minutes, ten at most, unless they were a very experienced cold-water swimmer.

Fiona gulped. She wished she had a waterproof watch she could wear, ensuring she didn't outstay her welcome. No chance of that. Her shivering body would tell her when her time was up.

Trembling at the prospect, Fiona unhooked her dressing gown off the back of the door and wrapped it tightly around herself as she headed downstairs, keenly followed by Simon Le Bon, who sensed an early breakfast. Though she didn't feel hungry in the slightest, she decided to prepare a sizeable first meal of the day to insulate herself from the cold, mostly influenced by an old TV ad she remembered from the seventies. She clearly recalled kids walking to school on a grim, drizzly morning, protected from the weather by an orange glow because they'd had porridge for breakfast. Either that or there'd been a leak at the local reactor.

With over three hours before she had to be at the beach, at least she'd have plenty of time to adhere to the rule of waiting an hour before swimming. Although, she vaguely remembered an episode of *QI* where Stephen Fry dispelled the myth. However, today wasn't the day to put that to the test.

After eating, she boiled the kettle and filled her flask with hot sweet tea to take with her — something she'd be in dire need of when she came out.

Sensibly, Fiona put on her new swimming costume first, so she didn't have to contort beneath a towel when she got to the beach. Over this, she slipped on several layers of the warmest and baggiest variety, anything that she could easily pull back on again with numb fingers after her swim. For the same reason, she picked her fur-lined shoes fastened by a Velcro strap. Then she took Simon out in the garden for a quick wee, deciding it would be better to leave him at home and pick him up on her way back. If she brought him to the beach, he'd only pine for her while she was in the water, an additional stress she could do without.

Eventually, she left the house, making it to the top of the zigzag with five minutes to spare. Leaning over the guard rail, she spotted a modest gathering of a dozen or so people beside the stone groyne, its pale-yellow boulders reaching out into the sea like a gnarled thumb. Huddled on the beach together, everyone sported bright oversized changing robes, appearing like a cluster of human–tent hybrids. All except one.

Impervious to the cold, a man strutted among them, clad only in a pair of skimpy red Speedos. Flitting from one person to another, greeting them each in turn, he appeared to be in charge, which seemed strange as Beth hadn't mentioned they had a leader, nor that he was a bit of a poser (although that wasn't the sort of information you volunteered on first meeting — *oh, by the way, there'll be a rakish fellow on the beach showing off a bit*). But it did strike Fiona as odd after what Beth had told them about wild swimming allowing you to cast off the restraints of dry land, with its dull rules and regulations. Telling people what to do was the main reason Colin had rubbed everyone up the wrong way, and perhaps got himself killed.

Fiona would question Beth about this down on the beach. However, as she descended the zigzag, scanning the people below, Beth didn't appear to be among them.

Finally reaching the promenade, Fiona trekked across the sand, the buzz of friendly chatter reaching her ears and growing louder as she approached. Collectively, the Southbourne Wild Things had that excited jitteriness about them. A small bubble of humanity fizzing with energy. Exactly the opposite of how Fiona felt at this precise moment. It took all her willpower not to turn around, head home and crawl back into the comfort of her warm bed.

The waiting swimmers all had orange lozenge-shaped changing bags by their feet and flasks wedged into the sand. They were of various ages, but she was heartened to see a couple her own age, matching yellow pompom hats atop their heads. Their flask was the largest of all, resembling a small barrel with a handle. Fiona cursed herself, realising that she'd left hers at home.

Before she'd had a chance to consider the implications of not having any hot tea to warm her bones when she emerged from the sea, Speedo man appeared in front of her, his hand outstretched and an enthusiastic grin on his face. "Hello. You must be Fiona." His handshake, like his jawline, was firm. In his early sixties, he was handsome in a Liam Neeson sort of way and had the body of a man half his age, toned and muscular, a six-pack popping from his stomach. "My name's Will. Beth told me you'd be paying us a visit. I thought there'd be three of you."

"There are, but it's just me today," Fiona replied. "Er, is Beth here?"

He glanced around. "She doesn't appear to be. Truth be told, this is the first swim we've had since Colin passed away. None of us felt like getting into the water after what happened."

"Oh, yes. I'm very sorry. I hope I'm not intruding."

"Not at all. Tell you what, you stay here while we have our swim. We won't be long. Then after we come out and dry off, you can fire some questions at us. How does that sound?"

Fiona's feet shuffled uneasily in the sand. "Oh, well, I was hoping to join you, er, for a dip."

Will's eyes glittered with enthusiasm. "Wonderful. Please do! It's a real source, isn't it?"

"A source?"

"Wild swimming. It's a source for whatever you want — peace, energy, healing, silencing those pesky demons in your head."

The last phrase caught Fiona off guard, and she wondered if he could sense Fiona's demon, hovering in the dusty corners of her mind. Dismissing this thought, Will was simply another evangelist like Beth, keen to extol wild swimming's many virtues.

"So, I take it you're used to swimming in the sea this time of year?" he asked.

The question threw Fiona for a second. "Er, no. I'm a complete beginner. Well, apart from swimming in the summer, but even then it's blooming freezing." She laughed.

Will didn't join in. His face lost all its positivity, becoming deadly serious. "That might be a problem. Sea's very cold this time of year. What about showers?"

Fiona wondered why he would be questioning her hygiene. "I have baths mostly."

"Sorry, I mean, have you been taking cold showers to condition your body, ready for the sea?"

She shook her head. Fiona felt every bit the rookie and incredibly naive. She should've done her research, but then, she hadn't thought there'd be any research to do, assuming that you just turned up and went in. To her further embarrassment, the swimmers around her began stripping off, discarding their changing robes and pulling on neoprene booties and gloves. The guy in the surf shop hadn't been giving her the hard sell — he'd been merely trying to prepare her.

Will spotted she was distracted by this. "The cold can take a toll on the extremities, which is why a lot of us wear gloves and especially boots. The shingle by the water's edge is like walking over broken glass when your feet are numb."

"How come you're not wearing any?" Fiona asked.

"I did but I've gradually weaned myself off them, and I've never used a changing robe in my life. I'm used to the cold, as you can see." He gestured to his well-toned body.

Fiona glanced down momentarily but kept her eyes above his Speedo region. "Did Colin wear any of that stuff?"

"No, like me, he kept it pure. It's all about calming your mind."

Fiona thought back to the telltale signs of hypothermia on Colin's face. Calming your mind wouldn't be much use if you were floating unconscious in water for any length of time.

"Okay, I suppose I'd better sit this one out," Fiona said, disappointed. "Maybe wait until I've acclimatised a bit under the shower."

"Oh, no. You should definitely go in. We just need to make sure you're safe. Buddy you up with someone, and I know just the pair." He called out to the older couple in the matching pompom hats. "Ahmed, Rani."

Smiling, the pair came trotting over with their bags and gigantic flask. Will introduced them to Fiona.

Ahmed gave a wide, bright smile. "Oh, yes. Beth told us all about you. You're going to—"

"Look into Colin's death." Rani finished off his sentence.

Ahmed's eyes became downcast. "His death really knocked us—"

"For six, it did." Rani finished another sentence. So, they were one of those types of couples. It was rather endearing.

"Certainly did," Will added. "But Colin would want us to continue swimming, I'm sure of it. Now, its Fiona's first time in these sorts of temperatures. Would you mind showing her the ropes, staying with her?"

"We'd be happy to." The pair smiled warmly.

"Thank you." Fiona returned the smile but inside she felt foolish, needing babysitters because she hadn't done her homework or any proper preparation.

"Do you have boots and gloves?" Rani asked.

Fiona shook her head.

Rani delved into her bag and pulled out a tatty pair of both items. Worn in places, they'd seen better days. "I always keep these spare, just in case."

She handed them to Fiona, who accepted them, overflowing with gratitude.

Will clapped his hands with delight. "I knew you were the right people for the job." He turned to Fiona. "I'll leave you in Ahmed and Rani's capable hands. Please excuse me. I'm off to swim out to the buoy."

Fiona spotted the tiny yellow dot, bobbing about three hundred metres offshore. She shuddered at the distance then plonked herself down on the damp sand to try on the borrowed items.

"Looks like we're about the same size." Rani smiled, revealing a gold canine on the left-hand side of her mouth. "They've got holes in them here and there, but they'll do for now. Better than nothing."

Fiona stood up, a tad more confident now she had a layer of neoprene protecting her hands and feet. "Thank you. They fit perfectly. I'll buy myself some new ones today."

"Shall we?" Ahmed gestured towards the water's edge, as if they were about to go fine dining. They began unzipping and removing their changing robes.

This was it, Fiona thought. Now or never. She shrugged off her coat and slipped out of her baggy clothes, glad she'd bought a new swimsuit for the occasion. Though it looked smart, it did precisely nothing to ward off the cold. The frigid February air coiled around her warm skin, giving her instant goosebumps. Every nerve ending in Fiona's body screamed at her to put her clothes back on. She ignored them and smiled at Ahmed and Rani. The three of them shuffled across the sand towards a petrol-blue sea and an equally dismal sky.

But something else screamed at her from deep within.

The *It* was back. Not with a hint or murmur, or the usual dark shadow, the *It* had become emboldened, dominating and besieging her mind, leaching all her hope and happiness. Her tinnitus joined in, screeching to warn her of the danger.

Halting abruptly, the menacing cacophony in her head made her giddy with fear. All her confidence fled, and she began to shudder, while her mind seized up, strangled by terror.

CHAPTER 7

A chorus of gasps and groans, and not a small amount of cursing, commenced as the swimmers eased themselves into the water — apart from Will, who dived straight in, his arms windmilling as he ploughed a watery furrow towards the buoy. It was all positive. A happy occasion as the members resumed their wild swimming once more after the tragedy of losing Colin.

Meanwhile, Fiona stood at the shoreline, immobilised by the *It*, her world crumbling into a pit of despair. In the past, she'd experienced the debilitating influence the *It* had over her, sometimes keeping its distance, other times dragging her down like an endless drizzly day in her mind, but this was different. The *It* had never been this strong before.

"Fiona? Fiona?" Ahmed's kind voice cut through the uproar.

She wanted to answer, but she had become mute. Silenced by fear.

Rani attempted to reassure her. "Don't worry. It's quite natural—"

"To have beginner's anxiety," Ahmed completed her sentence.

"It's just your mind's knee-jerk reaction—"

"At the thought of getting into cold water. That's all."

Inadvertently, the sweet couple had supplied Fiona with an explanation to her sudden debilitating state of affairs. It wasn't Fiona who was terrified. The *It* was. Like a cornered, frightened animal, her depression didn't want her going anywhere near the water because it sensed danger. This was the *It*'s survival response, a violent reaction to the threat, which meant only one thing — it must work.

"Maybe this isn't such a good idea," Ahmed said, tenderly.

"Why don't we go back and get changed?" Rani suggested. "Have some of Ahmed's famous soup."

"I use lentils as a thickener." Ahmed attempted to sell its wholesome credentials.

But Fiona didn't want soup, not just yet. She wanted to end the punishment going on in her head. "No," she snapped, reasserting some control over her mind, her resolve strengthened and renewed. "Sounds delicious." Her tone became gentler. "But I want to do this."

The *It* suddenly shrieked, stabbing her with guilt and anxiety. In response, Fiona would give it a dose of its own medicine with a bit of water torture.

"Good for you," Rani encouraged her.

"Now, first things first," Ahmed advised her, "we do everything gradually. Slow and steady—"

"Wins the race," Rani added.

"Get used to the cold a bit at a time, and don't stand on ceremony. If it's too much, we'll turn around and go in."

"Okay. Got it." Fiona took a step forward, eager to get in and drown the demon in her head.

"Just a minute." Ahmed held her back. "Second item on the agenda is breathing. That also needs to be slow and steady. You need to avoid cold-water shock—"

"Or you'll start hyperventilating," Rani added. "Try to breathe like you normally would."

Fiona nodded.

"Maybe no swimming today," Rani suggested. "Just see if you can get your shoulders under, then we'll get back out and get warm."

"But won't that ruin your swim?" Fiona asked.

"Oh, don't worry about us," Ahmed replied. "We're more your casual dippers anyway."

"We'll be by your side the whole time." Rani took Fiona's hand, as did Ahmed on the other side of her. Fiona felt like a two-year-old at the beach for the first time with her parents, but was immensely reassured by their presence while the *It* continued the assault on her mind.

The trio commenced a slow creep to the water's edge, one small, careful step at a time, until the sea swirled around their toes. Glad to have the barrier of rubber around her feet, she could feel the cold pressing against her, attempting to find a way in. A second later, it did. The holes in the boots allowed a small ingress of water. Little needles of pain everywhere. Fiona gasped.

"You okay?" Rani asked.

Fiona followed their advice and breathed through it. "Never better," she joked. "Onwards and upwards."

Two more steps and the water surged over the tops of her boots on unprotected skin. She gave another gasp. The cold was so far off the scale of what she'd ever experienced it felt like acid on her flesh.

Her breaths became uncontrollable, rapid and ragged.

Rani squeezed her hand. "Nice and slow, now."

Though her chest wanted to gulp down as many short, sharp breaths as she could, Fiona brought it under control, forcing herself to take unhurried lungfuls of air.

"We'll wait here for second," Ahmed advised. "Give you time to get used to it."

"Y-Yes," Fiona managed to say, juddering with cold. Soon, the breathing worked. "I think I can go a bit further."

"Right you are," Rani said.

They ventured forward, deeper now. Fiona tensed up, knowing that this would be the toughest part, when the glacial water would encircle her midriff. Fiona anticipated the shock and focused on her breathing, slowing it down even further but increasing the volume of each inhalation. The pain stabbed at her stomach but she ignored it.

"Are you okay, Fiona?" Ahmed asked. "Do you want to go back in now?"

They'd been in the water barely a minute, but she wanted to see how far she could push herself. She shook her head. "Just a bit more."

Gritting her teeth, she took two more steps forward until the water met her chest, the cold mauling her to the very core. Two steps more and her shoulders would be under. She set this as her goal.

One, two and she was up to her neck. Snatching her breath away, Fiona found herself laughing as she gasped for air. Partly because of the paralysing agony and partly due to the absurdity of it all. She was almost completely submerged in seawater in February, holding the hands of two strangers. Ahmed and Rani raised their arms in victory, thrusting Fiona's up into the air, as if they had crossed the finish line of a marathon.

"You did it, Fiona!" Rani congratulated her.

"Well done. Feels good, right?" Ahmed added.

"Er, I can't actually feel anything," Fiona gasped.

The three of them giggled. She had never felt so cold in her life. It was so deep and intense that it had become part of her, flowing through her, a powerful unstoppable force, and she was one with it.

"Okay, I think that's enough for today," Rani warned.

"G-Good idea," Fiona replied through chattering teeth.

"Who fancies soup?" Ahmed asked.

The humble offer had never sounded so irresistible.

CHAPTER 8

After much hurried fumbling to get back into her dry clothes, Fiona accepted a cup of Ahmed's famous soup. She immediately clasped it with both hands, luxuriating in its heat while he rattled off the ingredients. She couldn't retain what he said, the information immediately slipping from her ice-bound mind.

Slowly sipping the delectable broth, a hearty glow radiated out from her belly, gradually melting her frigid limbs. The welcome return of warmth felt euphoric in a way she'd never experienced before. A tingling spread across her body like thousands of tiny ballet dancers pirouetting over her skin.

As she stood on the beach gazing at the rest of the club members, somehow still frolicking in the biting sea, she attempted to unpack the blissful but strange sensation enveloping her. A personal achievement, perhaps? Maybe not to any onlookers, but for her, in the brief time she'd spent in the water she'd overcome a mountainous challenge and survived. It was as if the sea was the frozen lair of a great ferocious beast and she'd sneaked in while it slept, tiptoeing around it without rousing the monster and made it out unscathed. Well, apart from feeling colder than she'd ever felt in her life.

A grin spread across her face as something else occurred to her. She could no longer detect the *It.* The thing had been silenced, perhaps not for good, but for now it had retreated back into the deepest recesses of her mind. Immersion in the unforgiving sea was undoubtedly the reason, simply because, while submerged, she couldn't focus on anything else but the cold. The *It* and all the other rubbish floating around in her cluttered mind had been blown away by a blast of icy water. Would they be back to annoy and torment her? Probably, but for now she delighted in the respite that wild swimming had bestowed on her.

In the short time the three of them had been in and out of the sea and got changed, Will had swum to the buoy and back. Fiona watched him march onto the sand as if he were on a Caribbean beach. Incredibly, he ignored the temptation to dry himself off and slip into something warmer, which, she assumed, based only on their previous interaction, would probably be just a vest and shorts.

He made a direct line for Fiona and stood in front of her, stance wide, hands on hips and dripping wet, not shivering in the slightest. "Everything okay?" he asked.

"Yes, it was wonderful!" Fiona replied.

Will gave her a joyful smile. "I told you it was a source, didn't I?"

"I see what you mean now."

"Yes, you can't explain it. You have to experience it yourself. So, can we expect you back tomorrow?"

"Oh, definitely."

"Good for you!" And with that he was gone. Still neglecting to dry himself off, he called on all the others who'd recently emerged from the sea, checking they were okay and sharing their good-natured banter.

"He's a regular Wim Hof, that one," Ahmed commented.

"Wim Hof?" Fiona asked.

"The Dutch Ice Man," Rani replied.

Fiona remembered now. "Oh, is he the guy that swims under the ice and meditates in the snow in just his shorts?"

"The very same," Ahmed said. "Will's on his way there, if he's not already."

"So is Will in charge of the club?" Fiona asked, assuming that he was the most experienced cold-water swimmer.

Rani began putting her things away. "Gosh, no. We don't have a leader or anything like that, but when any group of people gets together—"

"A natural leader emerges," Ahmed finished.

"How does Beth feel about that, being the founder of the club?" Fiona asked.

"Oh, she's not worried in the slightest. I guess her role's more adminy."

Fiona glanced around. "I wonder why Beth's not here today."

"It's a very loose arrangement," Rani replied. "People turn up as and when they can."

"Does anyone ever swim alone?" Fiona asked.

Ahmed stared at Fiona. "You're referring to Colin, I assume."

Fiona nodded.

"We never recommend anyone swims alone. Not this time of year in these temperatures. It's different in summer, of course, but then you still need to respect the water."

"But to answer your question," Rani said, "it would be completely out of character for him. He was a stickler for doing things properly. But more to the point, Colin didn't have any friends apart from all of us. He was desperate for company. Swimming alone would have been pointless."

Beth had said something similar. Fiona took a different angle. "And how did Colin feel about Will's unofficial leader status?"

Neither of them answered immediately. Ahmed gazed into his soup, while Rani fiddled with the drawstrings on her bag.

Ahmed broke the silence. "I think Colin thought he had to compete with Will. Perhaps that's why Colin could sometimes be a bit bossy. He wanted to assert his authority."

"How did everyone else feel about that?" Fiona asked. "Aggravated? Angry?"

Ahmed shook his head. "We mostly ignored him. Maybe some were irritated."

"Anyone in particular?"

"None that I can think of, although you'll have to ask around, but not enough to murder him, if that's where you're heading. I think it was more a problem Colin had with himself than a problem people had with him, if that makes sense. Will is charming and isn't overbearing, which is why people like him. Colin was the opposite. A bit of a lummox. Awkward and abrupt. I think he couldn't understand why his words weren't being heeded."

"You can take the teacher out of the school, but you can't take the school out the teacher," Rani said.

From what Fiona could gather, Colin seemed to be a person of conflicting behaviours. On the one hand, eager for company and the warmth of friendship. On the other, an overbearing authoritarian who drove people away with his spiky attitude.

"Was Colin jealous of Will, do you think?" Fiona asked.

"Oh, yes, absolutely."

"Colin was an ex-sports teacher," Rani explained. "He had a bit of a chip on his shoulder when it came to swimming. Our club's not about competing with one another, far from it. However, I think he just assumed he'd be the best athlete here. But Will's an ex-county swimmer. Every session the pair of them would race out to the buoy and back, and every time, Will would beat him. I think that's what really annoyed him. Maybe it's why he started being bossy — you know, to vent his frustration. Which is ironic because Colin's therapist recommended wild swimming to help him with his feelings."

"Colin had a therapist?" This was the first Fiona had heard of it.

Rani and Ahmed both nodded.

"He was the one who recommended our club to him," Ahmed said. "For his issues."

"Do you know what issues?"

Ahmed and Rani both shrugged.

"This therapist," Fiona said. "I don't suppose you remember his name?"

CHAPTER 9

Euphoria still lingering, Fiona marched back to the top of the zigzag with renewed vigour. Having had an aquatic epiphany, she'd seen the light, or, more precisely, felt the agony of being dunked in freezing seawater and enjoyed it immensely. Did that make her a masochist? No — she hadn't relished the discomfort. It was more the relief afterwards, that she'd survived the ordeal, and now her head abounded with positivity. She felt as if she could do anything.

The strongest of bonds had been forged with her two woolly-hatted mentors — her new cold-water comrades, as she called them. On saying goodbye to Ahmed and Rani, they'd swapped numbers. A practicality in any investigation, but she hoped it would be more than that. Maybe they would become her regular swim buddies — if she eventually managed a stroke or two, instead of merely standing neck deep in deathly cold brine.

She pulled out her phone, eager to text Beth with an update on the investigation, but more to inform her that she'd had her first wild swim and loved it. Beth immediately pinged back a message, overjoyed but also apologising for her absence, promising that she'd be down at the beach tomorrow. Fiona couldn't wait to get into the water with her. Maybe she could persuade Daisy and Sue to join them. Yes! Wouldn't that be a marvellous thing! They could wild swim together before work. She could just see it now. Grinning at the prospect, her pace quickened as she worked out how best to persuade them. Daisy might be game but Partial Sue would take some convincing. Perhaps she could bribe her. Knowing how partial she was to a cooked breakfast, maybe the promise of a fry-up afterwards might sway her.

But first she needed to stop off at home to collect Simon Le Bon, and possibly another couple of layers of clothing. She'd underestimated just how penetrating the cold would be. Reaching deep into her core, it felt as if she'd swallowed a bowling ball made of ice. Warmth gradually crept back to her extremities, but it was a painfully slow process resembling the loading bar on her computer that was never in any hurry to get to the end. Maybe she could help it along a bit with a hot shower — was that anathema to wild swimmers? Would that undo all the cold-water therapy she'd just enjoyed? She had no idea. Probably best if she didn't.

After slipping on a thermal top under her clothes and a cardigan over her chunky-knit jumper — which didn't really go, but she was beyond caring at this point — she poured herself a quick cup of tea from the flask she'd left behind and downed it, burning her tongue. The rest she sloshed into a travel mug to drink on the way to work. Clipping on Simon Le Bon's lead, she left the house, her mind scheming with ways to get her colleagues to join her at the beach tomorrow.

She was only a few steps from the shop's front door when Fiona's conscience slapped her in the face for getting her priorities wrong. Since leaving the beach, her mind had been fixated on the religion of wild swimming and obsessed with ways of getting her friends to join its church, when it should have been focused on finding out what happened to Colin Barclay. She'd gathered some valuable intel at the beach and should've been analysing the facts, arranging the logic, ready to report back to her fellow amateur sleuths. Instead, she'd been like a child with a new toy, consumed and fascinated by it. Something had certainly shifted in her head if thoughts of dead bodies and possible murders were being superseded by those of cold-water dips. Maybe it was all the endorphins rushing around her system. Nevertheless, she still had a job to do. Fiona took a deep breath, refocused her mind and pushed the door open, the bell tingling above her.

Her colleagues were already in, busying themselves.

Daisy placed the chipped brown teapot on the table. "Morning, Fiona," she greeted cheerfully. "You're just in time for tea." Her face dropped when she saw the travel mug in Fiona's hands. "Oh, you've already had one."

Fiona stepped into the shop, keeping her coat on, and it would stay that way for as long as necessary. "Oh, don't worry about that. Room for one more. In fact, I'll be needing a lot of God's finest beverage to thaw me out."

Partial Sue abandoned a pile of donations, letting them topple in a heap. "You didn't go in, did you?"

"I did indeed." Fiona beamed, extremely pleased with herself but aware she had to rein in her zeal. Nothing in life was duller than an enthusiast.

"Oh, well done, Fiona. You must be freezing." Daisy handed her a cup of steaming tea.

"I am a bit." Fiona sat down, greedily clasping her hands around the mug's circumference, feeding off the heat it radiated.

A bewildered Partial Sue couldn't keep still. "But how? What, you just walked in the sea — in your swimming costume — in February?"

"That's about the size of it. Very slowly, I might add."

"Well, I think you're very brave." Daisy smiled.

"I can't believe it." Partial Sue perched awkwardly on the edge of a chair, clearly uncomfortable with what she was hearing. "How come you're not shivering like a dog?"

Fiona took a mouthful of tea. "Well, I was when I came out, but I'm warming up slowly. I still feel freezing." She got up and selected a man's overcoat off the rail and slung it over the one she was already wearing, relishing its extra warmth, then sat down again. "I have to tell you, it felt incredible. I can see why everyone's doing it." She desperately wanted to gabble on about her life-changing morning but bit her lip.

True to form, a cynical Partial Sue poured cold water on Fiona's cold-water experience. "I think it's just a fad like hula hoops or Wi-Fi — I'm still partial to ethernet cables at home — never drop out."

"Did you manage to question anyone?" Daisy asked. "Any possible suspects emerging?"

"Well, I have a couple of leads."

"Go on, spill the beans," Partial Sue urged.

Fiona outlined Will's status as the unofficial guru-slash-leader of the Southbourne Wild Things, and how Colin appeared to want to muscle in on his authority, and their unfriendly rivalry when it came to racing out to the buoy.

"I thought Beth was in charge," Daisy said.

"She is, sort of," Fiona replied. "But it's more running the website and answering emails. Will struts around on the beach in his Speedos, geeing everyone up, checking they're okay."

Partial Sue's eyes narrowed. "This Will sounds a bit proud to me. Guarding his status. For me, he's ticking all the murder boxes."

"Murder boxes?" Daisy chuckled. "Sounds like one of those monthly subscription goodie boxes, but for would-be killers. Each month they get a box full of murder weapons, poisons and gadgets to try out, and little booklets with step-by-step instructions."

Partial Sue took her suggestion seriously. "Yes, maybe he found one to murder Colin the usurper, and make it look like he drowned."

"I didn't get the impression he was the jealous type." Fiona was reluctant to paint Will as the killer. One, apart from strutting around in minuscule swimwear, she liked him (a terrible reason not to suspect him). But two, with the limited information she had, his motive didn't add up. "It's not an official role, just one he's naturally gravitated to. He seemed above all that pettiness, and from what Ahmed and Rani told me, it was all one-sided. Colin was jealous of Will, not the other way around. It would make more sense if Colin had murdered Will."

Partial Sue pulled a face. "I dunno. You never know what's going on in someone's head. Still waters and all that. Excuse the pun. Well, it's early days yet. More information may emerge, but I think this puts Will at the top of the suspects list."

"What's the second lead?" Daisy asked.

"Colin had a therapist. He's the one who advised him to try wild swimming for some issues he had."

"Do you know what those issues were?" Daisy asked.

Fiona shook her head. "Ahmed and Rani didn't know. They'd never met him but they said his surname was something like Mason, Maisel or Maple."

Daisy was on her phone, thumbs a blur, searching the internet. "What about Maplin? Ted Maplin's a counsellor in Southbourne."

"He sounds promising," Fiona said.

"He sounds like a character from *Hi-de-Hi!*," Partial Sue remarked.

Daisy scrolled through the therapist's website. "He deals with all sorts of phobias and issues — fear of flying, insomnia, panic attacks, anxiety. He'd definitely be able to tell us how Colin was feeling before he died. We need to talk to him."

"Not so fast," Partial Sue warned. "He'll be bound by client confidentiality."

"What, even though Colin's passed away?"

"Absolutely."

"Sue's right," Fiona agreed. "But it's worth a try. If we stress that Colin's death may have been suspicious, he may bend the rules a bit. Give us a few crumbs from the table. It's better than nothing. What's his email?"

Daisy flipped her phone around so Fiona could copy it.

"I'll ping him a message. Ask if Colin was his client and if it's possible to make an appointment."

Fiona got a ping back immediately.

"Wow, that was quick," Daisy said.

Partial Sue harrumphed cynically. "Can't be very busy if he replied that fast."

"Unless he's extremely efficient," Daisy replied.

"Yes!" Fiona cried. "He says Colin was his client and he's free after work."

It was only day one of the investigation and things were moving along nicely, and she was still basking in the afterglow of her wild swim, which looked set to last all day.

Then Sophie Haverford slithered into the shop, her condescending perma-smugness filling the place like mustard gas.

CHAPTER 10

With the panache of a Gestapo officer in her belted and flared black trench coat, Sophie was on one of her gloating missions. She never needed an excuse or a special occasion to cross the road and show off. Like an expert martial artist, she had to practise on someone to keep her skills sharp, usually the ladies of Dogs Need Nice Homes. Why them? It was a question that would never be answered.

"Greetings, one and all." Sophie sniggered at them derisively in the same way one might at an uncle dancing particularly badly at a wedding reception. Gail, her ever miserable and monosyllabic doormat of an assistant, followed behind, keeping her head low.

Partial Sue was having none of her patronising behaviour, not this early in the morning. "What do you want, Sophie?"

"Well, that's not very nice. I just popped in to see how you all were." She looked them up and down, appraising what each of them was wearing, possibly arming herself with sarcastic ammunition to use later. Finally, alighting on Fiona in her many coats and clothes, Sophie leaped back melodramatically, horrified, almost knocking Gail into a display of scarves. She threw the crook of her arm around her nose and mouth protectively. "Why are you wearing all those clothes? You haven't got flu, have you? Because it's irresponsible coming into a workplace if you have. I simply can't be ill. I have too many social engagements to attend."

"Fiona's been wild swimming," Daisy proudly announced on her behalf.

A delay hit the circuits of Sophie's brain. She always had an array of scornful comebacks lined up for every occasion, but not this one. "You? Wild swimming? In water?"

"That's usually the best place for it," Partial Sue mocked.

Sophie didn't bite, her eyes remaining fixed on Fiona.

"Yep," Fiona replied. "Little old me in the sea this morning."

Sophie didn't giggle or crack a sarcastic remark. Wrongfooted, she clearly didn't know what to make of this. Being an ex-PR maven (her words), every response, no matter how trivial, had to have purpose, had to be curated and considered, because it had a job to do — either to advance Sophie's cause or to put down her competitors, or both. She was probably weighing up what Fiona's wild swimming meant for her. How would it affect her status as Queen of Southbourne? Did it spell trouble, or could she use it against her? Judging by her blank expression, she didn't know which. She needed more intel, and her response was suitably economic. "What for?"

"We're investigating the death of wild swimmer Colin Barclay," Fiona explained. "I thought I'd join the local club. Not undercover or anything, just to see what makes them tick, and discover new leads."

Remaining poker faced, Sophie stared at Fiona unblinking, perpetuating the most uncomfortable of pauses. Then she turned to Daisy and Partial Sue. "And are you part of this wild swimming club?"

"No fear." Daisy shuddered. "I love the sea but it has to be really warm for me to go in."

"I'm not partial to the cold in any form." Partial Sue rattled off a list of her personal subzero bugbears. "Water, ice, sleet, frost, hail. I make an exception for snow and ice cream, but I don't like sorbets, slushies or—"

Sophie raised her palm to silence her. She stood in cogitative stillness, apart from her eyes hopping between the three seated ladies, as if one of them were hiding something from her and she was trying to work out who. This went on for several seconds, although it felt like hours, until she suddenly swished around dramatically, throwing the hem of her trench coat out in a wide arc, then marched out of the shop. Gail shrugged and smiled politely at the ladies, equally clueless as to Sophie's odd behaviour.

"Gail!" Sophie snapped. "Come on!"

Gail flinched then trotted after her mistress, closing the door behind her.

Fiona stripped off one of her coats, feeling a lot warmer after a brush with the woman who made the Cats Alliance more like *The Devil Wears Prada*. "What was that all about?"

"That was scary." Daisy gulped down the rest of her tea as if it were a shot of whisky. "I don't like it when Sophie's quiet. She's never quiet. Do you think she's okay?"

Partial Sue leaned forward. "She's probably plotting our downfall in her Eagle's Nest across the road."

"Well, no change there then," Fiona remarked. "But Daisy's right, that was out of character. I think I prefer it when she's talking about herself twenty to the dozen. She's definitely up to something."

CHAPTER 11

Finally, Fiona's body temperature returned to something resembling normal, allowing her to shed a couple of layers. The chunky-knit cardigan came off, but then her overcoat went back on again when she realised that she wanted to go out during her lunchbreak.

"Off somewhere nice?" Daisy asked.

"I'm going to get myself a changing robe and some booties and gloves. I had to borrow some this morning."

Partial Sue sniffed. "Doesn't that defeat the object of wild swimming, wearing protective gear? You might as well go the whole hog and get a wetsuit."

"The cold water's a bit harsh on your extremities, which makes getting changed a bit of a challenge. Boots and gloves stop them going numb."

Daisy made a *brrr* sound. "I imagine it's harsh on everything."

Partial Sue shook her head. "Numb is not a sensation I need in my life right now. Warm and snug is where I want to be."

"Me too," Daisy added. "Preferably with tea and cake on tap."

"Now you're talking."

Fiona left them to discuss their various warm and congenial scenarios involving open fires, hot toddies and fluffy slippers — both the mono, microwavable kind and the more traditional two-footed variety. She'd have an uphill battle trying to get these two to join her in the sea tomorrow, or any time for that matter. As she headed up Southbourne Grove, she resigned herself to the fact that it probably wasn't going to happen, and she wouldn't waste any more mental energy persuading either one of them. For now, she'd keep the wild swimming to herself, which was a pity. It had put a spring in her step, and she was sure it would do the same for them.

Pushing open the door to the surf shop, she expected a warm welcome from Roger, seeing as she'd come to spend more money. She'd offer her apologies to the struggling shop owner, admitting his advice had been sound, except for the part about flippers and goggles.

The sweet scent of coconut and pungent neoprene greeted her, but inside the shop, the atmosphere was distinctly bitter. By the counter, a large, suited man with perfect hair thrust a pointy little surfboard, sharp as an arrowhead, in the owner's direction. Roger didn't appear to want it and was reluctant to look the man in the eye. Sensing the gravity of the situation, Fiona quietly stepped sideways, making herself inconspicuous behind a display of sunglasses, where she could keep an eye on the situation without appearing nosy.

"You have to take it back." The man shoved the board in Roger's face again. "I can't get on with it."

"But you've used it. I can't put it back on the shelves in that state."

"Not my problem. And I've only used it once."

Roger examined the board. "But you've dinged the deck."

The man snorted. "Well, quality can't be up to much if it's already got dents in it."

Roger shook his head. "You said you wanted a high-performance board. Something light and fast. The glassing is thinner on these boards to keep the weight down. I did explain that to you."

"But I couldn't catch anything on it."

"Well, that's because it's a high-performance board. Only works in big, steep waves."

"Yeah, but we hardly get any big steep waves down here. I'd only use it a handful of times a year."

"I explained that as well."

"No, you didn't."

"Yes, I did."

"You didn't."

Fiona got the impression this argument had been going on for some time now, circling back to the same place again and again.

The man took the board, pushed past Roger and shoved it in an empty slot in the surfboard rack, then stood facing Roger, arms crossed. "You have to give me my money back. The board's not fit for purpose. I know my rights. Otherwise, I'll report you to trading standards."

Roger hesitated, stood his ground, staring at the man.

The pair remained deadlocked, neither one backing down or flinching until Roger eventually caved in and sighed. Reluctantly, he went around the back of the counter to retrieve the card machine, punched a few buttons, then held the device out to the man. "You'll need to put your card in for a refund."

Without speaking, he slipped his card out of his wallet and into the machine then punched in his PIN. It spat out a receipt. Roger tore it off and handed it to him. Snatching it, the man left.

Fiona emerged from her hiding place. "Difficult customer."

He brightened up a tad. "Oh! Hi, Fiona. Yes, you could say that. Sorry you had to witness that. Surf shops attract them, unfortunately. Some people want to be hardcore like the pros they see on YouTube. Trouble is, the sort of boards they ride won't work for the average surfer down here."

"You didn't have to refund his board."

Roger shrugged. "No, I didn't. But I hate selling someone a board they can't get on with. That guy knew what he was getting, though. I went to great pains to explain it to him."

Fiona could sympathise but was acutely aware that Roger might have also been desperate for a sale, telling the guy what he wanted to hear, just to get the till ringing.

"I bet you don't get customers like that in the charity shop," he remarked.

"Oh, you'd be surprised. We get people bringing in their own stuff from home, pretending they bought it in the shop, asking for a refund. They think I'm a soft touch and I'll give them a refund without a receipt."

"Really? Just for a few quid?"

"Oh, yes. I usually give it to them, truth be told. I think if they're that desperate they must really need it, so I guess I am a soft touch."

"Well, I suppose us retailers never have it easy. What can I do for you? Not bringing the swimming costume back, I hope."

"Nope, the opposite. You were right. I do need gloves, booties and a changing robe."

Relieved, his shoulders relaxed and a smile graced his face. "That's the best news I've had all morning."

* * *

Fiona left the shop, pleased with her purchases but feeling a tad sorry for Roger. It made her happy that she'd brightened his day, if only a smidge. However, something niggled her about his situation. No more than a gut feeling, a hunch at best, but she had a sneaking suspicion Roger was up to something. She was well aware that this might all be in her head, fuelled by witnessing his altercation with a customer. But desperate times called for desperate measures, and Roger was certainly desperate — his business was rapidly going down the pan. People behaved rashly when their backs were against the wall.

Did he have something to do with Colin's death? She could think of absolutely no reason why Roger would have wanted to murder Colin. Was there even a connection between Colin and the surf shop? Perhaps like her, the wild swimmers of Southbourne all bought their changing robes and bits and pieces there. But Colin was a purist and hadn't relied on these peripheries to enjoy his pastime, so why would he have had anything to do with Roger Masters?

Nevertheless, Fiona got an odd feeling when she thought about the two of them. Maybe she'd test out her theory tomorrow at the next meeting.

CHAPTER 12

Halfway down one of the many long avenues perpendicular to Southbourne Grove, the ladies stood outside Ted Maplin's house. Colin's therapist lived in a large, handsome red-brick home with white UPVC windows that had recently had a wipe down. Daisy looked impressed, especially as the block paving in front of the up-and-over garage had been de-mossed and pressure washed. Ted Maplin clearly ran a tight ship. Parked on the driveway was a smart new electric SUV, glistening in the afternoon light.

"The therapy business must be good," Partial Sue commented.

Fiona hesitated.

"What's the matter, Fiona?" Daisy asked.

"I wonder if we might have better luck if I go in alone."

"Oh, that's a good point," Daisy replied. "Don't want to overwhelm him."

"Are you sure?" Partial Sue asked.

Fiona nodded.

"Okay, we'll be right outside waiting for you in the car," Partial Sue reassured her.

On first inspection, Fiona thought the house had been divided into a couple of flats as there were two bells beside the front door. But on closer examination, she realised one was for his home, the other for his counselling practice. She pushed the latter.

Movement came from inside the house. Through the opaque glass, Fiona could see a shadowy figure heading towards her. After all the talk about *Hi-de-Hi!*, Fiona expected a rotund fellow with receding, badly Brylcreemed hair and a poorly fitting tartan suit. He was none of those things, although he did wear a suit, a grey number expertly tailored with a pristine high-collared white shirt secured with a Windsor-knotted pink tie, contrasting starkly with his swarthy skin and coal-black hair. His smile was warm but understated. "You must be Fiona, please do come in."

She followed him into a generous hallway of black-and-white harlequin floor tiles, scrubbed clean with a great deal of Flash. A grand, dark wooden staircase was off to one side, anchored by a large, polished newel post resembling a bishop in chess. Original pieces of modern art hung from the walls. The therapist clearly had taste and money.

Ted Maplin showed her into a room at the front of the house, sparsely but comfortably furnished. A large retro fifties sofa had its back to the wall, facing a couple of easy chairs separated by a low coffee table complete with a jug of water and several glasses on a neat circular tray. A stack of glossy hardback books sat next to it. However, dominating the room were packing boxes arranged in neat stacks, sealed with brown tape.

He caught Fiona curiously eyeing them. "This is only a temporary arrangement. I'm expanding, about to move into proper commercial premises, but I'm just ironing out one or two issues. Until then, my front room's doubling as my practice."

Fiona stared at the glossy books on the table. The titles on their spines had a distinctly Spanish flavour — *Seville*, *Granada*, *The Iberian Peninsula*. Then she turned her attention to the pictures on the walls. Lush, sweeping vistas of lakes and green mountains. "Is that the Lake District?"

"It is indeed," Ted replied. "My dad's from Cumbria, but my mum's Spanish."

"Oh, whereabouts in Spain?" Fiona asked.

"Cádiz in Andalucia."

"Oh, very nice," she gushed. "I mean, I've never been there. But it's a nice-sounding name, isn't it? Andalucia. Very poetic. Spanish is a very poetic language. I bet you get good poets from Andalucia, what with all those spectacular mountains and coastlines. Very inspirational . . ."

Fiona's nerves had started her talking and now she didn't know how to stop. Ted seemed to realise her predicament, politely stepping into the conversation. "Yes, it is. When I was young, we'd go back there every summer for our holidays. It was wonderful. Please, do take a seat."

Fiona perched on the sofa while Ted sat in one of the easy chairs, immediately crossing his legs. "So, I gather from your email you wish to ask me about Colin. Such a terrible tragedy."

"You must have been shocked," Fiona said.

"I was, especially as he was doing so well with his therapy. We hadn't had a session for over two months. He was in a good place, last time I saw him. I still can't believe he's gone."

"So your last session was over two months ago, you say?" Fiona asked.

Ted pulled out his phone and flicked at its screen. "Gosh, it was three months since our last session."

"What did you talk about?" Fiona asked.

Ted hesitated, sighed. "I'm guessing you're aware of client confidentiality in my line of work."

Fiona nodded.

"Why do you wish to know about Colin?" he asked.

Fiona took a deep breath. Better to be straight with him. "I'm investigating his death. Looking into the possibility it wasn't an accident."

"Not an accident? But he hit his head while he was swimming. I read about it in the paper."

Fiona attempted to be as delicate as possible. "Yes, it's just a possibility at the moment. I'm just gathering information to see if there's any support for an, er, alternative theory. Building a picture of his life before he died."

Ted sat up. "But if the coroner was satisfied that he died by misadventure, surely that's all there is to it?"

"And if I find no evidence to the contrary, then that verdict won't be challenged."

"But what would be the alternative if his death wasn't an accident?" Ted gulped hard, possibly knowing the answer before he'd asked the question.

"That it was murder."

His charming exterior slipped away. "M-Murder? Are you sure?"

"No," Fiona replied quietly. "That's what I need to find out."

Hands shaking, Ted reached out and poured himself a glass of water. He took a nervous sip.

"Are you okay, Ted?" Fiona asked.

"Sorry. Just a bit shocked, that's all. Losing a client is hard enough but to hear he might've been murdered — well, I'm going to need some therapy myself."

The guy looked as if he needed a hug, though Fiona didn't think that would be appropriate. "So sorry to spring this on you. But nothing's certain yet."

"What evidence do you have so far?" he asked.

"Well," Fiona replied, "after questioning some of his fellow wild swimmers, they claimed that Colin would've never have swum alone. I understand you recommended wild swimming to him."

Ted was reluctant to answer. Client confidentiality probably preventing him. Fiona gave him a verbal nudge. "It would really help to know just a bit about why he came to you."

Ted downed his glass of water and put it back on the tray. "I shouldn't really, but if there's any possibility he may have been murdered, I'd like to help. I can only give you broad strokes though."

"Broad strokes will help us paint a picture." The image of Tony Hart popped into her head, unbidden. A recollection of the beloved children's TV artist painting the outline of an elephant in a car park with one of those things that workmen used to draw lines on the road. Though nostalgic and comforting, it wasn't very helpful. She pushed it out of her mind.

After a beat, Ted collected his thoughts enough for a response. "Okay, I will tell you this much. Colin was having trouble adjusting to retirement. It's not uncommon in people of his age. In fact, it's extremely prevalent with retirees. People go from having structure to their lives and being needed, relied upon and valued, to feeling unwanted, a spare part with too much time on their hands and too many hours in the day to think about it."

Suddenly, Fiona had immense sympathy for Colin. This was precisely the same situation she'd found herself in when she'd given up work. It had left an uncomfortable hole in her life, which the *It* had inevitably filled. The main reason she'd volunteered at Dogs Need Nice Homes was to give her back some purpose in life. It had also given her two of the fondest friendships she'd ever had.

Ted continued. "He felt anxious, so we tried a few different therapies, talking about his feelings, getting him to open up. Nothing really worked, and I soon realised, being an ex-sports teacher, Colin was an active person and needed new challenges and a place to be each day, a reason to get up every morning. He was single, a bit awkward. Not great social skills. Had no friends or family. His fellow teachers had given him his daily fix of company in the staff room. Of course, that all stopped when he retired. It was clear he needed friends and something to keep his anxiety at bay. So, I suggested a few activities, one of which was to try the local wild swimming club. The cold water would help with his anxiety and give him a place to go every morning, and a ready-made friendship group. It worked like a charm. But I think the biggest surprise was the camaraderie. He'd never had a social life outside of work. The nature of our sessions changed. Instead of talking about his issues, he would talk about his fellow swimmers and how they'd meet up in the evenings for bowling and pub quizzes, always with a smile on his face."

"How did that feel for you?" Fiona asked.

Ted paused, a contented smile warming his face. "I always get a thrill when I've helped someone. That's why I do this, but I've never seen such a big improvement in someone. He'd completely changed from the defeated man who'd first walked into my practice. Now he held his head high. He'd got his confidence back. Our sessions grew fewer and further apart, until, like I said, they stopped altogether."

Fiona wondered how to broach the next topic, seeing as the mood had become so positive. "Talking about getting his confidence back, some of the wild swimmers have shared that Colin could be a little, er, overbearing at times."

Ted recoiled at this suggestion. "I never experienced anything like that. But then he came to me for help. He was always very humble and grateful."

"Did he ever talk about anyone in the club he didn't get along with?" Fiona asked. "Any conflict, altercations?"

Ted didn't answer. Eventually, he shook his head. "I'm sorry, but I think that's getting a little specific. Broad strokes, if you remember."

Fiona ignored the warning. "So there was someone he didn't get along with."

"I'd rather not say."

"I understand," Fiona replied. "You're in a difficult situation. But we are talking about a possible murder here. And this person might be a potential suspect. It would be really helpful if you could spare any crumbs from the table."

Ted frowned. "I think that would be irresponsible and unethical. What if this person is innocent and gets blamed for his death?"

Fiona attempted to allay his fears. "Well, of course, they'd be investigated thoroughly before any conclusions were made."

Ted steepled his fingers, contemplatively. "I tell you what, if you come to me with more evidence that Colin's death wasn't an accident, I might be more inclined to let the name slip."

"That will be very helpful," Fiona said.

Ted got to his feet to show Fiona out. "I'm so sorry I can't be of any more assistance in that regard. But if there's anything else you need to ask me, I'll help if I can."

"Okay, thank you for your time," Fiona replied.

She regrouped with Daisy and Partial Sue in the car outside, immediately relaying everything the therapist had uttered.

"You should've pushed him for a name," Partial Sue grumbled. "Although, to be honest, I'm surprised he told you anything. I thought confidentiality was a cast-iron seal with these healthcare types."

"It is, usually. I think I got lucky there," Fiona replied.

"I don't know," Daisy said. "Poor fellow sounded shocked. I think he just wanted to help find Colin's killer. I mean, if he even has one."

Fiona agreed. "Yeah, I think you're right, Dais. Pity he couldn't give us a name though."

"My money's on this Will chap. Has to be. Colin was muscling in on his status as sheriff of the Southbourne Wild Things, and Will wanted him out of the way."

"I'm trying not to make any snap judgements just yet. We need more evidence. Both for ourselves and so we can press Ted for a name." Fiona couldn't see Will as a murderer, but she had to keep an open mind. He had charisma, which had greased the way for murderers since time immemorial. But also, Colin's lack of charm meant it was quite possible he'd wound someone up who'd not yet emerged as a suspect.

Time would tell, she was sure of it. That was the thing about groups of people, whether they were co-workers or wild swimmers. You could always rely on them to gossip. Someone would know something. She just had to keep plugging away.

CHAPTER 13

Next morning, clad in her new changing robe and with her booties already on her feet, Fiona marched towards the beach, damp, early-morning air filling her lungs. She'd had the best night's sleep she'd had in a long time, deep, contented and unbroken. Unlike yesterday, Fiona had woken up with the alarm, not two hours before it. She felt infinitely more confident for her second wild swim, especially as she had double-checked that the most important item of equipment was safely stashed in her bag — the flask. Nothing gave you a boost like knowing you had a ready-made supply of tea on your person.

Making it to the bottom of the zigzag with plenty of time to spare, a small gaggle of swimmers huddled together in their changing robes, all happy chatter and bright smiles, brothers and sisters united by the cold. Fiona scanned their faces, seeking out Ahmed and Rani, but they weren't among them, and neither was Beth.

Today she needed to make some serious headway, hence her early arrival. As she approached, the gregarious group opened up to make space for her, everyone greeting her with a hearty, "Morning!" Though she hadn't spoken to any of these people before, they were keen to include her in their small talk about the weather, the temperature and the state of the sea: cold, grey and flat.

"How was your first dip?" one lady asked.

"I've never been so cold in my life." Fiona chuckled. There were sympathetic smiles and knowing nods. "But it was exhilarating. So I'm back for more."

"That's what we like to hear," another man said cheerfully.

As more people arrived, the group splintered into smaller clusters and Fiona had the chance to broach the subject of Colin with a few of them. They were happy to indulge her, but were initially reluctant to speak ill of the dead. However, after some prompting, they opened up about his personality.

"Bit of a know-all."

"Liked the sound of his own voice."

"Rubbed everyone up the wrong way."

"Had a bit of a superiority complex."

Fiona's assumption about people wanting to gossip had been correct. But that's all it was — gossip and griping. While consistent, their responses lacked any detail or depth. No one had any information about who the murderer could be, and there was no grievance they knew about other than Colin's rivalry with Will, which they were quick to point out was all one-sided. However, it still cemented Will as top suspect, but Fiona hadn't changed her mind about him being an odd fit as murderer. Would anyone go to such lengths because someone had coveted their spot in an amateur wild swimming club? It seemed ridiculously trivial. But then, people had murdered for a lot less, and who knew what was going on in Will's head? Behind his charming, unflappable persona might be a raging egotistical narcissist who had to be top dog at all costs. Before she headed down that road, though, she needed more evidence.

With one mind, as if a subconscious signal had been sounded, everyone began the ritual of shedding their changing robes and windmilling their arms to warm them up, ready for the plunge. She desperately glanced around for her two cold-water companions, but Ahmed and Rani were nowhere to be seen. She checked her phone and had a missed message from them. They couldn't make it to the beach this morning and apologised. Fiona began getting cold feet about her second wild swim, despite her new booties.

Ever the compassionate and conscientious leader, Will bounded up to her. He was wearing a different-coloured but equally skimpy pair of Speedos as the ones he wore yesterday. "You okay, Fiona? Do you need a swim partner? Rani and Ahmed not here?"

"Their car wouldn't start."

"Oh, that's a shame. If I'd known, someone could've given them a lift. Lots of people share cars to the beach."

"Did Colin ever share a lift?" Fiona asked.

"Gosh, no. He was a bit OCD like that. Always drove his car down here on his own."

Fiona seized the opportunity to put Will on the spot. "Can I ask you about your relationship with Colin?"

"Of course. What would you like to know?"

"I've been hearing that you and Colin had a bit of a rivalry."

He smiled. "Ah, I was wondering when that would come up."

She knew she'd have to rattle him to break through that slick exterior, so she prepared a blunt instrument of a question. "You didn't kill him, did you?"

To his credit, Will didn't take offence and remained calm. "I can see how it would look that way. But no. Ask anyone here and they'll tell you. I really wasn't bothered by him. I'm not here to be the best. But I think Colin was. He saw everything as a competition. Did that annoy me? Not really. Wild swimming's a great leveller and a pacifier. You can't really be annoyed about anything when you're in cold water. That's why we all do it."

Fiona partially agreed with his statement. "Yes, although Colin wasn't pacified by the cold water. He still wanted to beat you swimming out to the buoy."

"I was swimming out to the buoy long before Colin joined us. I've always swum like that. I used to do it in a pool every day. Now I do it in the sea. But Colin saw it as a challenge to try and beat me. Truth is, I wouldn't have been upset if he did. My racing days are behind me. But, yes, I think it did annoy him that I was faster than he was."

"You're seen as the leader of this group. What about Colin muscling in on that role?"

"Again, it's the same thing. I wasn't bothered. There's really nothing to muscle in on. We're just a bunch of people who wild swim every day. There's no leader. No structure. But I used to be a manager in the NHS. I can't help running around checking everyone's all right. It's in my nature. I think Colin misinterpreted it as me electing myself as the official leader. Saw it as another challenge."

"Do you know anyone in this group who wanted to kill Colin?" Fiona asked. If he was the killer, then this was the perfect opportunity to point the finger at someone else, but he didn't.

"I'd say you're looking in the wrong place. Like I said, cold water's a great pacifier. Colin may have irritated people before they got in, but any bad feeling was usually washed away afterwards."

His answers were smart but possibly a bit too well considered. Fiona wondered if he'd been through all possible angles, pondering the best way to respond so he could sound as convincing as possible.

"Do you want to know my take on his death?" he asked out of the blue.

Fiona nodded.

Will inhaled deeply. "No one here believes Colin would have swum alone, which is why they suspect foul play. Except me. I haven't been vocal about this because I know I'm in the minority. But I have a different theory: I believe he was regularly swimming alone, outside of the club meetings, getting in extra training. Secret solo sessions just so he could beat me out to the buoy. He didn't want anyone to know about it.

Probably because it would appear petty, childish. I think he overdid it on one occasion. Trained too hard or got too cold, or both. Got into trouble and banged his head. No foul play, just Occam's razor — the simplest explanation is usually the right one."

"That's an interesting theory," Fiona replied. Entirely plausible, it was indeed a perfect example of Occam's razor. However, Fiona was underplaying her response on purpose. She didn't want to appear too keen to let her number-one suspect off the hook. Besides, Occam's razor, though logical, was never a guarantee of truth. Crimes had an annoying habit of being immensely convoluted. Mostly on purpose, because complexity made great camouflage. For now, Will's name remained at the top of the suspects list, albeit written in pencil.

CHAPTER 14

Fiona waited for Will to select her a partner for that morning's cold-water swim. He pivoted on the sand searching out possible companions. There weren't that many options left to choose from. While they'd been deep in discussion about Colin, the rest of the club had begun the slow, excruciating descent into the frigid water, apart from one chap in his early fifties. About to disrobe, he had a thick mop of greying hair and a skeletal frame, on which hung a huge pair of tentlike swimming shorts secured by tightly pulled drawstrings almost garrotting his waist.

"George! George!" Will called out.

A bewildered George swung his gaze around until he found Will. He collected his things, which included a small yellow bodyboard, and trotted over. "Wotcha." He had a chirpy London accent and small glinting eyes. "Everything all right?"

Will introduced them. "George, I'd like you to meet Fiona. It's her second go at wild swimming. I was wondering if you would be kind enough to accompany her today."

"It would be my pleasure." George gave a gappy smile.

"That's very kind of you," Fiona replied.

Will adjusted the digital sports watch on his wrist. "I'll leave you to it." Wading into the water, he flung himself forward in a flat racing dive and took off like a power boat on full throttle.

"I dunno where he gets his energy from," George remarked.

"Yes, I wouldn't mind some of that." Fiona nodded to George's bodyboard as they stripped off. "Planning on catching some waves?" The sea was as flat as polished steel.

"Nah," he replied. "Got a frozen shoulder but it's not going to stop me swimming. I just do the kicking instead. But don't worry, I'll stay with you. Circle round you, if that's all right. Get my exercise in."

"Yes, indeed. I didn't actually swim yesterday. Just got my shoulders under, so I might try a bit of breaststroke today."

George gave her a reassuring smile. "Take your time, Fiona. There's no rush."

"Ready when you are."

Her second cold-water plunge wasn't any easier. At least she avoided the spike of pain in her feet thanks to her new watertight booties. However, once the water sloshed over her calves, the pain sledgehammered into her legs from every direction. She bit her lip to stop her breathing running out of control. Persevering, she pushed forward, the water encircling her midriff, forcing an almighty gasp. Shuddering, her ribcage tightened as if it had been cinched by the tightest whalebone corset.

Beside her, George wasn't faring any better. He panted hard and would have steamed up an entire patio door if he'd been facing one. Clutching his bodyboard in front of him, he kicked his legs, considerately keeping them below the surface so he didn't splash Fiona. He gasped again. "Good here, innit?"

Fiona laughed through the pain, alleviating the discomfort, but not much. "Remind me why we're doing this."

George gave a wheezy chuckle. "Cos we're all suckers for punishment."

"I'm going to try a bit of breaststroke." Fiona scooped her arms from her front to her sides and frog-legged her lower limbs, surprised that they hadn't seized up in the cold. The movement didn't exactly generate any warmth for her heat-starved body but felt better than just standing up to her neck, letting the cold assault her. "Oh, this isn't too bad."

"You're doing well," George encouraged her, cruising alongside, his head bobbing as he kicked. "'Ere, you're looking into Colin's death, ain'tcha?"

"I-I am," Fiona managed to reply between breaths.

George was brutally frank. "I didn't like the guy and tried to avoid him. I know he helped people and that, but he was an uptight so-and-so. You know, he asked me if I had insurance for this." He nodded towards his bodyboard. "I thought he was joking, so I laughed and said no, but it's fully taxed and MOT'd."

"And what did he say to that?"

"He started wittering on about any watercraft that goes in waves needs insurance. In the end I just swam away from him. Might have kicked my legs a bit hard and accidentally splashed him, if you know what I mean." George winked. He then continued listing all the things that irritated him about Colin, which were many.

Fiona didn't reply.

"You okay, Fiona?"

Her teeth were chattering. "I-I think I need to go in."

"Yes, sorry. I was going off on one. You go and get warm. I'll just do a little more, then join you."

Fiona swam a few short strokes to the shoreline, then staggered up the beach. Feet sluggish, the cold held on to her, possessed her as if wanting to drag her back down into the sea. This was the worst part, and she could feel her core temperature plummeting rapidly. She went straight for her changing robe and threw it on, the wonderful embrace of its fleecy lining soaking up the cold and wet. Next, she peeled off her gloves, thankful that her hands weren't too numb for the most important task of all — unscrewing the lid of her flask. Pouring herself a steaming hot cuppa, she took a greedy draught, wincing but not worrying that it burned her mouth and throat as it went down. Warmth radiated outwards from her belly, and she sighed blissfully. A beguiling sensation, heat slowly reasserted itself over her icy body, as if Fiona were being brought back to life.

George wobbled his way up the beach, a little unsteady over the shingle. Without a care, he dropped his bodyboard on the sand and snatched up his changing robe, nearly disappearing beneath its voluminous size. "These things are great, ain't they? Don't think I could do this without them."

"I did yesterday on my first swim."

"Yeah, same here. You do it once, then you never swim without one, eh?"

"Where did you get yours from, the surf shop?" Fiona asked.

"Nah, no one ever shops there."

"Why's that?"

"Too expensive. Everyone at the club gets their stuff online."

Fiona felt sorry for Roger at Ocean Masters. No wonder he was struggling, like all retailers who were constantly being bypassed for cheaper internet alternatives. But at least she could tick one thing off her list. There was no connection between the Southbourne Wild Things and the local surf shop.

George continued. "There's a site called Dippy Things dot something or other. Supplies everything you need for wild swimming at half the price. Changing robes, boots, gloves, dry bags, even flasks."

Embarrassed, Fiona wondered if this was a hint. "Oh, I'm sorry. Would you like some tea? I have a spare cup."

"Nah, you're all right. I've got me own. I'm very fussy about me tea. Mine makes builder's tea look anaemic, and you can stand a spoon up in it I add so much sugar."

Fiona's attention was suddenly caught by a striking fifty-something blonde woman striding out of the sea in a sparkling gold swimsuit clinging to her curvaceous body. She resembled a Bond girl, and as far as Fiona could tell she was the only one who'd been swimming with a full face of make-up.

"That's Hayley," George muttered. "Now, if you're looking for leads in your investigation, that's a good place to start."

"How so?"

"Colin had the hots for her. Was smitten, I'd say. He was always trying to chat her up."

"And how did that go down?"

"You heard of them monkeys trying to type Shakespeare? Well, they'd do a better job than Colin with his chat-up lines. It was painful to witness. But even if he did have the banter and looked like Brad Pitt, it wouldn't have made any difference."

"Why's that?"

George nodded towards the athletic figure of Will emerging from the sea like some scantily clad Poseidon. "She's only got eyes for him, that one."

Just as George had predicted, Hayley's gaze tracked his every move across the sand, her lustful eyes not blinking once.

"I think that's the real reason Colin was jealous of Will," George explained. "Not because he wanted to be leader or anything. But because Hayley fancied Will. To make matters worse, he's not interested in her. He's happily married."

"Is Will's wife here?"

"Gosh, no. You wouldn't catch her in the sea. Not for love nor money. She volunteers at the hospital. Nice lady, she is. The pair of them are devoted to each other. But that's not stopping Hayley from trying. She shows up every once in a while to try to tempt him, but Will never has any of it. Then we won't see her for months until she tries again. That's why we call her 'Hayley's Comet'."

Fiona got a hit of adrenalin to add to the euphoria of the heat returning to her body. Now she was getting somewhere. Nothing spelled trouble or had the potential for murder like a good old-fashioned love triangle, especially a lopsided one. A scalene love triangle, no less.

In her mind, Fiona went over Will's pencilled-in name with a biro.

CHAPTER 15

On her way home, Fiona got a text from Beth apologising for not showing up at the morning swim again. Fiona texted back, asking if everything was okay. She replied with a thumbs-up emoji, leading Fiona to wonder if everything was truly all right. The founder of Southbourne Wild Things hadn't attended a single swim since this investigation had started. Was that significant or was it Fiona's imagination running away with her, reading too much into it, conjuring up sinister plots where there weren't any? Analysing the situation objectively, Beth had missed only two swims. Hardly worth worrying about.

Her phoned pinged again. It was Beth, messaging to invite her to a pub quiz tonight in Southbourne with the rest of the club. Fiona could resist anything except a pub quiz. She texted back to say she'd be there. Beth replied, saying they could form a team. Fiona said that would be a great idea.

Simon Le Bon's tail whipped back and forth the second Fiona opened her front door, until he sniffed the aroma of sea air on her and was not happy that he'd missed out on a trip to the beach. Registering his displeasure, he took himself off to his bed, turning his back to Fiona. All was forgiven, though, once she'd changed into her work clothes and rattled his lead.

The pair headed to the shop, arriving late again. Daisy and Sue were already in, their attention focused on the table, which, for some inexplicable reason, was strewn with a variety of crackers and their opened packets. Daisy nibbled the edge of one like a hamster. Simon Le Bon wasted no time circling below to seek out any stray crumbs.

"Morning," Fiona said. "It's a bit early for crackers."

"I need a new cracker for lunch," Daisy replied. "I normally have cream crackers, but I want something different. So I'm doing a bit of a taste test."

Partial Sue held up a cylindrical navy-blue packet. "You should try my favourite next — a water biscuit."

Before she had mentioned anything, Fiona would have bet her life that Partial Sue's favourite would have been a water biscuit. Perfectly reflecting her as a person, they were thin and straightforward, and a bit on the hard side. But also honest and dependable.

Partial Sue ripped open the packet and offered one to Daisy. "Try one, Dais. I am partial to water biscuits because they don't upstage the topping. They're the perfect blank canvas."

Daisy took a nibble. "Urgh, more like bland canvas. They don't taste of anything. Why are they called water biscuits? That's drier than the lint trap in my tumble dryer."

Fiona supplied the answer. "They were designed to last on long sea voyages. Made with water rather than milk or butter so they wouldn't go off. Hence the name water biscuit. The Navy used to call them hardtack or ship's biscuits."

"Hardtack sounds about right," Daisy said. "What's your favourite cracker, Fiona?"

Fiona pointed to a red packet on the table. "I don't think you can beat a Ryvita. Tasty and very healthy."

Partial Sue wrinkled her nose. "Talk about dry. Ryvitas are like house dust that's been compressed into a rectangle."

Daisy slid one out of its packet and held up its pitted texture for close scrutiny. "Looks like the surface of the moon."

"See, I told you," Partial Sue remarked. "Moon's very dusty."

Daisy took a small bite. "Mm, I like these." She took another larger bite. "I think we have a winner."

Partial Sue continued to carry a torch for her favourite, waving the packet around. "You're making a mistake. Water biscuits never let you down."

"I'm good, thanks." Daisy continued to munch on the Ryvita, dropping crumbs everywhere, much to the delight of Simon Le Bon, who hoovered around her feet. "How did you get on down at the beach? Any more leads?"

"Yes, a big one. But first I need tea."

The crackers were moved aside to make space for the chipped brown teapot. The ladies gathered around the table to hear the latest, specifically the Colin–Will–Hayley love triangle.

"Unrequited love!" Partial Sue declared. "What bigger motivation is there for murder?"

"I adore a good love triangle," Daisy gushed. "*Pride and Prejudice*, *Twilight*, *Bridget Jones's Diary*. Except, in this instance, the love triangle doesn't work."

The other two ladies stared at her, keen to hear what Daisy had to say. Whether Georgian heroines or angsty vampires, she was an expert on three-sided affairs of the heart, both old and new, and they would default to her expertise on this one every day of the week.

"Why not?" Fiona asked.

"As you said, the triangle is lopsided. Actually, it's more of a love food chain than a triangle. Will is at the top. Hayley's next. She likes Will but doesn't like Colin below her. Colin's at the bottom because he likes Hayley but she doesn't like him. Hayley's spurned by Will and Colin is spurned by Hayley. However, Colin is the most spurned because no one in the food chain wants him. But if that's the case, surely Colin would be the one murdering Will, not the other way around. He'd want Will out of the way to get to Hayley, if that makes sense."

Partial Sue had a different take on the love triangle–slash–food chain. "It's more likely Hayley's the murderer. She killed Colin because he was cramping her style, getting in the way of her designs on Will."

"Trouble is," Fiona pointed out, "as I said before, Will's not interested. Shuns all her advances. He totally ignored her at the beach this morning. How would it benefit Hayley's predicament if Colin was out of the picture?"

"People have a habit of punching down," Partial Sue replied. "Blaming the person below them for their misfortune. Maybe Hayley's the same. She looked down on Colin. Vented her frustration on him, blaming him for the lack of progress with Will."

"Unless Colin tried to murder Will," Daisy said. "And Will turned the tables. Ended up killing him in self-defence. Hit him on the head and made it look like he'd drowned."

"Also very possible," Fiona replied. "I think I need to question Hayley. Get her side of things. Although she can be quite elusive. Apparently, she only shows up once in a blue moon to entice Will. Never works though. Always the same outcome. Will ignores her."

"Definition of insanity, according to Einstein," Partial Sue pointed out. "Doing the same thing and expecting a different result."

"Yes, but that's love for you. They say it's a form of insanity." Daisy glanced at her watch and jumped. "Oh, I nearly forgot. I have an expert witness coming in."

"An expert witness? Who's that?" Fiona asked.

"My neighbour Ralph. He's a surfer. He's very enthusiastic. Always telling me I should have a go at it. I'd love to but it'd have to be somewhere warm with clear blue water, cocktails at sunset and hula dancing . . ." Daisy's voice trailed off as her eyes glazed over at the thought of her dream holiday.

Fiona and Partial Sue exchange puzzled looks.

"Er, we're not looking into the death of a surfer," Partial Sue said. "Colin was a wild swimmer."

"Yes, I know. But Ralph said he has some information for us."

"What sort of information?" Fiona asked.

"Oh, I didn't think to ask. He said he'll pop by on his way to work."

Ten minutes later, a battered and noisy VW Transporter van halted outside the shop, held together by a plethora of bright surf stickers with no discernible pattern or logic, some of them upside down. Ralph sprang out of the cab onto the pavement looking every inch the archetypal surfer. His head was topped with thick, dry, sun-bleached hair that reached the tops of his broad shoulders. Wireless headphones were clamped to his ears. He jigged towards the shop, his body buzzing with energy, clearly high on life.

As he entered, he waved at Daisy, then lowered his headphones. "Hi, Daisy. You all right?"

"I'm fine, Ralph. Thanks for coming in." She introduced him to Fiona and Partial Sue.

He beamed a bright white smile at them, then his attention was off elsewhere, his eyes flitting in every direction. A puppy dog of a lad to whom everything was exciting. "Cool shop. Old-school wood panelling, like a gentlemen's club. Sick."

Simon Le Bon trotted out of his bed and headed straight for Ralph, sensing a playful, kindred spirit. "Hey, little fella." Ralph immediately dropped to all fours, his face level with Simon's. He let Fiona's dog drench his face with licks until Simon Le Bon suddenly rolled over on his back submissively. Ralph nuzzled his face in the dog's fur then came up for air. "Ha, he smells of popcorn! I love it!" He suddenly straightened up, his short attention immediately grabbed by a knitted Peruvian chullo hat on display. "Hey, I've been looking for one of these." He tried it on for size and checked himself in the mirror. "Kind of works." Then something else took his fancy, a long tweed overcoat. He pulled it off the hanger and slipped it on.

This might take some time, Fiona thought, *unless it's cut short.* "Ralph, Daisy tells us you have some information."

"Oh yeah, for sure, for sure." He slotted himself into a chair at the table.

"Would you like some tea?" Daisy asked.

"Nah, I'm good. I don't touch caffeine. Can you imagine if I did?"

Fiona could. He'd be spinning around like a whirling dervish on a waltzer.

Ralph zeroed in on Daisy's research project. "But I wouldn't mind a cracker or three. I'm starving. I get hungry when I'm nervous." He ignored the water biscuits and went straight for the Ryvitas.

Fiona wondered why someone as uninhibited as Ralph would be nervous around three older ladies who volunteered in a charity shop. She was about to press him for information when Partial Sue hijacked the conversation.

"What do you think of the movie *Point Break*?"

"*Point Break*?" Ralph replied with a mouthful of cracker. "I've not seen it."

Partial Sue harrumphed, muttered something derogatory about millennials, possibly still annoyed he'd rejected her water biscuits, then said, "It's only the greatest surf–crime crossover movie ever."

As far as Fiona knew it was the only surf–crime crossover movie.

Daisy googled it. "The one that came out in 2015?"

"No!" Partial Sue became impatient. "The proper one. The original with Patrick Swayze and Keanu Reeves. Came out in the early nineties."

"Oh, I like Keanu Reeves," Ralph said. "*John Wick* is awesome."

Fiona brought the conversation back on track. "So, Ralph. Tell us about this information you have."

"Oh, sure. So Daisy mentioned you're looking into the death of that wild swimmer dude, and you need clues, right?

Okay, I gotta clue for you." He paused dramatically. "Surfers and wild swimmers don't get along."

Fiona waited for the rest of the revelation to come, but judging by Ralph's expectant expression, that's all there was.

She responded slowly and politely, "Okay. Could you expand on that a little?"

"Yeah, so I don't mind wild swimmers. But when the surf's up, they have to mix with surfers in the waves, and they don't know what they're doing. They get in the way. I've never had a problem with them, but I've heard a few surfers who have. So, I'm thinking what if this Colin gets into a barney with a surfer. They have words with each other. Surfer gets all Jason Statham. Then boom!" Ralph punched the air. "Colin's face down in the water. Surfer's all like, 'Oh man, I just killed a dude.' Gets scared and runs away."

Partial Sue had a glint in her eye. "That narrative would certainly fit Colin's personality."

"How do you mean?" Ralph asked.

"Colin had a reputation for being bossy," she replied.

Ralph took a deep, pensive breath. "Oh, wow! So it could've gone down just like I said."

"Tell me," Fiona asked. "Where's the best place to surf around here?"

"Bournemouth Pier. That's where I surf."

"What about at Southbourne?" Daisy asked.

"A few surfers like the stone groyne at the bottom of the zigzag."

"Where the wild swimmers go?" Fiona asked.

"That's right," Ralph said.

Fiona continued. "Colin had an injury on the back of his head. If he was swimming near a groyne, and got in the way of a surfer, and that's where the barney happened, as you put it . . ."

Ralph gasped, grabbed the sides of his face dramatically. "No way! Someone shoved him. He fell back and clocked his head! Oh man! I think I just solved a murder. That's intense!"

Fiona wasn't a big fan of wry smiles, but she couldn't help one tickling the corner of her mouth. Ralph hadn't exactly solved the murder, but he had provided them with a very plausible version of Colin's death, and it didn't involve Will, Hayley or any love triangles, lopsided or otherwise.

CHAPTER 16

Ralph wouldn't sit still. In the end, the excitement got too much for him and he paced around the table, still clad in his newly acquired chullo hat and overcoat, muttering the facts to himself like a new-age Sherlock Homes. Halting his gabbling, he turned to the ladies. "Oh man. I can see why you guys do this. Solving a murder. It's like my brain can't hold it all in."

While not wishing to dampen his spirits, Fiona thought it prudent to manage his expectations. "We still don't know for sure. It's just a theory at the moment."

"It's a very good theory, mind," Partial Sue was quick to add.

"Yes, indeed. But for all we know Colin could've just slipped and hit his head. So we need evidence to support the theory that a surfer shoved Colin backwards onto the rocks after they had an argument. And then identify that surfer."

Ralph became a volcano of enthusiasm. "If you want me, I'm there for you. Hundred per cent. I can be your guy on the inside. Your undercover FBI agent. Sniffing out the perp."

"Like Keanu Reeves in *Point Break*," Partial Sue remarked.

"Seriously?" Ralph replied. "Is that what happens in *Point Break*?"

"Yep, he's an FBI agent who infiltrates a group of surfers who he suspects of robbing banks. It's a classic crime thriller."

Pogoing about, Ralph couldn't contain his energy, "Oh man! I am so watching that tonight. Get me some tips. I know I'd be good undercover."

"Well, technically, you wouldn't be undercover," Partial Sue pointed out. "As you're already a surfer."

"True but it's all about being subtle, yeah? Keeping a low profile."

Fiona didn't doubt Ralph's commitment, but wondered if subtlety or keeping a low profile were in his wheelhouse. However, she could imagine local surfers were a tight-knit community. If someone knew something, it'd be more likely they'd let it slip to one of their own rather than three retirees who worked in a charity shop.

Fiona was about to formally enlist Ralph's help when Daisy, who'd been strangely quiet amid all the excitement, raised her head. "Can I just check something, Ralph?"

"Sure," he replied.

Daisy thumbed the calendar on her phone. "So, Colin was last seen alive on Friday the seventh of January, then he shows up dead a week later on the fifteenth, which would mean this supposed barney with the surfer happened at some point in between."

Ralph stopped jigging, thought hard. "Yeah, s'pose so."

Partial Sue spotted where Daisy was going with this. "So there would have to be surf that weekend or in the week. You can't have surfers without surf."

Daisy nodded in agreement. "So my question is, were there any waves during that time?"

All eyes turned on Ralph. The expert witness in these matters, his tanned face turned a shade of puce. "Er, the old memory banks need a reboot."

"It wasn't that long ago," Partial Sue remarked, not exactly helping him.

Ralph swallowed hard, then gave a nervous laugh. "You know, I can never remember what I've done from one week to the next. I will remember eventually. It's in there somewhere."

"Take your time," Fiona said.

Suddenly he clicked his fingers. "Surf forecast websites record past conditions. Got no idea why, unless you wanna torture yourself by checking what waves you've missed."

Daisy was on it, checking in a flash. She whizzed through a site and found the answer. "Conditions for Southbourne were as follows . . . Oh!"

"What's the matter?" Fiona asked.

Daisy continued. "Northerly offshore breezes. Overcast skies. Temperature: two degrees. Clean conditions. Wave size: zero to half a foot. I can't imagine anyone would be out there surfing in those conditions."

Ralph became crestfallen. "No. I mean, the cold's not a problem. Surfers, like wild swimmers, go out in any temperature, but you couldn't even get a log going in waves that tiny."

"A log?" Partial Sue asked.

"A longboard. Massive nine-foot board. Like surfing a bus. They catch everything. Well, except zero to half-a-foot waves. Okay, stand down, ladies. False alarm." Ralph hung the chullo hat back on the display and shrugged off the overcoat, his shoulders immediately slumping as his dream of starring in Southbourne's version of *Point Break* died just as quickly as it had come to life. "I thought I had something there."

"Hey," Fiona said. "Don't worry. All information is welcome. We have to investigate every avenue."

"Yeah," Partial Sue agreed. "Anything you've got, no matter how insignificant, please run it past us. It's all useful."

"Helps to build a picture," Daisy added. "None of it goes to waste."

Ralph brightened a little. "Oh, okay. Yeah, for sure, I'll ask around and pop by if I find anything." He gave Simon Le Bon a last ruffle of his fur, then left the shop.

Fiona felt just as disappointed as Ralph. They were back to lopsided love triangles and food chains. Or were they?

"You know, something's just occurred to me," Partial Sue piped up. "I've just thought of a different angle on this whole thing."

CHAPTER 17

"We've made a big assumption about timings," Partial Sue declared.

"I don't understand," Fiona confessed.

"We're assuming Colin went down for a swim on the week of his death, possibly to get his extra training in, then crossed swords with a surfer. Passions ran high. The surfer shoved him, and we know the rest."

"But there was barely a wave to be had that week," Daisy pointed out.

"Yes, but Colin was a regular down there, swimming with his club in the morning. He wants to beat Will and impress Hayley, so he goes back there later in the day, when the club's not around to get in extra training. He likes having structure in his life, so we can assume his lone swimming sessions are at the same time, week in, week out. Plenty of time for him to have run-ins with surfers, every time the waves are up. One surfer in particular gets annoyed at him and decides to do something. He knows Colin's always there at the same time of day, training alone. Surfer picks a day when there's hardly any waves, just in case he needs an alibi. Goes down there, does the deed and makes it look like an accident."

"So our surfer planned it. A premeditated murder."

Partial Sue nodded. "I think so."

Fiona got a little tingle, as she always did when a theory sounded promising. "And if this surfer waited until the end of Colin's lone swim, he'd be cold and exhausted. He wouldn't put up much of a fight."

"Even more likely," Partial Sue enthused.

"What about witnesses?" Daisy asked.

"That week the temperature was two degrees," Partial Sue replied. "With northerly breezes that's going to feel more like zero degrees or lower. Not many people are going to be on the beach in those conditions, except Colin getting in his extra cold-water swimming practice. This surfer picked his moment."

"What about those surf webcams, can't you wind them back to see past footage?" Fiona asked.

"I did think of that," Daisy replied. "But they only go back the past twenty-four hours and there are only a handful of places they have them. There isn't one covering Southbourne beach, so we're in the dark, I'm afraid."

Fiona smiled. "Well, the surfer-killer theory is definitely still on the table. But first I'd like to get a second opinion." She pulled out her phone, dialled a number, then put it on speakerphone. It was answered immediately.

"Hello, Ocean Masters surf shop. Roger speaking," he said cheerfully.

"Hi, Roger. It's Fiona. I bought the changing robe from you the other day."

"Oh hi, Fiona. Everything okay?" The tone of his voice dropped into a minor key, possibly worrying that she wanted a refund.

"I'm good, thanks. I just wanted to ask you something. Have you ever heard of surfers and wild swimmers not getting along. Getting into arguments with one another?"

"Why, has a surfer been nasty to you?"

"Gosh, no. I was just wondering if there was a rivalry."

"Not really. I've never encountered anything. It's more likely surfers will have arguments among themselves. That's the only time I've ever seen any hassle."

"Really?"

"Oh, yeah. Down here, there are arguments in the water all the time. What you have to understand is we don't get waves here that often, but when we do, everyone gets a bit desperate. There are too many surfers and not enough waves to go around. It's easy to get frustrated and for tempers to flare."

"And this never extends to wild swimmers?"

"Not really. I've never seen anything. You have to understand a swimmer, even an Olympic one, is way slower than a surfer on a wave. When you're surfing it looks like they're not moving. Even a half-decent surfer can slalom around them without much trouble."

"Okay, thank you, Roger. You've been very helpful."

"My pleasure. Oh, before you go. I'm giving ten per cent off everything to all locals, just got to flash some proof of their home address."

"That's good to know. Would you like me to tell the other wild swimmers?"

"Would you? That would be fantastic."

"No problem at all." Fiona thanked him and hung up.

"Well, this is getting more and more interesting," Partial Sue remarked. "Who'd have thought laid-back surfers would be arguing over waves?"

Partial Sue had another angle on things. "I know what Roger said about wild swimmers being too slow to get in the way of surfers, but I can imagine Colin getting in the way on purpose just to spite them, and on many occasions."

Fiona had to agree. "Yes, he's the exception that proves the rule, and we've seen how that ends. Except instead of a spur-of-the-moment incident, someone has had enough of him. Bided their time. Planned to get him while he was alone."

"That's what I think happened," Partial Sue added.

"I'll run this past the wild swimmers. Get their take on it," Fiona said. "See if anyone remembers Colin having disagreements with surfers. Although, I'd bet my life on it that he did. You know, I was swimming with a guy today called George, who uses a bodyboard because he's hurt his shoulder. Colin started picking on him, asking if he had insurance."

"I can believe that," Partial Sue replied. "Being so bullish, there's no way he wouldn't start something with a surfer."

"We should ask his therapist," Daisy suggested. "What's-his-face."

"Ted Maplin. He might refuse," Partial Sue warned.

"It's worth a try." Fiona pulled out her phone, dialled him and put it on speaker. "Hi, Ted. It's Fiona."

"Oh hi, Fiona. How's the investigation going? Have you found any evidence yet?"

"No, still working on it. Listen, I know you're probably going to say this is against client confidentiality, but did Colin ever mention anything about surfing?"

"Surfing? How do you mean?"

"Sorry, did he ever get into any arguments with surfers?"

"Oh, er, in what context?"

"While he was swimming?" Fiona asked.

The line went quiet while they waited for Ted's response. It never came.

"Sorry, Ted," Fiona apologised. "I know this is probably a breach of confidentiality."

Ted sighed. "Yes, it is, but it's fine on this occasion, because he never mentioned anything about surfing or surfers."

"Are you absolutely sure?"

"Positive. He would have told me, I'm sure. He offloaded everything to me.",

"Including the person he didn't get on with in the club?"

"Yes, that too. But like I said, come to me with hard evidence that a crime has been committed and I'll happily tell you. Until then, I have to protect identities. I'm sure you understand."

"Yes, of course." Fiona thanked him and hung up.

"Well, that was a dead end, then," Partial Sue said. "But we can all probably guess that the person Ted's talking about is Will."

"Yes, has to be," Fiona replied. "As for arguments with surfers, I can get a second opinion with the wild swimmers tonight. I'm meeting them for a pub quiz."

"Oh." Partial Sue's face dropped. "I was going to suggest we go to the pictures tonight. All that talk of *Point Break* has made me partial to see a movie."

Daisy perked up. "Oh yes, I haven't been to the pictures in ages. We can get a nice big tub of sweet popcorn to share."

"I prefer salted," Partial Sue said. "But I'll bring my own. I'm not paying cinema prices. They want an arm and a leg for something that probably cost them ten pence to make."

"What about you, Fiona?" Daisy asked. "Are you a sweet or salty popcorn person?"

"I like the one that's both salt and sweet," Fiona replied diplomatically.

"So, do you want to come with us?" Partial Sue pressed her again. "I mean, you'll probably see the wild swimmers tomorrow for your early-morning swim. You can ask them then."

"Sorry, I promised Beth I'd be in a team with her. Why don't you two come?" Fiona knew how partial Sue was to a pub quiz.

Daisy looked worried. "Er, we don't really know anyone."

"You know Beth," Fiona replied. "We could all be on the same team. Be a good opportunity to meet the others in the club. Put names to faces. Maybe ask them about the case in between answering questions."

Daisy shook her head. "I'm no good at pub quizzes, unless I can use my phone, but I think it's frowned upon."

"Doesn't matter, it's just a bit of fun. What about you, Sue? There's a cash prize."

Partial Sue was also having none of it. "No, I'm in the mood for a film tonight. What do you say, Daisy?"

"Yes, why not?"

This was odd behaviour for the pair of them, passing up the offer of a pub quiz. She couldn't understand why they were being so standoffish. Oh, well, each to their own.

CHAPTER 18

With a few minutes to spare before the quiz started, Fiona turned up outside the Countess of Strathmore pub, named after the aristocrat and local Southbourne resident of the late seventeen hundreds. The swinging pub sign showed not an image of the regal countess but instead a wide-eyed pug, sitting at a table, a napkin knotted around its wrinkled neck, hungrily gazing down at a joint of beef and two veg. The eccentric Countess had spent the last years of her life caring for a large number of dogs, who'd dine with her, seated around the table, noshing on cooked meals, much to the annoyance of the hungry locals.

Warmth swamped Fiona as soon she opened the door, the air thick with laughter, the chink of glasses and the fug of alcohol. A crucible of conviviality. Antique timber frames held up low ceilings, and around the red-brick walls were more surreal pictures in ornate frames of dogs feasting on banquets.

Scanning the pub, Fiona tried to pick out anyone she knew but couldn't see the wood for the trees. She had that overwhelming sensation she always had when confronted with a roomful of people already ensconced in a social gathering, as if she were the interloper meddling with their enjoyment.

She fought the urge to turn tail and stepped inside, dodging people heading to the bar as she sought out a friendly face, or even just a familiar one. Then she spotted them. A large complement of the Southbourne Wild Swimmers propping up the end of the bar, Will at the centre of the group, holding court with what appeared to be a pint of soda and lime in his hand, presumably staying off the booze so he could keep that athletic figure of his.

Fiona became aware of a hand waving nearby, attempting to attract her attention. She was happy to discover it belonged to Beth, who'd managed to snag a table. Rosy-cheeked and still wearing her parka, she beamed at Fiona. "Excuse me for being presumptuous. But I had you down as a G&T kind of gal." Beth nudged the drink towards her.

"Good guess." Fiona joined her. "Thank you. I'll get the next round in."

"Sorry, I haven't been down to the beach, but my car's not working at the moment."

"Is it being fixed?"

Beth shook her head. "My mechanic said it'd cost more than the car's worth, so it's just sitting on my driveway. Besides, I haven't got the money right now."

"Do you want me to lend you some?"

"Oh gosh, no. It'd just be throwing good money after bad. But thank you."

Fiona wondered why no one had offered to give Beth a lift to the beach, seeing as Will had mentioned that a lot of the wild swimmers shared the driving. "I could come and pick you up in the mornings."

"No, that's fine. It's only temporary until I get the money to replace it. Get something better, more reliable. I just feel bad because I've abandoned you. I hope they've been looking after you down there."

"Oh, yes. They certainly have. Will's made sure I always buddy up with someone when I go in. I'm really enjoying it, by the way. Very painful but I can see why you do it. I wouldn't have believed it if I hadn't tried it myself. Who'd have thought jumping in cold water every morning would be so addictive?"

Beth's smile grew warmer. "People don't get it until they've tried it. I'm so pleased you're enjoying it. There's nothing like the endorphin rush afterwards. Sets you up for the day."

Fiona desperately wanted to tell her how the early-morning swims had driven the *It* from her mind, but she never told anyone about her depression and didn't want to start now. However, she did feel like she owed Beth for providing her with an antidote for a very nasty problem. Fiona didn't need to tell her the whole story. She could gloss over the darker aspects. "You know, I need to thank you. I always get a bit down at this time of year, once Christmas is over and we're still in the depths of winter, but I've never felt better."

"Room for a small one?" George turned up with a pint of Guinness in his hand.

"George!" Beth gave him a hearty welcome. "Please join us."

"Right you are." He pulled up a low stool and scuffed it towards the table.

"George and I swam together today," Fiona informed Beth.

"Oh, wonderful," Beth replied.

"Yeah, Fiona's doing well," George said. "It was only her second go today and she was swimming."

Beth raised her eyebrows. "Gosh, you are doing well. Took me a week just to get my shoulders under."

"I'm a glutton for punishment," Fiona joked.

George took a gulp of beer. "'S'weird, innit? Something so painful can make you feel so good afterwards."

"Yep, really gets under your skin," Fiona said.

"I'll say." George laughed. "And right into your bones. Then I'll be blowed, once you've warmed up, you feel like doing it all over again the next day."

Ahmed and Rani appeared at the table, minus their matching woolly hats, holding pints of Coke in their hands.

"Hello, my friends," Ahmed said warmly. "Mind if we—"

"Join you for the pub quiz?" Rani completed his sentence.

"Pull up a pew. The pair of you have just raised the IQ of the table," George joked.

Beth slapped him playfully on his upper arm. George grabbed it dramatically, cried out in pain.

Beth became alarmed. "Oh my gosh! That wasn't your bad shoulder, was it?"

"Nah, it's the other one." George giggled. "I think we have enough for a team now."

"Shouldn't we all be in a group with the other wild swimmers?" Fiona asked.

"There's always too many of us," Beth replied. "So we divide up into smaller groups."

A microphone squealed and everyone's attention turned to the landlord behind the bar. "Pub quiz will start in two minutes, folks. Two minutes. Get yourselves into teams. Pens and paper are on the tables. And remember, no looking up the answer on mobile phones. I'm looking at you, Tuckton Twitchers — remember what happened last time?" Fiona had no idea what had befallen the anoraked quartet in the corner. Probably disqualified, and possibly frogmarched out by the landlord, judging by the way they all sank down in their chairs.

"What shall we call ourselves?" Ahmed asked.

"We need something watery sounding," Rani suggested.

"The Big Drips," George giggled.

"Speak for yourself," Beth chided.

"The Water Babies," Ahmed proposed.

George frowned. "Water Babies? Have you looked at us in the mirror?"

Fiona had an idea. "What about the Briney Brainiacs?"

"Ooh, I like that," Beth said. "It's clever." Everyone else agreed. Beth grabbed a pen and paper and wrote the team's name at the top. "Speaking of water, how are you getting on with the investigation?"

"Good, thank you," Fiona replied. They all leaned in, eager to hear. This was always the tricky part. How much to divulge, especially as most of it was conjecture and unsubstantiated theories. She certainly didn't want to begin pointing fingers or mentioning that Will was their top suspect. Though no one would admit it, she felt sure many of the club members secretly suspected the squeaky-clean Speedo-wearing merman. She wouldn't reveal anything until she knew more. However, this was a good opportunity to steer the conversation in the right direction. "We're making headway and already have several promising avenues we're exploring. One in particular, which I wouldn't mind your opinion on — how did Colin feel about surfers?"

George nearly spat out his words. "Same way we all do. They're a pain in the behind."

"I'm sure they're nice people out of the water," Ahmed added. "But in it—"

"They rub us up the wrong way," Rani concluded.

"How come?" Fiona asked.

George supplied the answer. "We swim at the same spot at Southbourne, day in, day out. Always there, rain or shine. But whenever there are waves, which isn't that often, these surfers show up, acting like they own the place."

"We like swimming in the waves too," Beth said. "It's good fun. But they come along and behave as if we're not there. Flying past us. So many near misses. Reckless, they are."

Fiona remembered Roger's words, how even an average surfer could slalom around a swimmer. But from the opposite point of view, their actions would appear intimidating and dangerous.

"So, I'm guessing Colin gave them a piece of his mind," Fiona said.

George's eyebrows knitted together. "We all do, whenever it happens. Tell them straight."

"I'm always having words with them," Beth said. "I've tried to be polite, asked them to be careful, but all I get is a load of abuse. So now I give as good as I get. Tell them to sling their hook. Surf somewhere else, but they ignore me."

"They ignore all of us," Rani added.

"What about Will?" Fiona asked.

"He doesn't agree with us," Ahmed replied. "Will's all 'live and let live'. Sea's for everyone. We can't be water police, he always says. Deciding who can be in the sea and who can't."

"Can't you just find another spot?" Fiona suggested.

"Huh, that's what Will says," George replied. "But we all shut him down. That's our spot by the stone groyne. Always has been. If we move, that's like giving into a bully. Why can't they go somewhere else?"

Fiona knew the answer to this. "They would say that's where the waves break best."

"So what?" said Rani. "The waves only happen now and again. Like George said, we're there every day."

"Did Colin ever start a fight with a surfer or single one out in particular?"

"No!" Beth sounded shocked at the suggestion. "To be honest, it was the one time he wasn't outspoken, or rather, his outspokenness blended with everyone else's. We all voiced our disapproval. Well, apart from Will."

Fiona shrank a little, as the vengeful-surfer theory hit a setback. Colin's authoritarian attitude would have merged with everyone else if they'd all given these surfers the same short shrift. At least Fiona could cement one theory tonight. "So would you say there's a rivalry between surfers and wild swimmers?"

"Yes," came the unanimous reply.

The crackle of the microphone interrupted the conversation. "Right, folks. Grab your pens and put your phones away. First question in tonight's pub quiz: who invented the hovercraft? That's, who invented the hovercraft?"

Ahmed snatched up the paper and pen, and scribbled down the name Christopher Cockerell, a smug grin splitting his face. They were off to a good start.

CHAPTER 19

The pub quiz was drawing to a close and Fiona hadn't so much as uttered a suggestion. Her teammates had put her to shame with their general knowledge, jotting down answer after answer, sometimes all four of them providing the same one simultaneously. Being a veteran pub quizzer, Fiona considered her general knowledge to be fairly good — above average, in fact. However, tonight the right answers were eluding her, or perhaps it was just that the wrong questions were coming up. The law of averages had finally caught up with her, tossing out a mix of subjects she had no idea about. Although, it was more likely that her mind was on the most recent revelation — one she hadn't expected, not in a million years. When it came to quarrels with surfers, the whole club voiced their displeasure as one united front. Colin's normal forthright behaviour would've been rendered inconspicuous.

However, that still didn't rule out the possibility he'd had a separate altercation with a surfer on one of his lone training swims. But Fiona had to be careful and remind herself that these solo ventures into the water weren't based in fact — not yet, anyway. They only existed as conjecture, a theory put forward by Will. Though highly plausible, she had no proof

Colin had embarked on these secret swims, which made the whole premise a little shaky, and there was no surf on the week of his death. Question was, had he earned himself a reputation among the surfers — one that had got him killed?

Fiona posed the question again. "I know I've already asked this, but are you sure Colin never swam alone? To get in extra training to perhaps beat Will out to the buoy?"

"No way," George said, emphatically. "And I'll tell you why. He was bossy. He needed people to boss around. Thrived off it."

"Oh, he wasn't that bad," Beth replied.

"Yes, he was. I know what you're going to say. He would always help anyone that needed it. I'm not disputing that. But his help came with a price — a ton of mansplaining."

"That's true," Ahmed agreed. "He fixed our lawn mower once, which was very decent of him, but then he told me off for about half an hour for not maintaining it properly."

"Exactly," George said. "Benevolent but bossy. And bossy people need a bossee. That's why he wouldn't swim alone. He had to have people around him in the water to receive his unwanted swimming tips, and I can prove it. One time, I think it was Christmas Eve or the day before, everyone was busy, getting ready for Crimbo. Only me and him showed up at the beach. I wasn't feeling too great. Had a cold coming on and decided not to go in, but said I'd wait for him while he swam, you know, because we don't like anyone swimming unsupervised. He decided not to go in either, because he'd have no one to boss around, although, on the way back to our cars, he blathered on to me non-stop about why he never got colds. But my point is this — he wouldn't swim alone because he needed an audience to lecture."

"A teacher has to have a class," Rani added.

"I couldn't have put it better," George replied.

The microphone squealed. "Okay," the landlord barked. "Last question, folks. Last question. If I was eating hardtack, what would I be eating?"

Finally. A question Fiona knew.

Everyone around the table appeared blank. Fiona stole glances around the pub. Similar vacant stares. No one grabbed a pen or scribbled an answer. The whole place was clueless.

Quietly, Fiona took the pen and slid the answer paper in front of her, now cluttered with a disparate list of words and phrases numbered one to nineteen, some of them crossed out and rewritten. Feeling a little less like a spare part, Fiona wrote down number twenty at the bottom of the page. Her teammates leaned in, eager to witness what answer she would supply. In neat capital letters, Fiona wrote: *WATER BISCUITS*, then added *(OR SHIP'S BISCUITS)*, just to be on the safe side.

They all peered at the answer then at her.

"Is that right?" George queried.

Fiona nodded.

"Well, I never."

"I've never heard of hardtack before," Beth confessed. "Sounds like something you'd put on a horse."

The landlord gave the teams another minute then came out from behind the bar to collect the answer papers and add them up.

"How do you think we did?" Fiona asked.

"Hmm, not sure," Beth confessed. "Will's team usually wins. He's good at everything, that one."

"Somehow that doesn't surprise me." Fiona gazed across at the swimming star, still nursing the same pint of lime and soda water. He appeared effortlessly relaxed. One of those fortunate few who was happy in their own skin, having had all his numbers come up in the genetic lottery, winning the whole package of looks, brains, body and charm. A perfect and alluring combination, it would be easy for him to come across as smug and self-satisfied, but he even managed to avoid that pitfall. Fiona steadied herself, knowing that a lot of the traits she'd just listed were those of a psychopath. Especially as he did appear supremely overconfident at this precise moment, as if he and his team had this pub quiz all sewn up.

The landlord called out the answers then began listing the results in reverse order. The whole pub descended into silence, fizzing with anticipation. "In last place, we have the Tuckton Twitchers with five points. Not so easy without a smartphone, eh, chaps? Next, with six points — actually this team only scored five points, but I awarded you an extra point for your original team name — I Thought This Was Speed Dating . . ."

A flurry of sniggers spread through the pub. He continued to work his way through the list until only two teams remained. "So it's down to the Briney Brainiacs—" Fiona and her team cheered — "and Wet Wet Wet." Will and his slightly larger team produced a louder cheer.

"Okay, drum roll, everyone." On the landlord's command, a frenzy of hands slapped the edge of tables. "Winning by just one point with a score of eighteen out of twenty, beating Wet Wet Wet, congratulations to the Briney Brainiacs!"

The whole pub clapped and cheered.

"Can we have a representative come up to receive your prize?"

"You should go, Fiona," Beth urged.

Fiona shook her head. "No, I only answered one question."

"Yes, but that one answer—" said Rani.

"Pipped them to the post," Ahmed finished.

"You won't get any argument from me," George added.

Reluctantly, Fiona rose to her feet, then dragged them slowly towards the bar. Never comfortable being the centre of attention, she could feel countless eyes following her.

"Well done!" the landlord congratulated. "Now, as is tradition at the Countess of Strathmore, we have one more challenge." He fanned out three envelopes in front of her. "One of these envelopes contains the top prize of fifty pounds, another twenty pounds and the third a fiver. Which one will you go for?"

Fiona looked back to her team for guidance. They appeared to be mouthing the word *middle*, at her. Not wanting to linger, Fiona plucked the one in the centre and hurried back to her teammates. She wasted no time ripping open the envelope, only to find it contained a fiver. "Oh, looks like I picked the wrong one. Sorry."

"Don't worry," Beth reassured her. "Every week it's the same. Winning team always gets five quid, no matter which envelope they pick."

"That tight landlord must think we're daft," George said. "He stuffs a fiver in every envelope."

"Oh, that makes me feel a bit better." Fiona waved the bank note in the air. "Now, shall I get everyone a drink?"

"What, with a fiver?" said George. "That won't even buy a pint."

"Why don't you take it, Fiona?" Beth suggested. "Pop it into the till at the charity shop."

"Yeah, that's a good idea," George nodded. "Help the homeless dogs."

Ahmed and Rani both agreed.

"Thanks, everyone." She slotted the note in her purse. Looking up, she caught Will's eye from across the pub. He smiled and raised his glass in a congratulatory cheers. Fiona did likewise. Even in defeat, Will was a good sport with not a hint of bitterness. Suddenly, his face darkened, terror sweeping over his features like storm clouds. He appeared to be looking beyond Fiona, towards the entrance.

Fiona twisted around to see the source of his horror. Hayley stood in the doorway, her usual glamorous self, her sparkling eyes locked onto Will's, staring at him unblinking.

Fiona had never seen Will flustered before, but he was on his feet, chicaning around the tables trying not to barge into anyone. When he reached Hayley, Fiona could see the pair exchanging heated words. He must have suggested they go outside because the next second he had hustled her through the door.

George leaned over. "As I said before, if you're looking for leads, that's a good place to start."

CHAPTER 20

Next morning, after Fiona's wild swim, she stopped off at the bakery and bought three pains au chocolat. Smelling divine and still warm from the oven, the heat of the pastries radiated through the brown paper bag, pleasantly warming her hands. However, as she stepped into Dogs Need Nice Homes, the atmosphere felt distinctly frosty. Fiona quickly deduced that Daisy and Partial Sue weren't talking to each other. Sitting around the table with Fiona in the middle of them, they'd angled their chairs away from each other, the hot pastries doing nothing to melt the ice. Eventually, they were slowly devoured but in absolute silence, except for the delicate texture of the pastry crumbling with every bite, and Simon Le Bon snuffling below, seeking out any stray flakes.

"How was your film?" Fiona dared to ask.

"We didn't go," Daisy replied curtly.

"Oh, why not?"

"Couldn't decide what to see," Partial Sue grumbled.

The pair had wildly differing movie tastes. Partial Sue preferred dark thrillers, hardboiled cop dramas and action movies involving car chases, endless gun battles and punch-ups with characters who had outrageously camp nicknames. Daisy on the other hand was at the opposite of the cinematic spectrum: period dramas in polite society, heroines seeking love, romances in glamorous places, or underdog stories set in regional communities, usually involving a bunch of plucky fishermen slash factory workers slash miners who overcome the odds to provide the audience with a feel-good conclusion. Fiona had upset the social dynamics with her absence. She usually occupied the middle ground when they were choosing movies and would often arbitrate a compromise, suggesting a film they could all enjoy — a thankless task, but a necessary one, otherwise they'd never end up watching anything, as was the case last night.

With conversation blunted, no one had asked Fiona about her night, so she volunteered the information. "We won the pub quiz."

No verbal reaction from the pair, although Daisy did manage to flash her a brief smile.

Fiona decided it best to underplay the victory, as they clearly weren't in the mood to hear anything remotely positive. "We only won a measly fiver — which reminds me." She withdrew the note from her purse, got up and rang it into the till, then returned to her seat. "The team decided to donate it to the homeless dogs, which was nice of them."

Neither Daisy nor Partial Sue were moved by this small act of kindness. Their bust-up over the film must have been a serious matter. Maybe an update on the case would distract them from their feud. "I tested the water, excuse the pun, with our vengeful-surfer theory."

"And?" Partial Sue asked without catching her eye.

"Bit of a non-starter, I'm afraid. It's probably the one time Colin's outspoken attitude wouldn't have been, er, outspoken, as it were."

"How does that work?" Daisy asked.

"Whenever surfers show up, the whole club gives them an earful. Colin did too, but that meant he wouldn't have stood out. Wouldn't have been a target for any disgruntled surfers, as they all put up a united front."

"Unless he encountered them on his solo training swims," Partial Sue said.

"Still a possibility," Fiona replied. "But they were of the opinion he didn't embark on any solo swims — Colin was a compulsive authoritarian and needed a captive audience, which rules out any lone efforts."

Partial Sue huffed. "So, last night was a bit of a waste of time."

Fiona ignored her cynicism. What had got into these two? She tried to remain unruffled. "Well, there were a couple of interesting things that emerged. The first was Hayley showing up at the last minute, fixated on Will, as usual."

At least Daisy perked up at the mention of a juicy morsel of gossip. "What happened?"

"Well, let's just say Will's unflappableness flapped away. I've never seen him so uncomfortable. He marched straight across the pub and escorted her outside. Didn't see them again."

"Was he annoyed, angry?" Partial Sue asked.

"More worried, I'd say. She's clearly got him rattled."

Partial Sue tutted. "He should put a restraining order out on her."

"I don't think that's Will's style," Fiona replied. "He prefers diplomacy."

"Well, it's clearly not working," Partial Sue replied.

"Does his wife know?" Daisy asked.

"I asked them that. Apparently not. Club members have taken a vow of silence. But from what they told me last night, Hayley's obsessed with Will. They call her 'Hayley's Comet' because she disappears for a while, presumably after he's told her to leave him alone, but then returns, back to bother him a few months later. Never gets the message that he doesn't like her."

Partial Sue folded her arms. "Sounds like a stalker, and stalkers are capable of anything. Like I said, it wouldn't be beyond the realms of possibility that she blamed Colin for cramping her style. Murdered him."

"Yes, it's a definite possibility. We need to talk to her. Get her side of the story, but it certainly looks promising."

"What was the other thing?" Daisy asked.

"Oh, yes. Beth's car broke down, which means she can't get to the beach in the morning, which got me thinking. Where's Colin's car? We know that Colin always drove because he was a bit OCD and never shared lifts. So surely his car should still be at the beach, at the top of the zigzag. He drove an old pale blue Land Rover but it's not there."

"Maybe he swam somewhere else on that day?" Daisy suggested.

"Unlikely," Partial Sue replied. "If he was planning on beating Will out to the buoy and back, surely that's where he'd train."

"But then that contradicts what the wild swimmers were saying about him never swimming alone," Fiona pointed out.

"Okay, fair enough," Partial Sue agreed. "Maybe he was swimming with several others who turned out to be his murderers. Possibly other members of the club, who knows? But we do know he was found in the water in his trunks. That's a fact. So surely his car would still be there. Unless he swam at some other place. They lured him there."

"Maybe the police towed it," Daisy said.

"That's probably what happened, but before we make a nuisance of ourselves asking DI Fincher, who's probably not going to tell us anything, I think we should visit his house. Kill two birds with one stone — see if his car's there and question the neighbour. Ask about Colin's movements before he died. They might have seen or heard something."

Partial Sue perked up at last. "That's a good idea. I can't believe we didn't think of that sooner."

Finally, the ice had melted and all three of them exchanged warm smiles.

CHAPTER 21

After work, Beth texted Fiona the address of Colin's home, a modest bungalow near Iford playing fields with no memorable features, nothing that would prompt anyone to say, "Oh, I know that place. It's the one with the wooden plaque, or the black iron railings, or the tall chimneys." But what it lacked in kerb appeal was compensated with up-togetherness, being maintained to within an inch of its life, no doubt by Colin's fastidious hand. Not a crack in sight, a slipped roof tile, nor a wall joint that needed pointing. The only thing that stood out was the pale blue, old-school Land Rover parked on the drive, also maintained to obsessive standards.

"Well, at least we've found his car," Partial Sue said.

"Question is, how did it get back here?" Fiona asked.

"Must have been the police," said Daisy. "We should ask them."

Fiona didn't relish prising that information out of DI Fincher. She was tight-lipped in murder cases — that was to be expected — but this was a nice, neat case of accidental death. The dust had already settled on the death certificate, and she wouldn't want anyone disturbing it.

"Let's ask the neighbour, before we incur the wrath of DI Fincher," Fiona suggested.

They trooped around to an identical bungalow on the left, equally neat and tidy. A note written in biro had been sellotaped above the doorbell. The damp had got to it and the ink had run, but it was still legible.

Be patient. It takes me a while to get to the door.
Dave

Fiona pushed the buzzer. After a minute, through the frosted glass, a slow-moving shape appeared, gradually hobbling towards them. Another minute later, the door opened to reveal a man in his seventies, presumably Dave, the author of the blurred note. Red-faced and panting heavily, he resembled a flustered beetroot propped up with an aluminium walking stick.

"Sorry it took so long. My knees ain't what they used to be. Takes me ages to get anywhere."

"I'm so sorry to hear that," Fiona said.

Dave looked at them expectantly, wondering if all his effort had been worth it.

"We're from the wild swimming club." Fiona had thought it best to refer to themselves as this rather than amateur detectives. She didn't want to traumatise the poor fellow by announcing that his next-door neighbour might have been the victim of a murder.

Partial Sue was quick to qualify this. "She's the wild swimmer. We're not partial to cold water. You wouldn't catch us in the sea at this time of year."

Dave took a sharp intake of breath. "Me neither. God bless central heating, that's what I say. Mine's on the blink at the moment. Pressure keeps dropping. Pity my neighbour's not around anymore, God rest his soul. He used to fix everything for me."

"Was that Colin?" Fiona asked.

"Yes, indeed. You must have known him, being in his swimming club and all."

"Well, I've only just joined but I'm aware he died suddenly."

Dave shifted his weight on the walking stick. "Yeah, that was a shock, I can tell you. Completely out of the blue. He was a good sort, you know. Always ready to help. Mind you, he liked the sound of his own voice. But I'd tell him straight: 'I don't need a lecture, Colin.' He didn't mind. We're both thick-skinned. Not like these snowflakes you get today. All sensitive, with their oat milk and their allergies. I mean, there weren't allergies in the old days. We just had to get on with it."

"Well, I think there were," Daisy pointed out. "They just didn't know they were allergies."

He shook his head. "Nah, I think it's just people trying to be trendy. 'Oh, look at me, I've got an allergy. I'm special.'"

Fiona had to hold her tongue and not be goaded into an argument about whether allergies existed, and goodness knows what else Dave believed was made up by the media. "When was the last time you saw Colin alive?"

"Oh, yes. It was the Friday. I heard him go. He left the same time every morning, see. Seven thirty on the dot. I could set my watch by him. I'd hear his Land Rover start. That engine makes a proper rattle. Throaty exhaust, not like these namby-pamby cars they have today—"

Fiona cut him off. "And what time did he return?"

"Same time he always did. Back by nine o'clock every day."

"Did you see him after that?"

"Nope. And I never heard his Land Rover start up again. It's stayed put ever since."

"It hasn't moved?" Daisy asked.

"Nope, not an inch."

"Then how did he get back down to the beach?" Partial Sue asked.

Colin shrugged. "Search me, but it wasn't by car, that much I can tell you."

"What about cycling?"

"Nah, didn't like push bikes. He preferred his car."

"Did you see anyone give him a lift?" Fiona asked.

"Nah, he didn't accept lifts. I think he worried that he'd have to start reciprocating, and we all know where that ends. Next thing, you're taking people to the airport at four in the morning. Nah, I've never heard anyone pick him up, not even a taxi. And I'm here all the time."

Fiona wanted to double-check. "So you're positive he wasn't picked up by someone else after he got back on Friday?"

"Definitely not. I was here the whole time. I may be slow on my feet, but there's nothing wrong with my hearing. I never heard any cars pull up outside."

"I guess he must've walked to the beach," Daisy suggested. "Maybe his car wouldn't start."

Dave snorted. "Not a chance. Have you seen the state of his place? He'd be out there fixing it. He was obsessed with fixing things, even when they weren't broke. Bit like people. Barking advice at them when they hadn't asked for any—"

This time, Partial Sue cut him off. "Did he ever leave for an extra swim later in the day?"

Dave shook his head. "Nope. He only went out first thing in the morning. Never swam any other time. I guess once is enough when you're jumping in freezing cold water."

This was true, Fiona thought. Even for a hardy purist like Colin, who never required the comfort of a changing robe, one plunge in icy water a day would suffice.

Daisy altered the line of questioning. "Did he ever mention having a crush on anyone?"

Dave hesitated. Stared at her with two baffled eyes then guffawed so loudly that it triggered a hacking cough. "Colin? You're joking, aren't you? Women run a mile from him, and he had the charm of a bunch of stinging nettles. Nah, that guy was a singleton through and through."

Dave's boorish response prompted Fiona to push the questioning into a more delicate area. "Do you think what happened to Colin was an accident?"

"Do you mean someone had it in for him?"

Fiona nodded.

He shook his head. "Colin could be annoying. But he was always trying to do right by people, you know? Apart from not wanting to give them lifts." He chuckled. "So, I'd say no. I think the daft bugger had an accident."

* * *

On the way back home in the car, Daisy remarked, "I'm not sure I liked Dave. He was quite mean about Colin having a crush on someone. Everyone deserves to have a bit of love in their life."

"Spoken like a true romantic," Partial Sue remarked. "But you're right. I wasn't partial to him either. That was quite a nasty thing to say, and he wasn't exactly an oil painting himself."

"Yes, I didn't particularly warm to him," Fiona agreed. "However, he's been the most useful person we've spoken to so far. Ruled out quite a lot of speculation for us. Colin never embarked on any extra training sessions, because he only swam once a day, which also rules out the possibility he had any lone altercations with surfers."

Partial Sue grumbled as she changed gear. "But it's created more problems than it's solved. How did he get from his house to the sea? Why didn't he drive his car? And also, if he wasn't putting in extra training, what was he doing back in the water alone?"

"Could be a simple explanation," Daisy said. "He missed his morning swim on Saturday or whenever it was. Perhaps he had something important he had to do, or overslept, who knows? Like you said, Fiona, wild swimming's addictive, so he goes later in the day to get his fix. Decides not to take his car. Maybe it's broken down and he's waiting for a spare part. It's an old Land Rover, so it's harder to find spares. Or he just wanted to walk. He can stroll to the beach because he doesn't have to be there at any particular time. He goes in the sea, gets in trouble. Bangs his head. Death by missing adventure."

"It's death by *mis*adventure," Partial Sue corrected.

Daisy's phrasing may have been off, but her logic was impeccable. Alarmingly straightforward, she had a gift for seeing things unfettered by clutter and baggage. Fiona remembered Will mentioning Occam's razor and how the simplest explanation was the most likely. Daisy's explanation was the simplest of them all. No secret training sessions, no sinister conspiracies, no watery vendettas or floppy love triangles. Just a later-than-normal swim session and an error of judgement. He'd ventured out alone and no one was there to help him when he got into difficulty.

"But what about the scratches on his arms and legs, and the colour of his face?" Partial Sue asked.

"You remember what that forensics article said," Fiona replied. "Weird inexplicable things happen to bodies when they're in water."

Perhaps the biggest culprit in this investigation was the sea itself. That massive, mysterious and constantly shifting entity had an impetuous character. Prone to violent mood swings, there were signs all along the seafront telling you to respect the water. Even on the calmest of days it could be unpredictable. No matter how experienced or strong a swimmer you were, it could always get the better of you.

Was that the simple answer to Colin's death? Had he merely underestimated his killer, and how volatile it could be?

CHAPTER 22

Next morning, a keen breeze heckled Fiona all the way down the zigzag, while across the bay, a procession of white caps marched towards the beach. A cappuccino sea. Not exactly challenging conditions for swimming, just a great deal of froth to contend with, especially when it came to that tricky part of submerging one's midriff. Fiona liked to take her time at that point, easing herself into it slowly. It was painful enough at the best of times. However, today she'd have no control over the icy water sloshing up and down her body.

She spied Will on the beach. He was easy to spot. The only one stripped to his trunks, he flitted from group to group, doing his usual rounds, greeting everyone, checking they were okay. As she drew closer, Fiona realised once more that Beth was not among them. But she did notice a lone figure, separate from the various clusters of swimmers chatting on the sand. Standing in self-imposed isolation and clad in an unflattering changing robe, Hayley still managed to look glamorous, her laser-like eyes fixated on Will, following his every movement.

Fiona made a beeline for her, seizing the chance to question her alone before everyone took the plunge. "Hi, I'm—"

"I know who you are," Hayley replied abruptly, without taking her eyes off Will.

Her brusque response threw Fiona for a second. "Oh, er, well, I was asked by Beth to look into—"

"I know why you're here," Hayley snapped.

"Oh, okay. I hope you don't mind if I ask you a few questions."

"Depends what they are."

Fiona swallowed hard, desperately wishing she'd been more prepared for this moment, working out a careful strategy for her line of inquiry rather than fumbling into it *ad hoc*. No matter. An opportunity had presented itself and she had to grab it with both hands. She'd start small then work up to the uncomfortable stuff. "How well did you know Colin?"

"Not at all," came the economic reply.

"So you weren't friends with him?"

"Nope."

"Did he ever talk to you?"

"I've just said we weren't friends. Why would he talk to me?"

Fiona swallowed again. "Okay, so he never spoke to you?"

"That's what I just said, isn't it?"

Fiona knew this wasn't true. Colin had tried to chat up Hayley; George had told her so. Either he was lying, or Hayley was. Clearly defensive, the latter appeared to be the most likely. Fiona tried a different angle. "Can I ask you about Will?"

She tore her eyes away from him and glared at Fiona. "What about him?"

"Are the two of you friends?"

She shrugged.

"Sorry, does that mean yes or no?" Fiona asked.

"What has this got to do with Colin?"

"Just curious."

"I don't meet him for coffee, if that's what you're thinking."

"Oh, okay." Fiona thought for a moment, wondering how to gently probe her infatuation with Will, and the oddly skewed love triangle. She came to the conclusion that she should just rip the plaster off. "But last night at the pub quiz, you showed up and the pair of you disappeared together."

Hayley glowered at her. "That's none of your business!" She snatched up her bag and stamped off across the beach, passing within an inch of Will, almost shouldering him out of the way.

Fiona had triggered her, but she didn't have time to be shocked by Hayley's extreme reaction, or even analyse the reason behind it. A far more shocking proposition, bordering on terrifying, appeared, eclipsing anything Hayley had done.

Sophie Haverford sashayed across the sand, perma-smug grin on her blood-red lips. Draped in a black changing robe, she had somehow procured an expensive designer version of the practical garment, embellished with a gold filigree around the cuffs and hem. With her severely cropped bob of black hair and flawless pale skin, it was as if Dracula's bride had turned up for a dip, and perhaps to drain one or two swimmers while she was at it.

Hidden in her shadow, the diminutive form of Gail, her assistant, scuttled along behind her, wheezing and weighed down like a packhorse with a plethora of beach bags.

Sophie stood in the midst of everyone, greedily feeding off their curious stares. "I'm sure you all know who I am. But for anyone who's been living under a rock, my name's Sophie Haverford."

Fiona caught a few people muttering, "Who?"

Will approached her to extend his usual warm greeting. Sophie immediately unzipped her changing robe and flung it behind her, where it collided with Gail, almost engulfing the poor woman.

Sophie had a perfect body — of course she did. Gym-toned and moisturised, it was if it had been airbrushed into existence as she cavorted in front of Will. But it was what Sophie was wearing that alarmed Fiona the most. The exact same teal swimming costume that Fiona had under her own changing robe. This was no coincidence. Sophie would never wear a surf brand and probably had a separate rail in her dressing room (Fiona assumed she had a dressing room) dedicated to a collection of designer-label swimwear. Her rival's intentions were clear. Sophie had shown up this morning with the express intention of upstaging Fiona, donning the very same swimsuit so every onlooker could easily compare Sophie's perfect body to Fiona's far-from-perfect one. No wonder she had gone strangely quiet that time in the shop. The woman had been formulating a plan of water-based one-upmanship at that very moment. Why did she have this warped compulsion to beat Fiona at everything, whatever the cost? And where did she get the energy from? Fiona couldn't care less and would happily concede that Sophie was the better woman. Lookswise, at least.

The unofficial leader of Southbourne Wild Things introduced himself. "Hello, I'm Will. Welcome aboard." He extended his hand, but instead of shaking it, Sophie grabbed it, suddenly thrusting the back of her hand up to his lips to make it appear as if he'd kissed it.

"Oh, *enchantée.*" She giggled. "*Je m'appelle* Sophie."

Fiona had no idea why she had decided to greet him in French. Will quickly snatched his hand back but remained composed.

Sophie fluttered her eyelashes at him. "Charmed to make your acquaintance."

"And who's your friend?" Will asked, smiling at Gail, who had managed to bring Sophie's changing robe under control, like someone gathering up a spent parachute. Gail smiled back, pleased to be included in the conversation.

"Oh, that's Gail," Sophie replied off-handedly. "Pretend she's not here." Then her tone quickly reverted back to her clumsy flirtation. "I have a feeling you and I are going to become close." More giggling accompanied cheeky glances at his body.

Fiona rolled her eyes and amended her first thoughts. Okay, so she hadn't just come here to upstage Fiona. Sophie also had designs on Will. Presumably, she'd been spying on Fiona's wild swimming sessions and taken a liking to the dishy sixty-something with a six-pack. Lucky that Hayley had just left, or the pair of them might have been fighting over him on the beach.

"Have you been wild swimming before?" Will asked.

"Oh, yes. I swim every day. I have a beachfront penthouse." Sophie never missed an opportunity to inform anyone within earshot of her enviable address. "I'm always posting about wild swimming online. Encouraging others to reap its many benefits. You could say I'm a swimfluencer." More giggling.

Fiona followed Sophie on social media. Not as a friend, more to keep her enemy closer. She'd never once mentioned wild swimming in any of her posts. As for her claim that she was a regular cold-water swimmer, Fiona presumed she'd been cramming in cold-water dips since the moment she'd found out about Fiona's new pastime.

Sophie drew closer to Will, adopting a wheedling, victim-like tone. "But I've been doing it all on my own. And I'm desperate for company. Human intimacy is so important, don't you think?"

Will took cautionary step back. "Yes, let's buddy you up with someone, just to be on the safe side." He glanced around, seeking suitable candidates. Everyone's gaze dropped to the sand.

"What about you?" Sophie asked Will before he had a chance to pick someone. "I bet you're good at instructing people in all sorts of ways." She winked.

Fiona fought the urge to be sick in her mouth.

"I'd love to," Will replied. "But I swim out to the buoy and back at quite a lick."

"Oh, I'm a very good swimmer."

Will ignored her boast and locked onto Fiona. "Ah, Fiona. You've just started wild swimming. It's all fresh in your mind."

Ever since Sophie had turned up wearing the same swimsuit, Fiona had decided to give it a miss this morning. She wanted to keep her changing robe firmly zipped up, thank you very much.

Will's eyes pleaded with her.

Fiona caved in. "Yes, why not?"

"Oh hi, Fiona. We already know each other." Sophie sent her a sickly grin. Clearly happy with this arrangement, if she couldn't fulfil Plan A of swimming and flirting with Will, at least she could accomplish Plan B — showing up Fiona in her matching swimsuit.

CHAPTER 23

Reluctantly, Fiona unzipped her changing robe and slipped it off, bracing herself for the humiliating onslaught, engineered at the hands of her nemesis. She hadn't once felt self-conscious of her body since joining the wild swimming club. But now the fear of being body shamed in front of everyone made Fiona cower. She wished the sands would part and swallow her.

Louder than was strictly necessary, Sophie broadcast her fake surprise. "Oh, what a coincidence! We've got the same swimsuit!" Just to drive the message home that her body was far superior, Sophie hooked an arm around Fiona and pulled her close. "We're sea sisters!"

Face flushing, Fiona didn't dare look up. Sophie repeated the observation several times, each one more forced than the last. Her plan seemed to be faltering. Fiona plucked up the courage to raise her gaze and found that to her relief, nobody appeared particularly bothered or interested. Apart from Will, all the club's members were odd shapes and sizes, and weren't the kind of people impressed by toned bodies and polished skin. Besides, they were all too busy edging into the frothy water, their minds unable to concentrate on anything other than their plunging core temperatures.

Sophie huffed her frustration and unhooked her arm, then shouted, "Hat!"

Gail jumped and rummaged through one of the large beach bags, plucking out a black swimming hat, still in its packaging. She tore it open, then set to work, carefully stretching the balloon-like material over Sophie's shiny black bob, which wasn't easy, considering the height difference between the two of them. Sophie made no attempt to make it easy for Gail, forcing her to stand on tiptoe, stretching her arms to their full extent. "Ow! Careful, Gail! I am attached to every one of my hairs. I hope you're sorry."

"'S'right," Gail apologised, sort of.

Once the cap was tightly secured, Sophie examined Gail's handiwork using her phone, her fingers making nips and tucks here and there. "I suppose that will do." She tutted, then wasted no time marching towards the sea.

Fiona hurried after her. "Er, we're supposed to take our time. Avoid cold-water shock."

"Nothing shocks me, dear." Sophie strode in.

To Fiona's surprise, she didn't gasp or baulk at the freezing wavelets lapping around her and continued advancing forward, like a machine. Not even the most seasoned of wild swimmers in the club entered with such vigour. The only explanation Fiona could think of was that Sophie already had the cold heart of an international assassin, matching the frigid temperature of the water. Yet she still felt responsible as her swim buddy, and scurried after her. Forgoing her normal slow descent into the water, Fiona forced herself in, the pain stabbing every inch of her flesh like a thousand tiny needles.

Sophie had already begun swimming. Arms windmilling, her front crawl cut an impressive swathe through the water. With only her sedate breaststroke to propel her, Fiona had no hope of keeping up and a large gap opened between them. She wanted to shout, "Slow down!" or "Where are you going?" But she didn't have the spare breaths. All of them were engaged at the moment, gasping at the sudden cold assaulting her body.

Up ahead, Sophie had stopped and was now treading water, bobbed up and down by the little waves. Her intentions became clear. Will had already reached the buoy and was now on his return — which would put him right in Sophie's path, presumably so she could swim back with him, and continue her campaign of outrageous flirting. The last thing Fiona wanted was to be anywhere near her when that happened. However, as her designated swim buddy, Fiona didn't want to shirk her responsibilities. She had to keep an eye on her, even though Sophie, being supremely confident in the water, really didn't need it.

Curving her arms behind her, before they had a chance to seize up, Fiona resumed her slow breaststroke, heading out towards Sophie little by little.

As she neared, Sophie yelped and slipped beneath the surface.

"Sophie? Sophie?" Fiona searched the water for signs of her, but it was too murky to see anything. Panic gripped Fiona, crushing her breathing even more so than the cold. Her tinnitus rang in her ears as her eyes manically scanned the surface.

Sophie suddenly popped back up, coughing and spluttering, gulping down air. Her eyes were wide, and her arms thrashed wildly. Her timing was impeccable. A few seconds later, head down in the water, focused on his piston-like strokes, Will collided with her. He raised his head, disoriented and slightly annoyed by the sudden disruption. Sophie immediately threw herself onto him, hugging him around the neck, nearly sinking him. "You saved me!"

Will unravelled her arms. "What happened?"

Sophie spoke rapidly. "Something had hold of me. Grabbed me. Pulled me under."

Will examined her with disbelieving eyes, clearly suspecting a ruse. "Something grabbed you?"

"Yes, yes. It grabbed my leg. You saw it, Fiona."

"I saw you go under. I didn't see anything grab you."

Sophie threw herself at Will once more. It was hard to know if she was telling the truth. She seemed genuinely traumatised by the ordeal, but then Sophie knew how to switch on the melodrama when she wanted something.

"You must have scared it off. I was terrified."

Will kept her at arm's length, clearly fearing she might swamp him. "Okay, can you swim back?"

"Please, hold me," she said meekly, going limp and swooning as if she might slip beneath the water. Will darted around behind her and held her up, hooking his hands beneath her armpits. He swam back, dragging her along, with Fiona beside him.

Swimmers converged on their position from every angle, asking if Sophie was okay and to offer help.

"She's fine," Will answered. "Just had a little fright."

When they reached the beach, Sophie continued her limp fish act, forcing Will to lift her out of the water in his arms heroically. As he lay her down on the sand, she gazed longingly in his eyes and croaked, "Thank you."

More concerned swimmers formed a circle around Sophie. Gail was at her side, sitting her up and draping the posh changing robe around her shoulders. "You all right?" she asked.

"Oh, Gail. It was just awful."

Shivering, Fiona threw on her own changing robe and poured a hot cup of tea from her flask. She offered it to Sophie, expecting her to push it away, not wanting anything made by her rival's hands, but she accepted it with gratitude. After taking several small sips, Sophie embellished her tale, as if she were telling a ghost story to a pub full of superstitious villagers. "There I was, swimming through the dark water. While, unbeknown to me, something sinister lurked beneath the depths. Waiting, waiting, waiting. Suddenly, it grabbed me!"

There were as many gasps as there were looks of disbelief, as Sophie piled the melodrama high with a strong whiff of fabrication. "Down and down, I was pulled. The helpless prey of an unknown predator. I kicked and struggled, clawing to get away, but I couldn't break its deathly grip. I accepted my fate. To die in these cruel waters, like some drowned Ophelia.

But the strong arms of salvation lifted me, pulling me into the light. Will rescued me. Saved my life."

Will shifted uneasily on the sand. "Well, that's not quite how it happened. You were already on the surface when I collided with you."

Sophie held up a hand. "Please, Will. No false modesty. If it wasn't for your brave intervention, I might not be here." She added a tearful sniff.

"I wonder what it was," Fiona said.

"I reckon it was Henry," Ahmed suggested.

There were a few nods as well as confused expressions.

"Who's Henry?" Fiona asked.

"He's the local seal," Ahmed replied. "We nicknamed him Henry."

"He loves to play," Rani agreed. "Probably just got over-excited. Cute little fellow. Looks like—"

"A labrador without ears," Ahmed rounded off the description.

Fiona liked Henry already.

Sophie did not. "This was no seal!" she snapped. "Seals have flippers. They can't grab people." Her tone became wheedling once more. "You believe me, don't you, Will?"

"Er, well, I think we need to keep an open mind about these things. The main thing is that you're okay. Or do you need a doctor?"

"Yes, I think I do. Will you take me?"

Will sighed. "Okay, yes. Let's get you checked out. My wife works at the hospital," he was quick to point out.

This should have put the kibosh on Sophie's amorous efforts, but undeterred, she smiled impishly. "Then maybe we could get coffee and a bite to eat. I know this wonderful place by the river. The avocado on toast is simply to die for."

Any sympathy Sophie had earned with the gathered swimmers blew away in the onshore breeze, as her ulterior motive became clear. *There's many a slip,* Fiona thought, *between a cup and an invite to brunch.*

CHAPTER 24

Back at the shop, Fiona recounted the dramatic events of the morning — her spiky interaction with Hayley, and the tale of Sophie being pulled under the waves.

"Oh my, that's terrible." As Daisy listened, she nervously tapped her Malted Milk biscuits against her cup before dunking them in her tea.

Partial Sue had no such compassion. "I can't believe you're falling for it, Dais. That was clearly a stunt she invented so Will would come to her aid. The damsel-in-distress routine. It's pathetic."

Fiona was still in two minds. "Well, her initial shock did seem genuine."

Partial Sue scoffed. "Yes, initial being the key word. Sophie is nothing if not a good actor. She recovered pretty quickly, spinning a good yarn to get Will to take her to A&E so they could have brunch afterwards. And she didn't seem to be particularly bothered that Will's wife worked at the hospital. She's planning on stealing him away and probably scripted the whole thing."

"Yes, but she's also a natural-born opportunist," Fiona replied. "Spin is in her blood. It's a knee-jerk reaction for her.

I don't think a life-threatening situation would change that. If the world was ending, she'd be pouting into her phone and posting it on social media."

"Okay, so if she's telling the truth, what in heaven's name pulled her under?" Partial Sue asked.

Daisy nervously tapped another biscuit against her cup before dipping it and wolfing it down whole.

"Why do you keep doing that?" asked Partial Sue.

"Doing what?"

"Knocking your biscuit against your cup. You've been doing it all morning."

Daisy flushed. "Oh, it's just a silly little thing I invented to solve a problem."

"What problem?" Fiona asked.

"Biscuits falling into tea when you dunk them." Daisy selected another Malted Milk to demonstrate. "See, I lightly tap it against the cup first to test its strength. If the biscuit breaks, it's no good for dipping. However, if it stays together then it's good to go."

Fiona and Partial Sue both reached for biscuits, knocked them gently against the side of their cups. Partial Sue's broke but Fiona's stayed intact.

"Daisy, that's genius, that is," Partial Sue gushed.

Fiona dunked her biscuit safe in the knowledge that it would hold together. "I think you've just solved a problem that's been troubling tea drinkers since tea drinking was invented."

"Really?" Daisy flushed some more. "I mean, you still have to use your judgement and take it out before it gets too soggy."

"Yeah, but that's a given." Partial Sue snatched another biscuit and tried again. "I am partial to dunking a biscuit and, this way, you know the good 'uns from the wrong 'uns."

"I wish it was as simple with this case," Fiona replied.

Silence fell over the shop, apart from the gentle *tap, tap, tap* of Malted Milks being tested for their structural integrity.

"I did have one idea," Daisy said.

"If it's as good as the last one, then I'm all ears," Partial Sue enthused.

"I don't know about that, and it might be stretching things a bit. But what if Hayley pulled Sophie under?"

"Why would she do that?" Fiona asked. "And, more importantly, how? She left moments earlier."

"Yes, but did you see her actually leave?" Daisy asked.

Fiona thought back to earlier that morning. She'd seen her go off in a huff, but not actually leave the beach. "No, I got distracted by Sophie showing up. Everyone did."

"Exactly," Daisy replied. "She could've used the commotion to double back and slip into the sea unnoticed, maybe on the other side of the groyne. She swims back towards the club, then ducks under at the last moment and pulls Sophie under."

"I suppose it's possible," Partial Sue said.

Fiona had her doubts. "She'd have to get close without anyone seeing her, then swim underwater for a long time. Do the evil deed then swim away again, holding her breath all that time with the cold sapping her energy. Then get away without anyone noticing her. That's a big ask."

Partial Sue had other reservations. "Hold on, why would Hayley attack Sophie?"

"I don't think she meant to," Daisy replied. "I think she was after you, Fiona. She got angry when you asked about her relationship with Will. She stormed off but didn't see Sophie show up in the same teal swimsuit as you. I think you were her target, but she got Sophie by mistake."

Fiona gulped as the cold, hard logic lined up. "And peering through the murky water, she wouldn't notice the difference between my ample body and Sophie's trim one." The colour drained from Fiona's face as the dreadful possibility fogged her mind like toxic fumes. Tinnitus squealed in her ears. Had Hayley tried to kill her this morning?

"You okay, Fiona?" Daisy asked.

"Yes, I'm fine." Fiona wasn't fine.

For once, Partial Sue's bluntness came to the rescue. "Sorry, I'm still not buying it. Look, I know that Hayley was miffed at Fiona. But would she really go to all that trouble?"

"Depends how obsessed she is about Will," Daisy replied. "Desire makes people do silly things."

"See, I'm thinking my first theory was right," Partial Sue said. "She was jealous of Sophie. Plain and simple. Sophie was her target."

"But she didn't see Sophie flirting with Will," Daisy replied.

Partial Sue leaned in. "She might have done, from afar. Even if she couldn't hear them, she could've seen enough to fill in the blanks."

"What if she saw Will kissing Sophie's hand?" Fiona said.

"Exactly," Partial Sue replied. "Jealousy's a powerful motive. And, as you quite rightly pointed out, Hayley's obsessed with Will."

"I'd have to admit that sounds more likely," Fiona agreed, glad to be out of Hayley's firing line. "But either way, Hayley's stealthy underwater mission still feels like a big stretch to me. Just the time she'd need to hold her breath would make it tricky."

Daisy attempted to justify her theory. "But if she was in a rage, she could do it. Like the Incredible Hulk — he can do all sorts of things when he's angry, and you said she was really angry."

"Yeah, but I think even the Incredible Hulk would struggle to hold his breath for that long in freezing cold water," Partial Sue remarked.

The ladies were in familiar territory. In every case they encountered, they would hit a holding pattern. Arguments circling but never actually landing anywhere, and nothing to break the deadlock.

Fiona's phone buzzed.

"Anything interesting?" Partial Sue asked.

Fiona smiled. "Message from Ted Maplin. Says he's got some important information."

"Oh, lets pop over and see him after work," Daisy cried, excited about the possibility of a new lead.

"I think it would be better if I go alone, like last time," Fiona said. "I'll drive over there now, if that's okay. Hopefully he'll have something that will move this case forward."

Daisy and Partial Sue became downcast, wearing the same expression as Simon Le Bon when he knew Fiona was about to go out without him. But Fiona couldn't think of any other way. The therapist was already going over and above what was expected of him, and she didn't want anything to jeopardise that.

CHAPTER 25

On the way to the therapist's house, a broken water main had closed off Fiona's preferred route, sending her on a merry diversion around Southbourne's backstreets. The area was unfamiliar to her, and the sudden increase in traffic on otherwise quiet, suburban roads caused plenty of tailbacks. Her engine idled at yet another junction as she drummed her hands on the wheel, waiting for the queue of cars to edge forward. She was impatient to meet with Ted and extract whatever information he possessed before he had a change of heart. Her mind began to wander, conjuring up the possibilities of what it could be. Maybe he would reveal the person in the club that Colin didn't get along with, although that would be no great revelation or surprise. She'd bet her life savings that it was Will.

Speak of the devil. Out of the corner of her eye, Fiona spotted the athletic figure of Will, fully clothed for once, exiting a block of flats, diagonally across from where she sat. Strange — she didn't imagine him living in a flat with his wife. A second later, she amended her assumption as Hayley appeared behind him in the communal doorway and called after him. Will turned towards her. The pair had a brief word, then Will hugged Hayley and made a swift exit around the corner.

Fiona didn't hear their exchange but decided to seize the moment. Flicking the indicator down she pulled the car over to the side of the road and leaped out.

Hayley didn't notice Fiona approaching. She'd become momentarily distracted, stooping down in the open doorway to pick up the post from the mat. Straightening up to sift through it, she caught sight of Fiona. Her face became a mask of shock.

"Hello again," Fiona uttered with as much non-judgemental friendliness as she could muster.

Given their previous encounter, and Daisy's theory about her underwater stealth mission, Fiona expected a stream of expletives to pour forth from Hayley's mouth. But all she offered up was a brittle, "Hello."

Fiona smiled. "Sorry for the unexpected visitation. But I was just passing and saw you. I thought I'd come and say hi."

Hayley clutched the mail against her chest defensively.

They each stared at the other for a beat. An uncomfortable standoff.

Fiona wondered whether she should test out Daisy's theory and accuse Hayley of attempting to pull her under the water this morning, albeit grabbing the wrong person.

However, in the cold light of day, with Hayley standing in front of her, the whole idea seemed a little preposterous. Plus, it didn't help that Hayley's golden locks appeared to be perfectly coiffured and conditioned, as they had appeared earlier at the beach before Fiona had lost sight of her. Certainly not the look of someone who'd been submerged in freezing cold salt water, unless she'd rushed home and spent all morning washing, conditioning and drying her hair to salon standards. Fiona resorted to Occam's razor on the matter. The simplest explanation had to be that Sophie had engineered the whole drowning-damsel stunt to secure brunch with Will.

Hayley blinked a couple of times, then gazed at her feet humbly. She mumbled the last thing Fiona expected. "I'm sorry I was rude to you earlier."

"Oh, that's okay."

Hayley kept her head bowed. "I'm afraid I wasn't in a very good place."

"I hope you're in a much better place now."

"I am. Thank you."

Fiona waited for her to elaborate but she didn't volunteer any further information. She would just have to prod and jab it out of her. "I saw Will leave here, just now. I'm not here to judge or . . ."

Hayley's tone changed abruptly. "Good, because it's none of your business."

"You're right. It is none of my business." Fiona hated herself for what she was about to say but she had no choice. "I think Will's wife might beg to differ." She turned and walked away.

Hayley chased after her and grabbed Fiona by the arm. "Wait! It's not what you think."

Fiona arched a questioning eyebrow.

Hayley's body deflated. "I'll be honest with you, but you must swear not to tell anyone at the swimming club."

"I promise."

Hayley took a deep breath. "Will and I had a fling years ago. Just a one-night stand. We both regretted it. He's happily married with two kids, and I didn't want a relationship, not with him, anyway. It was purely spur-of-the-moment lust. We both admitted it was a mistake. However, that mistake had a consequence. I got pregnant. He wanted me to get rid of the baby, but I wanted to keep it. And I'm glad I did. Jacob is the best thing to ever happen to me." She beamed warmly.

Fiona blinked several times, taking a moment to digest this shocking new information. "I take it Will wanted to keep Jacob a secret from his wife?"

"That's right. But so did I. Maggie's a nice lady, and has two gorgeous kids. I didn't want to jeopardise what she had. I feel terrible about what we did. It'd destroy her if she found out. Probably end their marriage. I promised not to say anything, not for his sake, but for his wife and kids, as long as he promised to pay maintenance. By and large he does. But Will's not this whiter-than-white saint that everyone thinks he is. From time to time, he has to be reminded of his obligations."

"And that's why you turn up at the swimming club every now and then. To jog his memory."

"That's right. My mum looks after Jacob, gets him ready for school, while I make a nuisance of myself in front of Will at the beach in the morning."

"But everyone in the club thinks you're infatuated with Will. Like he's the innocent victim and you're stalking him. That's not right. Doesn't that bother you?"

Hayley sighed. "Since having Jacob, he's all I care about. I'm not bothered about what they think. Only that Jacob has everything he needs."

"Does Will ever see Jacob?" Fiona asked.

Hayley shook her head. "It's okay. I prefer it that way."

Fiona frowned. Will strutted around like some glorious, Speedo-wearing messiah when in reality he was an absent father, shirking his responsibilities to his own child. Others would have no qualms about broadcasting his infidelity. "So when I saw him just now, had he agreed to pay what he owes?"

"Yes, he did. Usually after I show up at the beach for a few days on the trot and it gets too awkward for him, he comes around and we thrash it out. He pays me some money, until the next time I have to twist his arm."

Fiona's fists tightened. She felt angry on Hayley's behalf, that the single mum had to go through that pantomime, playing the villain to protect Will's marriage, just to get him to cough up what he owed to take care of his own son.

Hayley must have detected the indignant rage in Fiona's eyes. "Please promise you won't say anything. If the club found out, it would get back to Maggie and then her whole world would end."

Fiona frowned. "I promise." She paused for a moment. "Can I ask you about Colin? I take it you knew he had a crush on you?"

Hayley nodded. "I did. Sorry I was so defensive when you asked me before, but I wasn't in the best of moods."

"Quite understandable."

"But I was telling the truth about not being his friend. I didn't want to lead him on, especially after what happened with Will, so I avoided him."

"What do you think happened to Colin?"

Hayley shrugged. "You know, I have no idea. Tragic accident. Who knows?"

"Did anyone in the club have it in for him? Will, perhaps?"

Hayley baulked at this suggestion. "God, no. He may be a shirker but he's not aggressive and certainly not a murderer."

"What about anyone else?"

Hayley thought for a moment. "Colin was a bit of a know-all. Had this compulsion to tell people what to do. Annoying, I'll grant you. But he was like that to everyone. It wasn't as if he picked on one person, and they decided to exact their revenge."

This was a point that Fiona hadn't considered before. If everyone was being harangued by Colin, then they'd all be in the same boat, which would sort of dissipate the effect. However, misery loves company. It was entirely possible that, united by their shared belittlement, they had all got together to end his life — a terrifying prospect.

"Okay. Thank you, Hayley. You've been very helpful, and I promise I won't divulge any of this to the club."

"Thank you."

"I suppose I won't see you for a while now."

Hayley smiled. "Nope, that's me done with cold-water swimming until the next time Jacob needs new shoes." She chuckled but it was laced with anguish.

Fiona left, satisfied that Hayley had nothing to do with Colin's death. She had bigger issues in her life. Fiona felt sympathy for the single mum, and more than a little annoyed on her behalf. She certainly didn't deserve that kind of treatment from the father of her child. Fiona's opinion of Will had plummeted, made worse by the fact that someone with such low moral standards was held in such high esteem by those around him. She felt as if she should set everyone straight. However, that wasn't her call to make, and a promise is a promise. But, as far as Fiona was concerned, the rakish lothario was still high on the list of suspects, despite Hayley coming to his defence. Anyone who showed such little care or interest in their own child and put on a good show of being the all-round nice guy also had the potential to be a cold, psychopathic killer.

Fiona started the engine and slotted the car back into the traffic queue, waiting to move forward. Her thoughts eagerly returned to where she'd left off before she'd spotted Will: just what was this information the therapist had for her?

CHAPTER 26

Ted Maplin, dressed immaculately in a suit and tie, crossed his legs and steepled his fingers, slowly gathering his thoughts.

As she waited uncomfortably, Fiona snatched glimpses around his lounge-cum-consultation room, to give herself something to do. The bright, sparkling covers of the coffee table books on Spain contrasted starkly with the brooding images of the northern countryside on the walls.

"I've been wrestling with something," Ted finally uttered. His eyes looked tired and puffy. Whatever was on his mind must have been keeping him up all night. "But I've come to the conclusion that telling you is the right thing to do, although it completely betrays client confidentiality."

Subconsciously, Fiona found herself scooching forward on the sofa, eager to hear. She desperately wanted him to get to the point but bit her tongue. Ted wanted to lay down the groundwork, fully justifying his decision.

"I'm no sleuth, and I know I'm probably telling you how to suck eggs, but I know that in murder cases, the first course of action is always to determine who stood to gain from the victim's death."

Heat gathered around Fiona's neck, spreading up to her face, as the rookie error became all too apparent. Neither she nor the other ladies had considered this crucial line of inquiry. They'd all been preoccupied with tales of vengeance and love triangles, ignoring the most blatant motive. Who, indeed, would benefit from Colin's death?

Ted stared at her, probably detecting her awkward expression and flushing cheeks. "Sorry, have I got that right?"

"Oh, er . . . yes, yes, absolutely," Fiona fumbled her reply, attempting to cover her oversight. "Please, continue."

Ted inhaled deeply. "Okay, so here's where I really overstep the mark. Colin wasn't short of a penny or two. It wasn't that he was a big earner or anything. He had his teacher's pension, but he hardly touched any of it. Told me as much. Never bought anything and was a keen DIYer, fixed everything himself and was very careful with his money. Now, here's the important bit. Colin had no family, and no real close friends, but he told me that there was someone in the club who was struggling. He told me how he would help her out as much as possible. Would go round and fix her car or her washing machine and pay for parts, because she couldn't afford them."

"I've heard that he did that with a lot of people," Fiona remarked.

Ted nodded. "Yes, he was kind like that. However, when he spoke about this person, I got the feeling he was worried about her, more so than the other people he helped, because she was in debt. Said he felt responsible for her."

"Who is this person?"

Ted raised his hand. "Before I get to that, let me just outline my thinking." He hesitated for a second. "Okay, this is where I stray into pure conjecture. Colin never mentioned anything to me about having a will. I mean, he had no idea he was about to die, so why would he? But I'm sure he had one. So I put two and two together and thought, it was highly likely that he'd leave his money to this person, or at least some of it. Now, if he'd mentioned that fact to said person and said person was struggling, desperate for money, you'd have a strong motive for murder, wouldn't you?"

Fiona swallowed hard. The therapist was a pretty good detective. Better than Fiona, in fact. She cleared her throat. "That's correct. Who is this person?"

Before he had a chance to utter the name, Fiona had a fair idea of the answer. "Someone called Beth," Ted replied.

The name rang out in Fiona's mind. Surely not Beth. She liked Beth. Although she hadn't seen much of her, Fiona would definitely consider her friend material.

Fiona attempted to put her personal feelings aside and think rationally for a moment. Only the other night at the pub quiz, Beth had informed her that her car was broken, and she didn't have the money to fix it. But then, almost in the same breath, she had mentioned that it would be okay because she would be getting money for another one. Fiona hadn't thought anything of that at the time, but how could Beth afford a new car if she was strapped for cash? Where would the money come from? Unless Colin had left it to her in his will, and she was just waiting for probate to complete.

"Do you know her?" Ted asked.

Fiona gave a devastated nod. "Yes, I do."

"What do you think of my theory?"

Reluctantly, Fiona said, "It makes a lot of sense. And it's definitely one I'll be pursuing."

Concern flashed in Ted's eyes. "Can I just ask how you'll go about that?"

Fiona read between the lines. "Don't worry. I won't mention your name or how I know about any of this. You've put your professional reputation at stake to give me this information. The least I can do is protect your identity."

Ted's shoulders relaxed, satisfied with her response.

"Can I ask another question?" Fiona said. "Did he feel anything romantic for Beth?"

Ted shook his head. "No, I got the impression he regarded her more like a sister. He said there was someone else he liked in the club, but she didn't pay him any attention."

Fiona decided to seize the moment and prod the therapist for more answers. "You also said there was someone Colin didn't get along with in the club."

She could see his reluctance to answer, but it was a little difficult to refuse now he'd already breached client confidentiality. "He mentioned a chap called Will. Although, with my therapist hat on, I'd say his dislike was fuelled by jealousy."

"How so?" Fiona already knew the answer.

"He told me the woman he liked had affections for this Will. I'm sure that was the source of his dislike for him."

Okay, no great revelations there. Fiona popped off a few more questions until Ted became uncomfortable and declined to divulge any more information.

She left his house preparing to have a very difficult conversation with Beth.

CHAPTER 27

Beth's shaking hand dumped a heap of brown sugar into her latte. Fiona watched as it refused to sink, buoyed by the dense foam. She attacked it with a spoon, creating a whirlpool of froth. Some of the sugar caved in and went under, but most of it remained captive on the surface, turning the froth a sweet bronzy colour.

Fiona took a sip of her own coffee. It tasted pretty good, much better than she had expected from an establishment specialising in alcohol. Like most hospitality outlets, from burger joints to sandwich bars, or even petrol stations, the Countess of Strathmore pub knew the importance of serving good coffee. People demanded it these days and could be put off a place for life if they were served something instant from a crusty jar.

The place was busy for mid-morning. Not packed to the rafters like the quiz night but busy enough for the low hum of people enjoying a natter and tucking into cake, and pretty good cake by the looks of it. However, the same couldn't be said for Fiona's table. Neither of them had the appetite for any baked delights and they sat opposite each other in momentary silence.

Fiona watched tears slowly gathering in Beth's eyes. She was about to offer her a tissue, but Beth snatched a napkin from a wooden caddy containing upright knives and forks and an array of condiments, their lids rimmed with dried sauce.

Beth dabbed her eyes and blew her nose. "I felt terribly guilty. Still do."

"What have you got to feel guilty about?"

Beth sniffed. "Because Colin left me all his money, his house, even that old Land Rover of his, and I don't know why."

"You said so yourself," Fiona replied. "He didn't have any family or friends. I know the swimming club gave him a social group but not what you'd call close friends."

"No, he annoyed anyone who got close to him." She managed a tiny but painful chuckle.

"Yes, except for you." Fiona smiled. "I think you were the closest thing he had to a friend. You understood him. No one else did. I remember you saying he reminded you of your brother, and I'm guessing he sensed a kindred spirit in you."

"But I don't deserve to inherit everything he owned. I'm benefiting from his death. It's horrible. That's why I kept it quiet. And I was worried if people found out, they'd think I killed him."

"Is that why you wanted us to look into his death?"

Beth wept, sniffed and blotted her eyes with another napkin. "Yes," she croaked. "I know what people are like. Even though I love the club, I know they'll think the worst, but I would never do anything like that. Never."

"They don't have to know you inherited anything. It's none of their business. I certainly won't say anything. Did you have any idea he'd planned to leave you everything?"

Beth shook her head. "No, not a clue. I had nothing to do with his death. I swear."

This rang true in Fiona's mind. If Beth stood to gain from Colin's death and she had killed him, then the last thing she would do was initiate an investigation into his possible murder. It'd be like a turkey voting for Christmas. Especially as Colin's demise had already been neatly tied up with the verdict of accidental death — a gift horse for any killer. Police were satisfied that foul play wasn't involved, so why make life difficult if she had murdered him?

Fiona reached out a reassuring hand towards Beth's and gave it a squeeze. "I believe you."

Without looking up, Beth mumbled a timid, "Thank you."

The pair went silent again. Fiona hesitated before asking her next question, preparing it as delicately as she could. "Beth, I know you said your car had broken down, but is there another reason you haven't been down to the beach?"

Beth fixed her with damp eyes. "What do you mean?"

"Please tell me if I'm out of order here, but has Colin's death put you off wild swimming?"

Fiona watched as Beth's gaze lowered, then she slowly nodded. "I just don't feel like it anymore. I'm scared to go in. But even if I did, it's like I'm being disrespectful to Colin's memory somehow."

"I know what you mean. But Colin would want you to carry on, I'm sure of it. You told me about the benefits of wild swimming, how it's good for mental health. And it is. I've tried it and it works. Right now, I think you could do with some of that. Blow all those nasty cobwebs away. Why don't you join me at the beach tomorrow? We'll have a swim together."

An uncertain smile finally broke across Beth's face. "I'll try, but I'm not promising anything."

"Good enough for me." Fiona gathered her thoughts. She needed to persuade Beth to be kind to herself and stop feeling guilty. "As for inheriting Colin's money, he wanted you to have it. That was his wish. He wouldn't want you to feel ashamed — far from it. The best thing you can do is respect his wishes. Use the money to pay off your debts and get anything else you need."

"Everything's tied up in probate at the moment," Beth pointed out. "Could take months."

"But when it's all done and dusted, no feeling guilty, okay? Accept what he's gifted you. That's the best way of honouring his memory."

"I'll try." The tears were back, but they were tears of happiness, of relief.

Fiona left Beth with a parting hug, and tried once more to persuade her to go for a wild swim the next day. She wasn't holding out much hope, but at least she'd left Beth in a better frame of mind than when she'd first sat down with her.

Fiona headed back to the shop, deciding to keep this little part of the investigation to herself.

CHAPTER 28

"What happened with Ted Maplin? Have we got a new lead?" Partial Sue asked before Fiona had even shrugged off her coat.

"No. Dead end, I'm afraid." Fiona was keen to move the conversation on and keep Beth's inheritance a secret. "But I did discover something else on my travels, which has put one area of investigation to bed."

"Ooh, that sounds interesting." Daisy placed the teapot next to a Victoria sponge, still in its box. Fiona had just had a large latte with Beth but could never say no to tea. However, she still didn't have the stomach for cake just yet.

When she had finished enlightening them about Hayley and Will and their illegitimate child, Daisy and Partial Sue let out deep and astonished gasps in perfect unison.

"So there was no love triangle," Daisy remarked, slightly disappointed. "Just an absent father not fulfilling his parental obligations."

"That's about the size of it," Fiona replied.

Partial Sue swore. "This Will sounds like a right egotistical hypocrite. Makes me sick. Swanning around pretending he's Mr Nice Guy."

"Don't forget the skimpy Speedos," Daisy pointed out.

Partial Sue's face became angrier. "Yes, I know it shouldn't matter what he wears, but somehow it makes him a lot worse. Stupid poser."

"I agree," Fiona said. "But I have to point out I'm under strict instructions not to divulge any of this to the swimming club. I made a promise to Hayley. It must stay between us three."

Daisy nodded.

"It's fine," Partial Sue replied. "I mean, me and Dais don't have anything to do with the club anyway."

Fiona detected a tone in her colleague's voice, one she wasn't sure how to take. It sounded like a little dig against Fiona. But before she had time to dwell on the possibly barbed remark, Daisy's face brightened. "Ooh, ooh, I forgot to say. I've discovered something you won't believe."

"This sounds interesting," Partial Sue remarked.

"It is. I've been researching surfing. I must confess, I got a bit sidetracked looking at all these tropical sandy white beaches, imagining myself cruising along the waves then snoozing in a hammock slung between a couple of palm trees as the sun goes down. But what I found's going to shock both of you. You'll never guess who was a surfer."

Judging by her demeanour, Fiona doubted this had anything to do with the investigation.

"Go on, guess. It's one of your heroes." Daisy shuddered with excitement. "I stumbled on it by accident."

"Not Martin Lewis from Money Saving Expert?" Partial Sue answered.

"No, go on. Guess again."

"Just tell me."

"You have to guess. It's a guessing game."

Partial Sue folded her arms defiantly. "I don't like guessing games. They're like jigsaw puzzles. Ultimately pointless. Just look at the picture on the box if you want to know what it will look like."

"You'll never guess." Daisy wanted to prolong the intrigue as much as possible.

"Just put us out of our misery," Fiona relented.

Daisy paused. "Agatha Christie."

"What?" Fiona said.

"You're kidding," Partial Sue snorted.

"Nope. She went on surfing holidays to Honolulu." Daisy thumbed her phone screen and showed them the photographic evidence, a selection of shots taken in the 1920s. The queen of murder mysteries was surfing in a bathing hat and a black swimsuit so thick and waterlogged it appeared to be knitted from squid-ink spaghetti.

"Well, I never!" Fiona blurted.

"Wouldn't you just love to do that?" Daisy stared longingly at the images.

"If she can do it, so can we," Fiona agreed.

Partial Sue grumbled, but before she could voice her opinions on the matter, Ralph burst through the door, a dishevelled ball of jittery energy.

"Hey, Ralph," Daisy said immediately. "Did you know Agatha Christie was a surfer?"

"Agatha Christie?" Ralph muttered. "Is she one of the Sugababes?"

"No," Partial Sue snapped. "She's *the* most famous crime writer in the world."

Ralph's eyes suddenly became as wide as glitterballs. "Oh man! Speaking of crime, have I got something for you!"

Simon Le Bon immediately launched himself at Ralph's legs, wanting to play. Ralph was happy to oblige and immediately dropped to all fours. The pair became an entangled maelstrom of fur and sun-bleached hair. When Ralph finally came up for air, clawing at his damp locks, which had been plastered to his face with dog licks, he stared at the ladies blankly. "Sorry, what was I saying?"

"You have something for us," Fiona informed him.

"Oh, that's right!" Ralph's limbs immediately became animated, acting independently of one another. A scarecrow brought to life in baggy surf clothing, he approached the table and pulled up a chair. His eyes suddenly locked onto the Victoria sponge, still in its packet. "Is that cake up for grabs?"

"Help yourself," Fiona said.

"Oh, cheers. I'm absolutely hollow." He slid the cake out of its box, forgoing the usual ritual of transferring it to the large plate, leaving it on its circle of cardboard. Grabbing the knife, he hacked away at it as if he was sawing firewood, resulting in an odd number of roughly cut and grossly unequal segments, some as wide as doorstops, others no more than slivers. Daisy shifted in her seat, her fastidiousness about cake etiquette not liking this one bit.

Ralph shoved the largest wedge into his mouth. "That's amazing."

"Would you like some tea to go with it?" Daisy asked.

"Nah, I'm good. Got my water bottle in the van."

Partial Sue screwed up her face, presumably offended that anyone would pair water with cake.

They all watched expectantly, urging him to finish so he could divulge some new and hopefully beneficial information. Thankfully he demolished it in just three mouthfuls.

Ralph wiped the crumbs from his mouth, then he suddenly turned to Partial Sue and shot off on a further distraction. "Oh! I watched *Point Break* the other day."

Partial Sue became bright and attentive. "What did you think?"

"It's totally awesome. It's now my favourite movie, after *Toy Story* and *The Exorcist.*" Ralph had eclectic tastes, it seemed.

"So many cool lines in it," he continued, overflowing with enthusiasm. "I love that bit when Keanu says, 'I am an FBI agent!' Just awesome." Ralph didn't have to work too hard to pull off a better-than-average impression of the kind-hearted Hollywood action star.

Fiona grew mildly impatient, wondering if Ralph actually had something for them or had just come here to scoff cake and trade movie opinions. "Speaking of investigations into surfers, did you have any luck?"

"Yeah, okay. So, I asked around if anyone had seen a surfer and a wild swimmer having a barney that weekend in January. No one heard or saw anything. But I guess we already knew that, 'cos there weren't any waves down here."

"How many surfers did you speak to?" Partial Sue asked.

"About thirty, maybe forty."

Fiona was impressed. Not a bad sample size. "That's good work, Ralph."

"Thanks. But a few of them did mention something interesting. When your guy disappeared, it was a spring tide."

"But it wasn't spring," Daisy replied. "It was January."

Ralph shook his head. "I don't know why it's called a spring tide because it's got nothing to do with spring. They happen every month. But spring tides are high. Really high and powerful."

Fiona mused on this. "So even if there weren't any waves, the sea would still be dangerous. Perfect conditions for getting into trouble."

"It's possible. I can't say for sure, but you have to be careful with spring tides. Sea doesn't behave like it normally does. But that's only half the story. Get this. When the tide goes out, it's just as strong as when it comes in. And it goes out really far, sucking everything out to sea. Would've pulled a body right into the Channel, no problem."

Suddenly everything lined up and the accidental death by misadventure verdict seemed more likely than ever. Had they been reading too much into the sinister circumstances surrounding Colin's death, pointing fingers at everyone, when the biggest suspect was nature itself? They'd pondered on this before. But now they had some serious evidence to back it up — the precarious conditions caused by an extreme tide.

Fiona summarised. "So, oblivious to the fact it was a spring tide, Colin went for a swim. High currents maybe swept him onto the rock groyne, where he hit his head, and then dragged his dead body out to sea until it got washed up on Hengistbury Head a week later."

Ralph had an awkward expression on his face. "Yeah, I suppose you could say that."

"Do you have a different take on it, Ralph?" Partial Sue asked.

His face gurned. "Well, maybe I've got into this detective thing a bit too much, but I was thinking if someone wanted to kill Colin and dump his body in the sea to make it look like an accident, a spring tide would be the best time to do it. Freak tides cause a lot of deaths each year. It'd be chalked up to another one."

The ladies became silent, digesting all the information. Fiona felt her mind going back to that blessed holding pattern again. A fifty–fifty stalemate situation where nature could be the cause as much as premeditated murder. But no real evidence to say one way or the other. "And exactly when would be the best time for that to happen?" Fiona asked.

"Right at the point where the tide changes," Ralph replied. "Once that happens, the tide would go out really fast. Take the body with it."

Daisy was on it in a flash, seeking out a tide table website for Southbourne. "Well, on Saturday the eighth of January, for example, high tide was at 11.30 a.m."

"That would fit with our theory," Partial Sue enthused. "We think Colin missed his morning swim with the club for some reason. So, he went down to the beach later. Club would have gone by then, weather was cold and miserable. Just two degrees. Nobody's going to be hanging around in those conditions, except Colin — and his murderer, who bashes his head in and dumps his body on the outgoing tide."

"Where it stays for about a week," Fiona added. "Conveniently mucking up the evidence. Remember what that article said: *Water is a particularly suitable medium for camouflaging foul play.*"

"There's something else," said Ralph. "I don't know if it's important or not."

"Believe me, everything's important." Fiona smiled.

"Well, the guys I spoke to told me there was surf that weekend."

"But we checked those forecast websites," Daisy pointed out. "There was barely a wave."

"Yes, down here," Ralph replied. "But not at Kimmeridge."

"That's west of here, isn't it?" Partial Sue became excited. "On the Purbeck Hills. The Jurassic Coast, with the giant sea monster skull. I saw it on David Attenborough."

"We love David Attenborough," Daisy added, warmly.

Ralph nodded. "But what most people don't know is Kimmeridge is a legendary surf spot. A lot more exposed than Bournemouth or Southbourne. Picks up loads more swell. Conditions have to be right, though, and it rarely works, but when it does, the place can be chest high while there's barely anything ridable here."

"And was it like that on that weekend in January?" Fiona replied.

Ralph looked downcast. "Yeah, apparently all week. Not classic Kimmeridge — I'm told the waves were a very doable waist high. But I missed it. Can't believe it. I think I was working. But the place would've been packed with surfers and bodyboarders. Can I have another slice of cake?"

"Please, have as much as you want," Fiona said. "What if Colin had known about the waves at Kimmeridge and wanted to wild swim there? I know the club told me they love swimming in waves. Are there CCTV cameras over there?"

Ralph shook his head, his mouth full of sponge. "No. Place is old-school. You have to drive over and see for yourself. But there are a ton of rocks over there."

"So he could've bashed his head. But how would he know there were waves there?" Partial Sue asked. "He's not a surfer. And would he really drive all that way just to frolic around in some waves? It seems unlikely. I mean, it's an hour's drive from here."

"He didn't drive anywhere, remember?" Daisy reminded her. "His nosy neighbour said his Land Rover hadn't moved since Friday the seventh."

Ralph swallowed the last bit of cake and eyed up another. "He could've checked swell forecast sites, and a lot of surfers share lifts over there. Maybe another wild swimmer picked him up."

"His neighbour would've heard a car pulling up," Partial Sue said.

"And Colin didn't like sharing lifts, either," Fiona added.

Ralph shrugged. "Fair enough." He took another slice of cake without asking.

"Okay," Fiona said. "Let's just assume he did go over there and banged his head, either by accident or by design. You said the place would've been packed."

Ralph stopped mid-munch, as something occurred to him. "You're right. It gets so crowded in the water at the weekend you can hardly get a wave to yourself. If he got into trouble, someone would've helped him. Okay, surfers don't usually like wild swimmers, but when it comes to water safety, they're all over it. They would have pulled him ashore, no doubt."

"What if he went there really early on the weekend, when no one was out?" Partial Sue asked. "He usually swims at eight o'clock with the club."

Ralph shook his head. "Dawn patrol would've been out."

"Who or what is a dawn patrol?"

"Surfers who get up at like four or five in the morning," Ralph answered. "To get down there before sunrise, to catch clean, empty waves. Trouble is, everyone has the same idea these days and turns up at the crack of dawn. It's just as busy as the rest of the day." Ralph finished his cake, then checked his watch. "Aw, shoot. Gotta get to work."

"Ralph, thank you so much for dropping by," Fiona said.

The other ladies agreed. "You've given us lots to think about," Partial Sue added.

"No worries, and cheers for the cake." He jumped to his feet, but on his way out, Ralph's short attention span got the better of him. He spied a bright red Rip Curl sweatshirt hanging on the men's rail. Priced at only five pounds, it was catnip to a cool cat like Ralph. He snatched it from its hanger. "Oh man. I gotta try this on before I go."

Unhampered by any self-consciousness, he stripped off his top in front of them, revealing his naked torso. Politely, the ladies immediately averted their eyes, but not before Fiona noticed something about his body and it was nothing to do with his surf-toned muscles.

It was a key piece of evidence.

CHAPTER 29

Ralph tugged on the sweatshirt and checked himself in the mirror. It only took him a second to decide that it suited him, although it was a little short on the arms. "I'll take it!" He dug into the pocket of his jeans, fishing around for some money. His hand emerged, dislodging spent ticket stubs and protein bar wrappers, plus some earbuds and a Hot Wheels car, but no money of which to speak. He switched to the other pocket. Again, no luck, except lint and litter.

Fiona halted him. "Ralph, don't worry. The sweatshirt's on the house."

He ceased his rummaging and looked up, his face child-like. "Really?"

"Of course. You've helped us out immensely. It's the least we can do. But I've one last request before you go."

Ralph wobbled with excitement. "Sure, whatever you need."

"Would you mind taking your top off again?"

Ralph ceased his happy cavorting, as if someone had switched him off. He swallowed hard. "Er, is this some kind of *Magic Mike* thing? Because I'm really not into that. Although, you three are very nice ladies."

"Sorry," Fiona apologised. "I'll rephrase that. I noticed something on you that matches Colin's dead body."

Alarmed, Ralph pulled the sweatshirt over his head and tossed it to one side, then frantically examined himself all over as if looking for evidence of some deathly lurgy.

Partial Sue and Daisy spotted it immediately. Not hiding their shock, the pair sucked air into their lungs at a rate of knots.

"What is it? What have I got?" Raph contorted in front of the mirror, hoping to catch a glimpse of his ailment.

"Relax," Fiona said. "It's nothing to worry about. But your head's a slightly different colour from the rest of your body."

Ralph had a healthy glow to his face, but it ended abruptly in a well-defined line at the base of his neck. Below this, his skin was as pale as milk.

He ceased his twisting and turning, relieved that he hadn't come down with some tropical disease. "Oh, that. It's a surf tan."

"Surf tan?" Partial Sue asked.

Ralph turned to the ladies and pointed to the stark line around his neck. "That's where I've been wearing a wetsuit. This time of year, your whole body's covered in neoprene, even your hands and feet. Head's the only thing exposed to the elements. All that salty sea air, your face gets weather-beaten." Ralph threw his top back on and picked up his newly acquired sweatshirt from off the floor. "Did Colin have a surf tan, then?"

"I'm not sure," Fiona replied. "Beth from the wild swimming club had to identify his body. She told us his face was brownish, while his body was pale. He also had lacerations on his arms."

"We checked it on the internet," Partial Sue said. "We thought the colouring on his face could have been caused by hypothermia and the lacerations were where the body was dragged along the seabed."

Ralph raked his fingers through his hair. "I don't know about lacerations or hypothermia. But if he had a tan mark like mine, that's from wearing a wetsuit. Hundred per cent."

"Don't people who work outside a lot get tanned faces?" Partial Sue asked.

"Yes," Fiona agreed. "But I doubt working outside or hypothermia would produce such a sharp, well-defined line."

"Yeah," Ralph said. "Only a wetsuit does that. Which means it's unlikely your guy's been wild swimming. Those dudes don't wear wetsuits. He must have been surfing."

"Can you surf without a wetsuit?" Daisy asked.

"Not in the winter. Maybe for about fifteen minutes, then you'd definitely die of hypothermia. There's a lot of sitting on your board in surfing, waiting for the right wave. Wetsuit keeps you warm for hours, protects you too and gives you buoyancy. Helps you pop to the surface if you wipe out." Ralph glared at his watch. "Oh, man. Now I really am late for work. Thanks for the sweatshirt. Call me if you need anything else."

The ladies repeated their thanks and said their goodbyes. Ralph shambled out of the shop and was gone.

Fiona started texting.

"Are you messaging Beth?" Partial Sue asked.

"Yes, I've just asked her if Colin's body had a tan line around the neck."

Beth pinged back a reply immediately. Fiona grinned. "She said it did. Like he was wearing a white turtleneck."

"But did Beth ever notice it when he was wild swimming?" Daisy asked. "Or anyone else?"

Fiona quickly texted Beth the question. The answer pinged back. "She said they didn't."

Daisy grumbled. "Surely if he'd been surfing, wouldn't the whole club have noticed his surf tan when he stripped off to go wild swimming?"

"I don't think they would," Partial Sue said. "Colin had a reputation for bending people's ears. You wouldn't want to look in his direction in case he gave you a lecture. It's like Downward Doug at the shoe repairers. Don't ever catch his eye, otherwise, before you know it, he's moaning away and sending you in a downward spiral of despair. I bet club members were the same, averting their eyes whenever Colin was around."

"True," Daisy said. "But surely Beth would've seen it. She was his friend. Must have looked him in the eye all the time."

"Maybe she just didn't notice." Fiona knew this was a weak argument. Had she not noticed on purpose? She thought back to Ted Maplin's words about who stood to gain from Colin's death. But for the life of her, she still couldn't see Beth as the killer.

"I think we're getting sidetracked," Partial Sue said. "Why would Colin be wearing a wetsuit at all? He didn't like surfers, remember? Gave them an earful along with everyone else in the swimming club — well, except for Will."

"Doesn't mean he was surfing," Daisy suggested. "He could've been snorkelling or scuba-diving."

"But he wouldn't have a tan line if he was mostly underwater," Fiona pointed out.

"And his body was found at Hengistbury Head, not Kimmeridge. It's nearly thirty miles away. And his car hadn't moved since the Friday before he died."

"I know, I know," Fiona replied. "But I have a gut feeling that the key to all this is over on the Purbecks at Kimmeridge. I think we need to have a nose around. See what's what."

"I'm not sure I agree. I can't see the connection." Partial Sue smiled. "But I'm always partial to a jolly on the Purbecks."

CHAPTER 30

No one argued about closing up the shop for the afternoon. With a homogenous grey sky hanging low over Southbourne like a grotty suspended ceiling, it wasn't a day for mooching around charity shops. It wasn't a day for mooching around anywhere, it seemed. As they left Southbourne Grove behind, its eclectic mix of quirky cafés and boutiques were bereft of visitors, apart from the odd schoolchild nipping into a newsagent to stock up on unhealthy snacks.

Exactly one hour later, Partial Sue's car buzzed around the tightly cinched lanes of the Purbeck hills. The majestic landscape was a mixture of dark woodlands and sloping green fields, dotted with cloudlike sheep and divided by drystone walls. All it needed to complete this perfection was a blast of Vaughn Williams, but Daisy couldn't get a signal for her Spotify. Instead, Simon Le Bon grizzled all the way, his wet nose pressed against the side window as he watched acres of good walking country pass him by.

The car followed a narrow passage of hedgerows until the road kinked abruptly into a hairpin bend. The steering rack strained as it negotiated yet another tight corner, providing Fiona with her first proper glimpse of Kimmeridge village.

"It's so pretty," Daisy remarked.

Comprising of little more than a single road lined with cottages, the diminutive hamlet had everything needed to be classed as quaint. Ancient stone church: check. Tumbledown thatched roofs: check. Medieval-sized doorways: check. Red phone box: check — not functional, of course, but standing in someone's garden, sprawling with potted plants. Fiona was sure there would be a plaque somewhere announcing that Kimmeridge had won prettiest village several years ago. However, missing from the essential checklist was a local pub, but there was a sweet, ivy-strewn restaurant with a courtyard and garden, advertising a hearty welcome and home-cooked food. Fiona didn't doubt it for one second, judging by the look of the place.

Strangely, Daisy and Partial Sue hadn't zeroed in on the little eatery, earmarking it for tea and cake once they'd completed this evidence-gathering mission. Their attention had been ensnared by the building opposite — the Etches Collection — a smart, new stone-built museum housing fossils from the local area.

"That's where the sea monster lives!" Daisy gushed.

"Well, technically, it's a pliosaur," Partial Sue corrected. "And it died 150 million years ago."

Fiona craned her neck as they passed. "Gosh, car park's packed."

"That's the Attenborough effect for you," Partial Sue replied. "That fossil's world famous now."

Leaving the village behind, a long, sweeping road bisected two fields, leading them down to Kimmeridge Bay and its two distinct headlands separated by a wide square inlet of water.

"This is nearly shaking the fillings from my teeth," Daisy complained, as the car rattled and bumped its way towards the base of the headland that guarded the left-hand corner of the bay. Round yet another sharp corner, they passed a modest-sized boat park scattered with small dinghies. Beyond it, a cluster of squat fishermen's huts topped with rusted corrugated roofs, hunkered down among the rocks and vegetation. Eventually the road ended in a deserted gravel-strewn car park, commanding spectacular views over a dark and ominous sea.

Partial Sue wrenched on the handbrake and the ladies exited the car. Fiona gazed at their surroundings, taking in the full eeriness of the place. Whereas Kimmeridge village had been all hanging baskets and cutesiness, Kimmeridge Bay had a bleak, foreboding beauty about it. Towering muddy black cliffs, rich with oil and laden with fossils, plunged to a beach scattered with giant grey boulders and ashen slivers of sedimentary rock. There were no waves today, just gentle lapping at the strands of slick kelp languishing by the shoreline. Above this, the drum-like Clavell Tower watched over the sea from the clifftop. The place had all the ready-made components for doubling as an alien world in *Dr Who*.

"You know, you can rent that place out." Partial Sue pointed up at the lonely tower. "We should stay there one weekend. I'd be partial to staying in a tower."

"Not if it's haunted." Daisy took a cautionary step in the opposite direction.

"It's not haunted," Partial Sue scoffed. "But I've heard P.D. James used it as inspiration for her book *The Black Tower*."

"Really?" Fiona replied. "I can see why. This place has a mysterious charm to it."

"Gives me the creeps, if you don't mind me saying," Daisy quivered.

Just to add to the unsettling atmosphere, an almighty thud rang out across the bay, echoing off the hills and low cloud.

The ladies all jumped. Simon Le Bon whimpered.

"What the hell was that?" Partial Sue spun around, searching in every direction for the source of the disturbance.

"Maybe it's thunder?" Daisy said timidly.

"There are no thunderstorms forecast for today," Fiona replied.

Another boom blasted over the air.

"I don't like this." Daisy's eyes were wide with fear. "This is like one of those stories where everything's fine then the weather turns nasty because evil forces are at work."

"Maybe they are," Partial Sue warned, not particularly helping Daisy's fragile state of mind. "Maybe they're trying to stop us discovering the truth about Colin's death."

In the distance, a *rat-a-tat-tat* reverberated over the landscape as if a giant woodpecker were drumming its beak against the side of an enormous tree.

Daisy was ready to leave. "Oh my gosh! Can we go?"

"Don't venture t'other side of the bay," a piratical voice growled from behind them.

Jumping out of their skin, they turned to see a stocky fellow, who'd somehow sneaked up on them undetected. Dressed in scuffed yellow wellies and a battered wax jacket, he had a face like a discarded chamois with a beard trimmed to a sharp point. Large glasses perched on his nose and a fisherman's cap was pulled tightly down over his ears. He glared at them intensely, resembling Roger Whittaker's more sour-faced brother. A name tag pinned to his chest identified him as Bill the coastal warden.

Simon Le Bon growled at him, not liking his sudden appearance one bit.

CHAPTER 31

"Why, what's over there?" Daisy asked nervously. "Is that where the noise is coming from?"

Bill the coastal warden gazed ominously across the bay to the opposite headland. Fiona half expected him to say, "There be dragons." But his answer was oddly sedate and nostalgic. "VG are training."

"VG?" Fiona wondered why a now defunct convenience store chain would be making such a racket.

"Vehicle gunners," he informed them. "Tanks, in other words, from the gunnery school at Lulworth Camp. Practising with live rounds, they are. Wander over there and you might die! Blown to smithereens." He arched one grey eyebrow for dramatic effect. "Hit by a shell or a machine gun."

Daisy shuddered. "Er, are we safe here?"

Rubbing his beard and sizing up their location, he delayed his answer, presumably to further heighten their peril, clearly relishing the chance to spread his dour pessimism.

Partial Sue had had enough of his doom-and-gloom shenanigans. "Well, we must be safe, otherwise you wouldn't be standing here."

"Aye, 'tis a fair point you make. We're fine on this side of the bay. But keep your wits about you."

"Tell me," Fiona said. "Were they firing on the weekend of the seventh of January?"

He whipped out a dog-eared leatherbound notebook secured with an elastic band, flicked to a page and scanned down it, then nodded. "Aye, firing all that weekend and into the next week."

"On both sides of the bay?"

"No, just over there." He nodded to the other headland.

"We've heard there was some nice surf that weekend," said Partial Sue.

"Aye, that there was. Car park was full of surfers and their campervans. I remember 'cos it was a spring tide. Big 'un."

Despite him leaning into his old salty seadog routine so much that he was in danger of toppling head over his Wellingtoned heels, Fiona felt confident he knew what he was talking about. "Did anyone get in trouble that weekend or the days following?"

"Er, no." He looked disappointed at not having a woeful tale lined up to drag them down. He clearly thrived on being a merchant of despair.

"Are you sure?" Partial Sue asked.

"Aye. We have to report any accident or misdemeanour in the incident log. If someone sets one foot on the firing range, it goes in the log. Well, we drag them off the range first pretty sharpish, I can tell you."

"Can we see?"

The eyebrow was raised again. "You want to see me drag someone off the range?"

"No, can we look at the log?" Fiona thought he'd put up a fight. Make all sorts of jobsworth excuses, but he didn't seem to mind.

"Step this way."

They followed him to a small cabin with a corrugated roof next to the fishermen's huts. Little more than a garden shed but surrounded with large windows, it had a hefty door and emergency phone mounted on the outside, along with a defibrillator. Inside, several binoculars mounted on tripods pointed out to sea in different directions. There was a range of electronic equipment, marine instruments and displays, plus a laptop on a small desk, next to a tin mug with dried coffee in the bottom and the ledger in question. He pulled the hefty tome towards him. "Incidents get recorded digitally, but we're still required to write everything longhand. Maritime traditions don't die easily."

Daisy pulled out her phone, stared at its screen, then at the warden's laptop. "Do you have Wi-Fi here? Because I can't get a signal."

Bill grinned impishly, flicking at a white cable going into the side of the laptop. "Still got an ethernet cable. My secret weapon."

Partial Sue suddenly warmed to the warden. "That's what I'm always saying. I've still got them in my house. Never drops out."

"Aye, that they don't. Not like that wussy Wi-Fi. Best-kept secret, if you ask me." Bill winked. Partial Sue smiled back, happy to have found a fellow retro-technology fan.

The warden snapped open the ledger and wetted his index finger, then flipped through its pages. He stopped and swivelled the ledger around so they could all see. "Look. Nothing logged for that weekend or the days after."

They peered down at Bill's swirling copperplate writing. Each report was a masterpiece of misery, a novella of nastiness, going into great and grisly detail with dates, times, exact locations and plenty of graphic descriptions. One incident outlined a male walker who'd twisted his ankle on the path up to the tower. Bill had drawn a diagram, annotating all three ligaments the poor chap had probably torn. He'd also attempted to articulate the guttural sounds uttered every time the walker had tried to put weight on his foot. They ranged from gasps to splutters and a great deal of onomatopoeias such as "awk", "yowl" and, of course, "argh". Warden Bill clearly took a lot of pride — although, some might say, a little too much pleasure

— in recording other people's misfortunes. However, no incidents were recorded for the weekend of Friday the seventh of January, and nothing for several days afterwards until the following Friday, when someone's car wouldn't start, and the AA had to be called.

"Okay," Fiona said, satisfied. "What if someone, say, a surfer or a swimmer, got in trouble, and you missed it? Maybe they strayed over to the other side of the bay. Maybe a shell landed beside them in the sea. The explosion didn't kill them, but they got knocked against a rock." She was spitballing, prodding Bill to gauge his level of vigilance. Although she'd wager he had the eyes of a hawk when it came to detecting near-death situations.

"Impossible," he snapped, clearly offended at such a notion. "We'd haul them back before they ventured anywhere near the firing range. When the red warning flags are up, we monitor the land and the sea around the area. Anyone heading in that direction, on foot or by water, gets stopped if they get too close. And it's not just me monitoring things. A patrol boat goes up and down the coast stopping anyone getting close to the danger zone — boats, surfers, kayakers." His seafaring accent diminished somewhat as he explained the importance of keeping people safe when live ammunition was flying around. "Thing is, it's not likely anyone would get hit, even if they did go over there. The firing range is well away from here, at Lulworth, surrounded by high barbed wire fences. It's just a safety precaution in case a stray shell overshoots. No member of the public has ever got hit."

Partial Sue wasn't about to let his earlier scaremongering go unchallenged. "So when you declared we'd be blown to smithereens if we wandered over there, that was just for effect."

Bill shrugged. "Better to be safe than sorry."

Fiona changed the subject. "So I'm guessing you know this place pretty well. Are you originally from around here?"

He wouldn't catch Fiona's eye and mumbled something incomprehensible.

"Sorry?" Daisy asked.

"No," he replied quietly. "I'm originally from, er, Milton Keynes."

Geographically, it was about as far away from the sea as you could get in any given direction.

"Ah, so you moved here to be closer to the briny," Partial Sue chirped. "Got the sea in your blood."

He shook his head and sighed. "I know all there is to know about water, and love being beside it, but I can't stand being in it or on it. Makes me seasick."

Bill the coastal warden was the most ironic person Fiona had ever met. His salty seadog image was a pantomime, masking his contradictory aversion.

The room grew quiet until he regarded the three ladies curiously. "Can I ask why you're so interested in that weekend in January?"

"A wild swimmer washed up on a beach near us at Hengistbury Head," Fiona explained. "This was the weekend after. His body had been in the water for a week, so we think he must've died the weekend of the seventh."

This piqued Bill's macabre interest. "I hadn't heard about that. Tell me more, and don't spare any details."

For one moment Fiona thought he might whip out his little black book and start making notes.

"He drowned after he hit his head on a rock," Partial Sue said. "And he had scratches on his body."

"Ah, travel marks," Bill interjected, a little too enthusiastically. "That's what they're called when the body is dragged along the seabed."

Fiona was impressed, although a little unsettled by the extent of Bill's morbid knowledge. "That's correct. We had a silly hunch that he'd been out at Kimmeridge."

"What makes you think that?" Bill asked. "As you can see, no incidents were logged."

Partial Sue explained. "His face was brownish but his body was pale. At first, we thought this was due to hypothermia.

But now we think he'd been wearing a wetsuit and his face had been exposed to the elements."

"A surf tan," Bill added, rubbing his beard, clearly enjoying the sleuthing process. "Yep, I've seen a fair few of those with all the surfers getting changed in the car park."

"Exactly," Fiona continued. "Thing is, he never wore a wetsuit when he was wild swimming at Southbourne. So we thought he might have been out surfing, but there was no surf at Southbourne that weekend. The only waves were over here. But it's a silly idea because he wasn't found in a wetsuit. He was found in his swimming trunks.

"And he wasn't found on the Purbecks either," Daisy added. "He was discovered at Hengistbury Head, which is very close to Southbourne beach, where he would wild swim. So it's more likely he died there alone, but then he never swam on his own, so it doesn't make sense."

"Makes perfect sense to me," Bill mused. "Well, some of it."

Fiona got a hit of adrenalin.

"It does?" Daisy asked.

"Oh, aye. Come with me."

They followed him out of the cabin, up towards the boat park, which was little more than a grassy clearing connected to the water by a rough concrete slipway. A handful of small boats and dinghies were arranged haphazardly, some on trailers and some resting on the grass leaning over at awkward angles, but they were all secured to the ground by hefty chains. He pointed to a grubby-looking vessel in need of some desperate TLC. It had faded blue-and-white paintwork and a tall wheelhouse, giving it a top-heavy appearance. The boat was named *Job*, and, appropriately, looked as if it had been tested to breaking point, like its biblical namesake.

"Last October, a storm came up the Channel," Bill told them. "Not a big storm, certainly not big enough to have one of them daft names. However, it was combined with a spring tide, so high that this 'ere boat was lifted up and pulled out to sea. Guess where it washed up?"

"Not Hengistbury Head?" Daisy gasped.

CHAPTER 32

The three ladies stared at the pocket-sized vessel. It looked a little sorry for itself, like a stray dog that had been lost and found.

"That washed up at Hengistbury Head?" Partial Sue asked, incredulous.

"Aye," Bill replied. "Took a bit of a beating, mind. But she's a tough old tub, that one. Owner got a lift over there with an outboard, fixed it on the back and drove her home. Now we secure all the boats with chains to stop that happening." He tapped the nearest one with his boot. "Thing is, a westerly swell combined with an outgoing spring tide would've done the same to your man. Pulled him far out to sea, swept him along the coastline. Prevailing currents would've eventually dumped him at Hengistbury Head, thirty miles away."

"That's if he went in the water at Kimmeridge," Partial Sue pointed out. "But if he went in at Southbourne, surely the same thing would happen. He'd just end up at Hengistbury Head."

Bill shook his head. "Process would be the same. Body gets sucked far out into the Channel, swept up the coast probably the same distance. He would've ended up at maybe Calshot, near Southampton, or on the Isle of Wight at Compton beach."

This was a breakthrough. A solid one. Fiona steadied herself. She didn't want to get too excited. But the evidence appeared to be coming together in a very rough sense like the drystone walls they'd passed. However, it was all still a little precarious, missing some large key pieces to hold it in place, as Partial Sue was about to point out.

"Hold on. We've got a contradiction here. Red flags were up all that weekend and the week following. The sea was being monitored by you and the patrol boat. Plus, all those surfers in the water, confined to the left-hand side of the bay because of the firing on the other side. Someone would have spotted him, surely?"

Bill responded immediately. "Kimmeridge isn't the only place on the Jurassic Coast where there are waves. There are secret spots at Dancing Ledge, Chapman's Pool, Durlston Head, Ringstead Bay. Most surfers who drive down here from inland don't know about them, which means they're uncrowded. I only know about them because I've done this job for so long. There are probably other spots I don't know about. However, a lot of local surfers don't bother with them, because of the time and hassle it takes to get there. You have to hike for an hour across countryside, over walls and stiles. Not easy carrying a surfboard. Then hike an hour back. That's why Kimmeridge is so popular. You can park beside the beach, probably one of the few places you can do that on the Purbecks."

"Secret spots," Daisy said, gleefully. "That sounds almost too good to be true for a murder investigation."

Fiona wondered why Ralph hadn't mentioned this. Unless, being an avid surfer, he wanted to keep them a secret even from a trio of ladies who chatted to a lot of customers. He probably feared word would get around, especially as a lot of surfers lived in Southbourne.

"This fellow who died," Bill said.

"Colin," Daisy replied. "His name was Colin."

"This Colin, how good a surfer was he?"

"Well, we don't even know if he was a surfer," Fiona replied. "It's just a theory at the moment. There's an equal amount of evidence that says he wasn't. His wild swimming club didn't get along with local surfers, so we might be barking up the wrong tree. Why do you ask?"

"Well, Kimmeridge isn't a place for beginners, and these secret spots even less so. They're reef breaks. You're surfing over rock and it's hard to get in and out. Not a place for the inexperienced. If he knew about these places and had the confidence to surf them, he'd have to be a pretty decent surfer. An expert or at least intermediate."

The ladies had no answer to this. No evidence to back it up either way, and no way of finding out. If Colin had been a surfer, then he'd kept it quiet.

CHAPTER 33

"Can you text Ralph?" Fiona asked Daisy. "Quiz him about these secret spots."

She got on it straight away. Ralph pinged her back immediately. "Yes, he's confirmed everything but sworn me to secrecy. Surfers aren't supposed to talk about them — that's probably why he never mentioned them. He's just asked how I know." Daisy thumbed back her reply. "I said it was the coastal warden who told us."

"What did he say to that?" Partial Sue threw the car around yet another blind corner with wild abandon. Fiona wondered how her tyres were holding up under so much abuse.

Daisy's phone pinged again. "Ralph says everyone's scared of him. They think he's sinister."

Partial Sue snorted. "No surprise there."

Daisy nodded. "He said the warden has the power to hoick them out of the water at any time. Stop them surfing."

"But he doesn't like the water," Partial Sue pointed out.

"I suppose he can summon the patrol boat to do it for him," Fiona surmised.

Partial Sue ground the gears. "Well, I think he's a good guy."

"Is that because he uses an ethernet cable?" Daisy asked.

"That did put him up in my estimations, granted. But he gave us some great intel. The dinghy washing down to Hengistbury Head means there's a strong possibility Colin was out at Kimmeridge, or at least over on the Purbecks somewhere."

Fiona sighed. "But it's made things more confusing and contradictory. For this to make sense, Colin has suddenly become an expert surfer, when by all accounts he hated surfers, like the rest of the club, and no one I've spoken to has ever mentioned anything about him being a surfer."

Daisy looked up from her phone. "Unless he was keeping it quiet because he didn't want to fall out with them."

"Excellent point, Daisy!" Partial Sue drummed the wheel excitedly. "Makes sense. He's going surfing without their knowledge because he doesn't want to lose his friendship group, so he keeps schtum."

Fiona had a reservation. "My problem with this secret-surfer theory is that I'm sure his nosy neighbour would've seen Colin popping out with a surfboard under his arm, or at least heard him."

"That's true." Partial Sue was still undeterred. "Maybe he knew how loose-lipped he was and didn't want to risk it getting back to the club, so he found a way to sneak out undetected."

"But he would have heard his noisy Land Rover starting up," Daisy replied.

"He probably got a lift."

"Colin didn't like giving or accepting lifts," Fiona said.

Nothing would dampen Partial Sue's spirits. "Okay, so the theory needs a little finessing. But I think we're making major progress, which calls for a minor celebration. A pie and a pint at the George, and further discussion. Nothing gets the old grey matter going like meat and pastry drenched in gravy, washed down with ale. They've got a two-for-one offer on at the moment."

"I can never say no to a pie." Daisy grinned at the prospect. "Who can? It's physically impossible. I just never know whether to go for meat, veggie or vegan. Everything tastes better in pastry."

"I couldn't agree more," Partial Sue said. "It's like cheese. Everything tastes better with cheese on top. Soup, chilli, mashed potato, salad, curry . . ."

"You put cheese on curry?" Daisy asked.

"Yeah, why not? You should try it. It's not that different from a dollop of yoghurt. Hey, I might go for their cheese and veg pie tonight. Or I wonder if they do a curry pie?"

"With cheese on top," Daisy giggled.

"Now you're talking. What about you, Fiona? Will you have your usual chicken and leek, or are you going to push the boat out? Or should I say, the gravy boat?"

The pair of them tittered in the front while Fiona shrank in the back seat. She swallowed hard, preparing to let the side down. "Sorry, I can't tonight. I'm seeing Beth."

The stereo tittering halted abruptly and the atmosphere turned decidedly frosty. No one said anything until Fiona broke the uncomfortable silence. "Why don't you come with us? We're going bowling."

"We wouldn't want to tread on your toes," Daisy replied quietly.

"You're not treading on anyone's toes. Come on, it'll be fun with all of us."

Partial Sue squeezed the steering wheel harder than was strictly necessary, turning her knuckles white. "We have things to discuss. These new revelations. We need to make sense of them. Figure out the logic. We can't do that if we're sitting in a noisy bowling alley."

"We could do that afterwards." Fiona knew this was a weak suggestion.

"Might not be appropriate discussing the case in front of Beth," Partial Sue replied coldly.

Fiona became increasingly fidgety in the back seat. "But she's the one who asked us to investigate in the first place, remember? She might be able to shed some light on the things that don't make sense. She'd be a good addition to the conversation."

"Sounds like you want her to become the fourth member of our detective agency," Partial Sue growled. "Or maybe you'd prefer to start your own one with just you and Beth."

The bitter suggestion surprised and hurt Fiona deep in her core, snatching all the air from her lungs. "What's that supposed to mean?"

"You tell us," Partial Sue snapped. "Ever since joining that swimming club, you've given Daisy and I the cold shoulder."

"No, I haven't. When have I ever done that?"

"The pub quiz and tonight's bowling."

"What, just two occasions?" Fiona fumed. "I'd hardly call that the cold shoulder."

Daisy made an attempt at diplomacy. "But we're worried it's the thin end of the wedge. That you're starting to go off us."

Despite her gentle delivery, Daisy's remarks still smarted like a hot poker. "Utter nonsense!" Fiona exclaimed.

"Then why do you keep interviewing suspects and witnesses without us?" Partial Sue asked.

"Who?" Fiona demanded.

"Ted Maplin, Hayley."

Fiona sighed. "You know why I interviewed Ted Maplin alone. We needed him to turn a blind eye to client confidentiality and it wouldn't have helped if we all turned up *en masse*. As for Hayley, that was by accident. I saw her on the way to Ted's house. I decided to strike while the iron was hot. I think you're making mountains out of molehills."

"You're mixing your metaphors," Partial Sue chided. "You always do that when you're nervous, so you must have a guilty conscience."

Fiona wanted to glare at her, but it was a bit difficult when Partial Sue was sitting in front of her in the driver's seat. "Well, I also mix metaphors when I'm upset. So now you know." Fiona sat back in her seat, crossing her arms harshly and huffing loudly. Simon Le Bon grumbled and licked his lips, sensing the conflict.

Fiona didn't know whether to scream or burst into tears, or perhaps a snivelling, hiccupping combination of both. What had got into these two? Why had her closest and most trusted two friends decided to turn on her over something so trivial? She had no idea, but she couldn't stay in this situation any longer.

Fiona banged on the side of the door. "Stop the car. I want to get out."

"But I'm on the dual carriageway," Partial Sue said.

"I don't care. Anywhere's better than in here."

"We're miles from home," Daisy said.

"I'll call for a taxi."

"Don't be stupid," Partial Sue replied.

"Oh, I'm the one being stupid, am I? You mean I should sit here while the two of you criticise and make me feel small? No, thank you. Pull the car over, now!"

"Please don't do this," Daisy pleaded.

"Sorry, but I'm not putting up with this nonsense any longer. Pull over."

Partial Sue obeyed, drifting over to the hard shoulder, until the car came to a stop.

Fiona flung the door open and climbed out onto the grassy verge with Simon Le Bon, who seemed to be the only one happy with this arrangement. She slammed the door and began trudging along the unkempt grass verge. A few seconds later Partial Sue's car sped past her, belching an oily cloud of smoke in her face.

She wiped several tears from her eyes, which were nothing to do with the exhaust fumes, despite what she told herself.

Her phone pinged. She thought it might be Daisy attempting to apologise, but it was Beth cancelling tonight's date. Today just kept getting better and better.

CHAPTER 34

That night, Fiona slept on a bed of nails. Every time sleep's intoxicating embrace came for her, she was jabbed awake by the upsetting exchange in the car. Nothing troubled her more than falling out with her friends, not even a murder case. Analysing and reanalysing each and every word, her brain churned away, thoughts folding over themselves again and again. Never fully making sense of what happened, her mind buzzed incessantly. Whenever it calmed enough to permit her to perhaps snatch a modicum of sleep, off it would go again. A delirious heat coiled around her. She kept throwing off the covers and nervously popping to the loo, even though she didn't really need to go. Striking the final nail, her tinnitus joined the fray, whining in agony. At least the *It* didn't make an appearance, but any hope of rest was put well and truly beyond her reach.

Finally, she did what all insomniacs do and gave in to the inevitable. She got up, slid her feet into her slippers and threw on her dressing gown. Envious of Simon Le Bon snoring on the bed, she went downstairs and made herself a cup of tea.

As she waited for the kettle to boil, the kitchen clock above the cooker mocked her with its sluggish hands, reminding her of the time: 4.40 a.m. Fiona attempted to comfort herself that it wasn't such a bad time to get up. Lots of people were up at this time. Mostly bakers and holidaymakers catching budget flights to the Canaries. Admittedly, not charity shop workers.

Ever the optimist, or, more accurately, desperate, she made herself a caffeine-free rooibos tea in the hope she might doze off on the sofa. To help lull her into a snooze, she flicked on her DAB radio, tuning it to Radio 4. The soporific tones of the five o'clock shipping forecast might do the trick. Slowly sipping her herbal tea, she sank into the sofa, letting the mysterious names of lonely, faraway seascapes wash over her — Viking, German Bight, Faeroes, Lundy, Rockall. She always thought they sounded like an encrypted message sent by a World War Two spy from an occupied country. She imagined the courageous operative, billeted in an upstairs bedsit, radio in a briefcase open on the bed, frantically transmitting secrets vital to the war effort. Of course, conjuring up such a thrilling scenario did nothing to calm her mind.

She should forget sleeping. Write it off for now and go the other way. Maybe a wild swim was what she needed. A spot of cold-water therapy would blow away the cobwebs and put her in a more positive frame of mind for the day ahead. Despite knowing all this, she really couldn't face dunking herself in the icy sea this morning. Besides, she didn't feel comfortable meeting up with the club. It was partly — well, mostly — the reason she'd fallen out with Daisy and Partial Sue in the first place.

They'd felt threatened by her new-found pastime, but more so by the instant friendship group that had come with it. The same reason Colin had taken to it so quickly. However, Colin was a loner with no close friends to feel jealous or insecure about his cold-water companions. Unlike Daisy and Partial Sue, whose noses had been well and truly shoved out of joint.

Rationally, Fiona knew she'd done nothing wrong. She was free to see whomever she pleased, whenever it suited her.

She didn't need their permission. However, her heart told a different story. Her insides ached constantly whenever she thought back to the altercation in the car. Her friendship with these two meant so much to her. Going beyond friendship, they were a fixed point in life. An anchor embedded in rock. Reliable, unshakeable. But right now, its permanency was under threat. Big cracks were showing, and she was in danger of being set adrift, washed away, cold and alone like Colin's body. She didn't dare think about where she'd end up.

Fiona made a decision. Their friendship meant too much for her to fall out over a petty squabble. She didn't want to give up Beth or her wild swimming, but she would if that's what it took to make amends and save what she had with Daisy and Partial Sue.

The hours dragged, but finally she got ready and set off for work with Simon Le Bon trotting by her side. First to arrive, she made herself a proper cup of tea this time and sat at the table, contemplating what she'd say, arranging and rehearsing the words she'd extend as a peace offering. Only an unequivocal apology would do. She'd been in the opposite situation before — on the receiving end of someone's apology, only for them to attach conditions that undermined their sincerity. Saying, *I'm sorry — however, you did this or that*, or *I apologise, but you have to take some of the blame*, was not an apology at all. Sorry not sorry. Fiona made up her mind. This would be an unconditional apology. Clean, simple and genuine.

She gazed at yesterday's Victoria sponge on the table, or what was left after Ralph had demolished most of it. Just three small, oddly cut, stale slices sat on a white, circular cardboard base among a sea of crumbs where he'd hacked away at it. In their hurry to get over to Kimmeridge they'd forgotten to box it up and store it properly in a cool dry place, as the instructions always advised. She was tempted to have a piece. A bit of comfort food before facing the music, but she wanted to wait. If all went well and her apology was accepted, they could have it with tea, and put the matter behind them. But if it was unresolved, then she'd be in desperate need of some jam-and-sponge solace.

The doorbell went. Fiona's heart flew up into her mouth.

Partial Sue and Daisy bustled in.

Before Fiona had a chance to speak, Partial Sue held up her hand, signalling that she wished to speak first. "We both owe you an apology."

"A big apology." Daisy nodded rapidly. "We feel terrible about what we said yesterday."

Fiona got to her feet. "I was about to apologise to you."

"What for?" Partial Sue asked. "You haven't done anything wrong."

"I've been taking your friendship for granted and for that I'm sorry."

"No, no, no." Partial Sue shook her head. "We're the ones who need to apologise. We were being selfish and oversensitive."

Daisy was on the verge of tears. "We had no right to speak to you like that or make demands on who you can see. We're very sorry."

"No, I'm sorry." Tears pricked at the corner of Fiona's eyes. "You two are my best friends in the world, and I've been neglecting you."

"Stop apologising." Partial Sue was at her side. "You're our best friend and we feel dreadful, especially abandoning you on the dual carriageway."

Daisy joined her. "Yes, that was beastly of us."

"No," Fiona replied. "That was my fault. I put you in a terrible position."

Partial Sue was having none of it. "No, that was our fault. We're so sorry."

"No, I'm sorry."

"No, we're sorry."

"No, I'm sorry."

It carried on like this for several minutes, each side demanding to take full responsibility. A battle of the sorriest with neither side giving any ground in this stalemate of contrition. So in the end they agreed to an amnesty and hugged it out in the middle of the shop with much sobbing and a great deal of relief.

After falling out, the triangle of friendship was healed and much stronger for it. Although, to really seal the deal they needed tea. They assembled around the table, clutching the world's best liquid comforter in their hands, and helping themselves to a slice of yesterday's cake. Everything was right with the world again.

"I'm so glad we're back to being friends." Partial Sue gave Fiona's knee a squeeze. "This feels so nice."

Fiona relaxed her shoulders. "Oh, it's such a relief. And this cake's not too bad, although it was left out overnight."

"Apart from Ralph making such a mess of it." Daisy's compulsion for cleanliness wouldn't allow her to sit still. Gently, she lifted up the spent cardboard base strewn with fragments of cake. Holding it beside the edge of the table, she used it like a makeshift dustpan, with her other hand sweeping stray crumbs onto it. She slowly rose to her feet and tipped them into a nearby bin, then tossed the cardboard base into the recycling.

Something caught Fiona's eye. "Wait!"

She leaped up and fished out the piece of cardboard.

"What's the matter?" Daisy asked, worried. "Did I use the wrong bin?"

"No, far from it." Fiona took the cardboard base, now clean of crumbs, and placed it on the centre of the table. "This is a clue. A big one."

CHAPTER 35

The three ladies sat around the table, staring down at the circular piece of card that had once supported a delicious Victoria sponge.

"Sorry, what am I looking at?" asked a baffled Partial Sue.

"Ralph's handiwork," Fiona replied. "Or, should I say, his lack of it."

Resembling a miniature ice-skating rink, the white cardboard circle was criss-crossed with long, thin, wobbly blade marks where Ralph had slashed away at the cake.

"Okay, so he's not great at slicing up sponge," Partial Sue remarked. "It's not exactly a hanging offence."

"No, but it might be a drowning offence."

Daisy gasped. "You don't think Ralph had anything to do with Colin's death?"

"I have no idea," Fiona replied. "That's not what I'm getting at. Beth said that Colin had lacerations on his arms, and the coroner informed her they were also down his legs."

"Travel marks," Partial Sue said.

"Yes, but what if they weren't travel marks? What if they were made by a blade cutting his skin, like these marks on the card?"

"But why would someone cut Colin's skin like that?" Partial Sue asked.

Daisy looked equally puzzled.

Fiona attempted to explain. "Okay, we're pretty sure Colin had been wearing a wetsuit because of the tan mark around his neck. Let's assume he was out surfing at one of these secret spots in the Purbecks. His killer knocks him unconscious, and maybe he wants to make it look like Colin drowned wild swimming. Wild swimmers don't wear wetsuits, or at least Colin never did. So the killer has to remove his wetsuit. It'd be too difficult peeling it off him if he's unconscious, and even harder if he's floating in water. Quickest way to get it off him is to cut it off. But the killer's in a hurry, isn't careful enough with the blade. Knife slices through the rubber, catching Colin's skin beneath, creating those lacerations up and down his legs and arms. Once the wetsuit's off, Colin's body is left to the mercy of the outgoing tide and swept out to sea. He's washed up in only his trunks. Coroner doesn't bother to examine the cuts in any great detail because he thinks they're travel marks. Besides, the body's been in the sea for week, distorting them. Easy verdict for him: death by misadventure."

A wide grin split Partial Sue's face. "Oh my gosh. That's it! Has to be."

Daisy wasn't buying it. "But for all that to happen, and since Colin was found in his swimming trunks, the killer must've cut him out of his wetsuit then put him in his trunks to make it look convincing."

"That's not impossible," Fiona replied. "Okay, it's a bit awkward."

"And how would the killer have got hold of Colin's trunks?" Daisy asked. "Unless he broke into his house."

Fiona immediately pictured the bizarre scenario. Colin returning home to find his door ajar. Rushing inside, panicking, only to discover that nothing had been taken or disturbed except perhaps a drawer, ominously left open and, bizarrely, his one and only bathing suit missing. (Colin struck Fiona as someone who'd only invest in one pair of trunks at a time.)

"Maybe he already had them on under his wetsuit," Partial Sue suggested. "You know, like underpants."

"That sounds more plausible," Fiona said. "Do surfers wear swimming trunks under their wetsuits? It seems a bit surplus to requirements."

"Let's ask Ralph," Daisy said. "He'd know." She dialled his number and put it on speakerphone.

Ralph answered amid much rustling of paper. "Hey, Daisy. What's up?" It sounded as if his mouth was full. "Sorry, just having a breakfast burrito. Oh man, you gotta try them. Totally sick. They're doing two for one at the moment."

Partial Sue, being a sucker for anything buy-one-get-one-free, suddenly became interested. "Ask him where he got it from," she whispered.

Daisy didn't even need to relay the question.

"Hand car wash in Pokesdown has an offer on. Guy cleaned my van then made me a couple of burritos. Happy days!"

The more Fiona heard, the less appealing these burritos sounded.

"We have a little question to ask you," Daisy said. "Er, what do surfers wear under their wetsuits?" She blushed a little. It was a bit like asking a Scotsman what he had under his kilt, Fiona thought.

The line went quiet. Fiona worried that Ralph would think a pattern of inappropriate requests was forming, after the last time he was in the shop and she'd asked him to remove his top.

Thankfully, Ralph thought it was a wind-up. "This isn't a prank call, is it?"

"No, I wouldn't know how to do one of those," Daisy said without a hint of guile.

Ralph seemed satisfied with her answer. "Oh, okay. Well, we don't wear anything."

"Nothing?" Daisy asked.

"Nope."

"So nobody ever wears swimming trunks underneath?" Partial Sue asked.

Ralph sniggered. "No, no way. No one would be seen dead wearing budgie smugglers."

"Budgie smugglers?" Fiona asked.

"Yeah, you know, Speedos. They'd get the mick taken out of them, big time. Nah, only people that wear them are kooks."

"What's a kook?" asked Daisy.

"A beginner. Everyone wears swimming trunks under their wetsuit when they first start. Even me. But after a while you clock that no one else bothers. There's no point. Plus, it's dead uncool."

"Okay, but if Colin was a beginner, would he have a surf tan?" Fiona asked.

"Oh, sure," Ralph replied. "You can get a bit of a tan after two or three surfs, no problem."

"Okay, thanks, Ralph. That's really helpful." Daisy said goodbye then hung up.

"Maybe that's why no one at the club noticed Colin's tan," Partial Sue suggested. "It was lighter than Ralph's because he'd only just started, but after his body had been in the water for a week, it exaggerated the colour. Made his face darker and his skin paler."

"Definitely possible," Fiona said. "Strange things happen to bodies in water."

Partial Sue rubbed her hands gleefully. "Now we're getting somewhere. Colin wore trunks under his wetsuit because he hadn't been doing it for long."

Daisy still had her doubts. "But if he was a beginner that doesn't explain why he would be over on the Purbecks when it's only for advanced surfers. But why bother cutting Colin out of his wetsuit in the first place? People can still drown wearing a wetsuit."

"But then it looks like a surfing accident," Fiona pointed out. "This killer has gone to great lengths to make it look like

Colin died wild swimming, presumably to stop the finger of guilt being pointed at a surfer."

"Because the killer is a surfer themselves," Partial Sue added.

"Exactly."

"So we're back to surfing rivalry," Daisy said. "Wild swimmers versus surfers."

Fiona shook her head. "I don't think so. This is different. Colin's a surfer, albeit a closet one. A learner, judging by what he wears under his wetsuit."

"Well, if he's a learner he'd need a teacher," Partial Sue put in.

"A surf instructor," Daisy suggested.

The three ladies stared at one another, prompting small, confident smiles across their collective faces. A shared meeting of minds, that they'd reached a point they all agreed on. Fiona got a delicious spike of adrenalin, a surefire sign they were on to something.

"Are there any surf instructors around here?" Partial Sue asked.

"I know one, and I think he may have a motive." Fiona grinned.

CHAPTER 36

Surfing on the south coast was not like surfing in Devon or Cornwall. The north coast of the West Country was perpetually bombarded by Atlantic swells dumping their energy, rewarding its surfers with a seemingly never-ending conveyor belt of waves. Sometimes big and overhead, other times little knee slappers, there were always waves to ride, apart from the odd flat day, the likes of which you could probably count on one hand. However, the more sheltered south coast didn't fare so well. Most days were a wave-barren wasteland apart from small wind slop to feed its hungry surfers, unless a deep swell in the Atlantic forced its way up the Channel to bless it with proper waves. Surfing in the English Channel was a labour of love. A waiting game. Like patiently hanging on for the sun to come out. It did happen, just not that often.

Therefore, the profession of surf instructor was not one you could build a lucrative or meaningful career on. Sure, people wanted to learn how to surf, but offering this service was unpredictable, and could only happen when nature played ball. No full-time surf instructors existed in the area, not even part-time ones. The only way to provide the service was as a casual sideline to supplement a more consistent business, which is why just one surf instructor could be found in the area — Roger Masters, owner of the local surf shop.

The ladies gathered around the laptop as Fiona scrolled through the Ocean Masters website, specifically the page advertising Roger as a surf instructor. Beside a big onscreen button instructing visitors to BOOK NOW, an image showed Roger in a wetsuit with a rash vest over the top, emblazoned with the words INSTRUCTOR, in case anyone had any doubts. He clutched a large, spongey surfboard, as did the smiley wetsuited teenager next to him, though the lad's face had been pixelated out, presumably because Roger hadn't obtained permission to use his image.

"That looks like a weird ransom picture," Daisy commented.

"The parents have to pay up," Partial Sue said. "Otherwise, the kid will be forced to learn how to surf, which he looks quite happy about."

While the other two were distracted by the sinister promotional imagery, Fiona read the blurb. "*As well as running and owning Southbourne's only surf shop, I've been an experienced surf instructor for over fifteen years.* Blah, blah, blah. Listen to this: *I only provide one-to-one tuition, as it's safer and more effective. The student gets more attention, learns quicker and will improve their technique better than they would in a group setting. I can supply all the equipment, including wetsuit and surfboard, and with my local surf knowledge, I can pick you up and take you to the best spot to suit your surfing abilities.*" There was an asterisk after this with a heavy disclaimer, stating that bookings were subject to change, and would be rescheduled if conditions weren't favourable.

"He comes and picks you up in his van," Fiona said.

Daisy didn't like the sound of this. "Isn't that a bit creepy?"

"Yes, but it would answer why Colin's car hasn't moved from his driveway. If he had a lesson booked, Roger would've picked him up, then possibly killed him while they were out surfing."

"But Colin never accepted lifts or gave them," Partial Sue was quick to point out.

"This is different," Fiona replied. "Technically, it's not a lift. It's all part of a service he's paying for, so in Colin's mind he'd be fine with that because he wouldn't have to repay the favour."

Daisy had other reservations and pointed to a smaller picture on the page. "That nosy neighbour of Colin's would've surely heard that pulling up outside." The image showed the surf shop's long-wheel-base van with its sliding door open, revealed an interior stuffed with boards and wetsuits. The Ocean Masters logo was plastered all over the side in bright letters, together with a host of other surf brands, leaving no doubt as to the nature of the vehicle's business.

"Not the most inconspicuous vehicle to use for a murder," Partial Sue agreed. "But my question is, why would Roger Masters have wanted to kill Colin?"

"One of the biggest motives there is," Fiona replied. "Money, or the lack of it. Ocean Masters is struggling financially. Spend five seconds in his shop and you'll see he's in trouble. Empty shelves and racks everywhere. His business is nose-diving and whenever anyone's desperate for money you can bet murder's not far behind. One thing we know about Colin is he had lots of disposable cash. Ted Maplin told me he wasn't short of a penny or two, but never spent it on himself."

Daisy clicked her fingers. "And Colin would always help anyone who needed it."

"Yes, my thoughts exactly." Fiona nodded. "Maybe Colin offered to lend him the cash or invest in his business. Roger thinks all his money worries are over. But what if Colin got cold feet at the last minute or they fell out?"

"That's not difficult to imagine, given Colin's abrasive personality," Partial Sue said.

"Yes, so he pulls out of the deal," Fiona continued. "Roger might have already promised his suppliers and debtors they'll be paid. Has to go crawling back to them and explain it's not going to happen. He's humiliated. Left high and dry, while he knows Colin is sitting on a big pile of cash he's not using.

Roger's fuming, incensed at Colin reneging on the deal. So much so that he kills him."

"That sounds very believable," Daisy said. "But Roger won't get any money if Colin dies, will he?"

"No, but that doesn't matter," Partial Sue replied. "Lots of people kill in business if a deal goes south, out of vengeance. Blood on the carpet, or beach towel in this case. Especially if they don't get the money they've been promised. Would almost feel like you've had it stolen from you. Been double-crossed."

"But who will get Colin's money now he's dead?" Daisy asked. "Surely they'd be the biggest suspect."

Fiona's jaw clenched. She'd hoped to avoid mentioning anything about Beth being Colin's sole beneficiary because the poor woman didn't want anyone to know. But on the other hand, it was key to the investigation. She had no idea how these two would react when they knew she'd purposefully withheld evidence, especially as the subject of Beth had been so sensitive. And this latest revelation would make it look like Fiona was going soft on her because they were friends. She swallowed hard and decided to come clean. "It's Beth. Colin left all his money to Beth."

Partial Sue flinched, almost sending the laptop flying. "You're kidding?"

Fiona shook her head. "I'm not, I'm afraid. Sorry I didn't say anything, but she didn't want anyone to know, and I promised I wouldn't mention it to anyone. Colin left her everything, and she was worried that people would immediately put two and two together and think that she'd killed him."

"Is that why she hired us to investigate?" Daisy asked. "To put her above suspicion?"

Fiona nodded. "Partly, but she's also carrying around this terrible guilt that she's profiting from his death."

"And do you believe her?" asked Partial Sue. "I mean, getting all his money sends her straight to the top of the suspects list."

"I do," Fiona replied. "It's not her fault that he left her all his money. She had no idea. Was completely oblivious. But she seemed genuinely distressed by the whole situation, and I know what you're thinking. That could all be an act, crocodile tears. But if she killed him, why would she ask us to look into his murder? Especially since she'd got off scot-free with a nice, neat verdict of accidental death? It doesn't make sense. Surely she'd let sleeping dogs lie."

The air in the shop became cold, quiet and uncomfortable, as her two colleagues chewed and digested this unexpected new twist.

Eventually Partial Sue said, "You're right. It doesn't make sense. No one would do that."

"I agree," said Daisy.

Relief spread through Fiona's body. She didn't think she could take another disagreement with her two best friends. "Should we pursue our theory of Roger being hungry for revenge after being left out of pocket?"

"Yes, definitely," Partial Sue agreed. "But I still have one little problem with it. Colin must have had more than one surf lesson with Roger, if it had got to the point where they were comfortable enough to discuss business."

"And for Colin to get that surf tan," Daisy pointed out.

"Yes, quite," Partial Sue continued. "So, Roger must have picked up Colin in his van more than once. Now, I can imagine his nosy neighbour might have missed this on one occasion, but not several."

"Yes, that is a problem," Fiona agreed. "Law of averages says he would've heard Colin leaving in that van at some point. But he told us no one ever came to pick him up."

"Okay, the theory has its problems," Daisy said. "But we still need to question this Roger."

"I think so too." Fiona nodded. "Let's see how he reacts."

"It's still early," Daisy remarked. "Should we wait until the end of the day to pay him a visit?"

Partial Sue gave a mischievous grin. "No time like the present. Besides, if he's a possible murderer it would completely justify shutting up the shop to question him." She grabbed her car keys and rattled them. "Let's see him pixelate his way out of this one."

CHAPTER 37

Roger Masters leaned against the counter, staring into space, his eyes vacant and unfocused. When the three ladies walked in, his whole body jerked to life as if he'd been hooked up to a couple of jump leads. Automatically switching to friendly shopkeeper mode, the horseshoe moustache dangling below his nose kinked as he broke into a smile. But his face really lit up when he recognised Fiona, presumably because she had a habit of spending money whenever she visited, and, as a bonus, had brought two friends along. Fiona could almost see the pound signs flashing in his eyes.

"Hello, Fiona," he said warmly.

"Morning, Roger," Fiona returned the greeting. "This is Daisy and Sue."

"Let me guess," he said hopefully, but stopped short of rubbing his hands together. "Two new recruits for wild swimming who need kitting out with changing robes and booties."

"Not likely," Partial Sue informed him. "Me and cold water don't get along. Unless it's the tonic variety mixed with gin on a hot summer's day."

A textbook salesman, Roger attempted to build empathy. "That's a favourite tipple of mine too. I like sloe gin. You know, I used to think it was called that because they distilled it very slowly. Didn't realise there was such a thing as a sloe berry."

"An easy mistake to make," Daisy said. "I always thought Welsh rarebit was made from rabbit so I never ate it. I couldn't stomach eating a bunny." Realising she'd strayed into an odd subject for this early in the morning, Daisy quickly changed tack. "I like your shop. It feels like I'm on holiday, like being in Hawaii. I'd love to go one of these days. Have a flower garland put around my neck when I get off the plane, so romantic. Maybe give surfing a try. What is that lovely smell, by the way?"

"That's the coconut wax for the surfboards," Roger replied. "A lot of people buy it for their homes for the fragrance. We're doing two blocks for the price of one at the moment and you don't have to go to Hawaii to try surfing. You can do it right here."

Daisy smiled. "I'd love to try surfing. My neighbour's a surfer. He's always saying how wonderful it is."

Sensing a possible sale, Roger drew closer. "He's right, and I can sign you up right now for lessons."

Daisy backed off. "Oh, no. It's too cold here. Wouldn't agree with my asthma."

"Don't worry about the cold," Roger reassured her. "Wetsuits are amazing at keeping you warm."

"I don't fancy squeezing this body into a wetsuit," Daisy giggled.

Before Roger had the chance to launch into a sales pitch about wetsuits, Fiona cut him off. "We are interested in surf lessons. But not for us. We're enquiring about someone called Colin Barclay."

"Oh, is he a friend of yours? Because I sell lessons as gift vouchers. If you buy a block of six you get ten per cent off."

"We're not here to buy surf lessons," Partial Sue clarified. "We just wanted to know if you gave any to someone called Colin Barclay."

This appeared to stump Roger. "Name doesn't ring any bells. To be fair, I don't give that many lessons. It's tricky to get the right conditions. We get a lot of flat spells on the south coast."

"Could you check for us?" Fiona asked.

"Er, customer details are confidential."

"It's okay, we don't need any details," Daisy reassured him. "All we want to know is if he had lessons."

"Can I ask why?"

The three ladies looked at one another. Time to let the cat out of the bag and see if Roger had an allergic reaction.

Fiona cleared her throat. "Colin Barclay was the wild swimmer whose body washed up on Hengistbury Head. We're looking into how he died."

If Roger was the murderer, then he covered it well, saying all the right things, wincing and contorting his face in the right places. "Oh, no. I heard about that in the news. Poor guy. What a terrible thing to happen."

"We believe he wasn't just a wild swimmer. We have a theory that he was also a surfer." Fiona examined Roger for the minutest flicker of recognition or guilt.

To his credit, or perhaps his wily powers of concealment, Roger didn't offer up so much as a twitch or a tic. "I'll be honest, I know all the surfers around here, and he wasn't one of them."

"We think he might have been a beginner," Partial Sue said. "Hence the surf lessons."

Roger was happy to cooperate. "Let me check my diary. Lessons are booked online. Records all the names and dates." He went behind the counter and logged into a sleek silver laptop. After dabbing a few buttons, he swivelled it around so they could see. The screen showed a page divided up into a grid of days of the month represented by a stack of different rectangular blocks. It was devoid of any names. "This has been a slow month. Let's try the previous one." This time, a handful of blocks were coloured pink, presumably to signify bookings. The same name appeared four times: Simone Davis. "She was a good student. Picked it up real fast. Helped that there was plenty of surf that month. I sold her a board and wetsuit right after her last lesson." Roger smiled wistfully as he reminisced about such a sizeable sale, then he scrolled back another month, then another and another. Random names in pink rectangles popped up here and there, some only once. Many were coloured red, where Roger had had to cancel and rebook the lesson because conditions weren't favourable. However, one thing remained consistent throughout the search — Colin's name was nowhere to be found, despite Roger taking them back a full year.

The ladies left the surf shop, collective tails between their legs, as another theory backed itself into a corner.

"Doesn't mean anything," Partial Sue grumbled as they got back into the car. "The guy's not stupid. If he did kill Colin, he's hardly going to leave his name up there for all to see. Might have erased it while the laptop was turned away from us. He hit quite a few buttons before he showed us the screen, probably deleting any record of him."

Save for the grinding of the engine at the hand of Partial Sue's gear changing, the car went quiet as the ladies contemplated yet another dead end.

Eventually, Fiona said vaguely, "Nothing ever gets deleted."

"What?" Daisy asked.

"Freya's always saying it. Online, nothing ever gets deleted. A record of it always remains somewhere. It's just how deep you're willing to go to find it."

"We need to call her," Partial Sue blurted enthusiastically. "Get Freya to do some digging on this Roger, preferably with a big shovel or a big yellow JCB. I am partial to a JCB."

Daisy shrunk down in the back seat, uncomfortable at the mention of Freya's name. The owner of the unassuming local computer repair shop was an accomplished weightlifter and kickboxer, and an even more formidable hacker. Brains and brawn in one very capable package. When her powerful hands weren't choke-holding an opponent into a quick submission in a cage fight, they could be used to equally devastating effect hacking into someone's digital life. But her approach was less shovel and more scalpel, never leaving so much as a scratch or a scar even after she'd had a good poke around. None of which was legal, of course — hence Daisy's discomfort at the prospect of enlisting Freya's shady skills. But sometimes rules had to be bent to advance a case, especially one that refused to budge in a forward direction.

CHAPTER 38

The customer ummed and ahhed, debating whether to buy a beige polo shirt or a grey one for her husband. Holding them aloft, her gaze shifted between the two, scrutinising both options. "He's learning to play golf, you see," the lady volunteered. "I don't want him turning up on the pitch looking like a dog's dinner. Honestly, if it were up to him, he'd wear a bin liner."

Growing impatient, Fiona fought the urge to correct her that it was a course, not a pitch, and she doubted it would matter if he wore a polo shirt or a bin liner at this time of year. Any garment, plastic or otherwise would be covered up by several layers to keep out the cold while wandering across the bleak, wintry golf links. But there was another reason Fiona grew impatient and wanted the woman to finalise her purchase. Freya had promised to call them back at around 4 p.m. with information about Roger and Colin. It was now ten past, and Fiona really needed this indecisive individual out of the shop. She didn't want any distractions when they gathered around the table to hear what Freya had to report, and certainly no members of the public eavesdropping on the conversation and its not-strictly-legal content.

"Why don't you take them both?" Fiona suggested. "We're doing two for a fiver." They weren't, but anything to get her out of the shop.

"Well, that does sound like good value for money. I'll take them."

Fiona relieved her of the shirts, in case she changed her mind, and bustled towards the till. Partial Sue began ringing in the sale to speed up the process, while Daisy hovered, unsure how she could help.

Worryingly, the woman's gaze idly drifted around the shop. "Are you doing two for a fiver on any other items?"

"No, just polo shirts." Partial Sue shoved the card reader under her nose, prompting her to complete her purchase and get out.

Fiona hurriedly folded the shirts, shoved them into a bag and handed them to the woman. "Thank you very much for your custom."

"You know, I might be back for more. All being well, if he likes playing golf, and I hope he does — truth be told, I need something to get him out of the house — he'll need more than just two. The price of new ones is extortionate. I tried the golf shop, and they wanted forty-five pounds just for a shirt because it was embroidered with a stupid chicken or penguin or whatever it is. Daylight robbery." Clearly, she wanted to stay and have a moan.

Fiona's phone rang. She glanced at the screen. Freya was calling. She needed to make something up that would force the woman out of the shop, preferably of her own volition. She thought quickly. "Sorry, this is the pest control company. I have to take this. We have a little infestation of, erm . . ."

"Spiders," Partial Sue offered.

"Moles," Daisy blurted at the same time.

The woman eyed them suspiciously.

Daisy was the world's worst liar, doubling down on her initial fib. "We think the moles and the spiders have joined forces."

Partial Sue attempted to salvage the tall story with a bit of *ad hoc* logic that sort of made sense. "The spiders come into the shop from above ground and the moles from below. It's a pincer movement."

"But you have solid floors." The lady stamped her foot to demonstrate. "Moles aren't going to get very far."

"Actually, it's wood," Partial Sue replied. "Original floorboards, so I'm told."

The woman's face soured. "Then they'd need to add woodpeckers to their alliance. To get through it."

"I think beavers would be a better fit," said Fiona, wondering why she had become embroiled in such a bizarre debate, which wasn't helping to eject the woman from the shop.

Daisy became excited. "Oh, yes. I can imagine beavers and moles working well together. Like a Disney buddy-up."

At that point, the woman had had enough. She gave them a parting glance as if the three of them had lost the plot and left the shop while the going was good.

Partial Sue locked the door behind her and turned the sign around to "Closed", then faced Daisy. "A mole and spider alliance?"

Daisy shrugged, red-faced. "It just popped in my head."

"Don't forget the beavers." Fiona examined her phone. Freya had hung up. They all gathered around the table while she called her back. Freya answered first time.

"Hi, Freya. How did it go?" Fiona put the call on speakerphone.

"Not great, I'm afraid."

The ladies uttered a collective "Oh."

"I've accessed Roger's online booking system. It was pretty easy, if I'm honest. Surf lessons aren't exactly a high target for hackers. But there's not a trace of Colin Barclay signing up, or anyone of that name being deleted. There are plenty of cancellations and rescheduling but it's all completely innocent."

"Could he have booked himself under another name, an alias?" Partial Sue asked.

"Entirely possible. I'm not sure why Colin would do that, but I did have a snoop through Roger Masters' emails, phone calls and texts. Nothing there either. No communication between the two of them whatsoever. Only thing I did find was a bunch of final demands from his suppliers. Poor guy's struggling. Business going down the pan. I'm sorry, but I think your surf shop owner was telling the truth. He's never had anything to do with Colin Barclay as far as I can tell."

"Well, thank you for trying," Fiona spoke in a small voice. "We really appreciate it."

"Hey, no worries. Sorry I don't have better news. But if you need anything else, just let me know." Freya hung up.

All three ladies shrunk in their chairs. They'd pinned their hopes on Freya uncovering a thread of steel linking Roger to Colin. That they'd had some shady financial arrangement gone sour, resulting in Colin's death. But Roger was just another high street retailer drowning in an ocean of online competitors.

"What if Colin paid Roger in cash for his lessons?"

"That's entirely possible," Fiona replied. "But if he invested in Roger's business or lent him money, surely there'd be some sort of communication back and forth, either by text or email, to make it official."

Partial Sue harrumphed. No matter how they sliced it, Roger would not slot into the hole marked "suspect", despite his obvious money troubles.

Quiet descended over the shop, accompanied by a dull, energy-sapping cloud of pessimism.

For something to break the silence, Fiona stated the obvious. "I think someone else had it in for our ex-sports teacher."

"My sports teacher always had it in for me," Daisy muttered. "Always criticising me. The worst part was being picked for teams. I was always the last girl standing."

"So was I." Fiona remembered the humiliating experience well, watching the numbers slowly dwindle, and realising once again you were everyone's last choice. "Why did they make us do that?"

Partial Sue was strangely quiet. Having a killer bowling arm and the peppy energy of a swallow, she probably got picked first for everything.

"Sports teachers are all sadistic," Daisy declared. "That's why."

Fiona experienced a dropping rollercoaster in her stomach. A heavy, shocking anxiety. A neglectful realisation, like leaving a baby in a pram outside the supermarket. "Oh my gosh! We've been so obsessed with wild swimmers and surfers that we've overlooked the obvious. Colin's old pupils."

Partial Sue screwed up her nose. "But they would have been from years ago."

"I don't know how long Colin had been retired," Fiona replied. "But it doesn't matter. Sadistic teachers stick with you. As we've just demonstrated."

Daisy agreed. "From what we've heard about Colin, he sounds like just the type."

Fiona texted Beth. A reply came back immediately. "Beth says she doesn't know how long he'd been retired. But she did give us the address of his old school. Hartley Upper in Southbourne."

"I know it," Daisy said.

"Did you used to go there?" Partial Sue asked.

"No, but the boys from our school used to have fights with theirs at lunchtime."

"Sounds about right," said Partial Sue.

Fiona glanced at the time. "It's only four thirty. Kids will have gone but the staff will still be there."

Chairs scraped back as the ladies rose as one and made for the door. Fiona's initial embarrassment at overlooking such an obvious line of inquiry was washed away by a flood of optimism, and the prospect of having a new lead. Butterflies pinged in her stomach, but a few of them stuttered and failed to take off, grounded by fear. Although she was a grown-up and had left school in another lifetime — a lifetime in which she never stepped out of line, never handed in homework late and never dared to talk when she wasn't supposed to — the thought of going into a school to see the headmaster sent a shudder through her core.

CHAPTER 39

Schools had changed a lot since Fiona's day. Hartley Upper was new and shiny, and from the outside almost resembled a shopping centre, with its big windows and bright blocks of colour. Nothing like the funereal Victorian pile she had attended as a shy young girl. Where she had sat day after day, not daring to speak at a boxlike wooden desk with a redundant hole in the corner for an inkwell. These days, pupils were more likely to write on an iPad than they were with a pen and paper. Fiona hoped it was a less scary environment for youngsters. More inclusive and understanding. In her day, you were just as likely to be bullied by a teacher as you were by another pupil, whacked across the knuckles with a ruler for writing with your left hand, or being struck in the temple by a flying blackboard rubber for talking. (Did they even have blackboards anymore?) Teachers nowadays seemed to be a lot more, well, educated. Enlightened that everyone was different, and that was okay. Yes, thankfully a lot had changed for the better. But one thing had not, and that was the smell.

A familiar, pungent odour enveloped her as they pushed open the main entrance door. What could only be described as a cocktail of adolescent sweat and budget disinfectant mingled with the odour of overcooked food. It seemed to pervade the airless corridors of every school regardless of the location of the canteen.

"I hope we get the nice one," Daisy said as they followed the arrows to the reception area.

"What do you mean?" asked Partial Sue.

"Well, both of Bella's schools, including the one I worked in, had two receptionists — a nice one and a mean one. Whenever I had to drop off a form or phone in to say Bella was sick, I'd always get the mean one, who'd tell me off because the form was late or make me feel guilty for keeping her off school. You mark my words, there'll be a nice one and a nasty one. It's the universal law."

As they turned the corner, it appeared that Daisy's prediction was right. They were confronted by a large double reception desk fitted with a glass partition reaching up to the ceiling. On the left, a sweet-faced receptionist patiently helped a parent pay for a school trip because he couldn't get the online portal to work. While on the right, free to take enquiries, perched a hawklike receptionist with a ghostly chalk-white face and bifocals on the end of her nose. Her hair had been scraped back in a tight, headache-inducing bun, with a fringe so straight it must have been cut with the aid of a spirit level.

"That'll be the mean one," Daisy whispered.

Fiona edged forward, accompanied by Partial Sue, with a timid Daisy bringing up the rear, using her two friends as a human shield.

"Hello," Fiona said as pleasantly as possible. "We were wondering if we could have a word with the headmaster."

"Do you have an appointment?" The receptionist's voice was cold and monotone.

Fiona shook her head. "Er, no."

"Do you have a child or a grandchild at this school?"

Fiona shook her head again.

"Then it's simply not possible." The receptionist stared without blinking.

"Hold on a minute, you don't even know why we're here." Partial Sue was not going to be intimidated.

"And why exactly are you here?" the receptionist sneered.

"To enquire about one of your ex-teachers."

"Then it's certainly not possible."

"Why not?" asked Fiona.

"Well, isn't it obvious?"

Fiona glanced at her friends then back to the receptionist. "No, it's not."

The woman sighed and rubbed the bridge of her nose. "Because you don't have a child here. We can't give out information to any Tom, Dick or Harriet who wanders in off the street."

"Doesn't matter." Partial Sue leaned in, her face almost pressing against the glass. "We need information about a teacher called Colin Barclay. He died recently and we're investigating his possible murder."

The parent next to them took a slow, deliberate step sideways, clearly not comfortable with all this talk of murder, when he'd only popped in to pay for a trip to somewhere innocent like Salisbury Cathedral or Corfe Castle. The receptionist helping him appeared equally nervous. By contrast, nothing troubled her colleague's face. It remained cold and firm like the white cliffs of Dover, except with bifocals and a fringe. "Did Colin Barclay die on school premises?" she asked.

"No, he—"

"Then it has nothing to do with the school, and that's the end of the matter." Twisting her seat away from them, she busied herself with paperwork that didn't appear to be particularly urgent, judging by the way she butted it together then shoved it back into the tray she'd just retrieved it from.

"Is there someone else we can speak to?" Fiona asked, aiming her question mainly at the nice receptionist, who pretended that she hadn't heard.

"Asked and answered," the mean receptionist replied without swivelling her chair around.

"You haven't answered anything," Partial Sue protested.

This time she turned to face them, pointing to a sign sellotaped to the glass, informing visitors that abusive behaviour would not be tolerated.

"I don't think we're being abusive," Fiona disagreed. "We haven't raised our voices. We just asking about the possibility of—"

"Asked and answered," the receptionist snapped once more.

Daisy suddenly barged between her two friends. Years of unresolved, pent-up frustration with gatekeepers like this woman flooded out in an angry rant. "Now, you look here. I know your type. I had a daughter at school and there was always someone like you on reception, being a bully and making parents feel small. Well, I'm not frightened of you, sitting there all high and mighty in your fish tank, like you're the queen of . . . fish. You haven't answered any of our questions. In fact, you've been obstructive. Which makes me think you've got something to hide. Now, get someone down here tooth sweet — please."

Caught in the blinding headlights of Daisy's wrathful diatribe, or perhaps her mispronunciation of *tout de suite*, the stunned receptionist sat perfectly still, eyes unblinking. Then, slowly, she reached over and picked up the phone.

In Fiona's head, a triumphant fanfare blew. Their normally mild-mannered friend had unleashed her seldom-seen fiery side and had got the job done in no uncertain terms. But Fiona's internal celebrations ended abruptly when the receptionist spoke into the receiver. "Can I have security to the reception desk please? There are three women here who need to be ejected from the premises for antisocial behaviour."

* * *

"I'm really sorry." Daisy hadn't stopped apologising since they'd been thrown out by school security, although this title was a tad generous. A weary-looking janitor in droopy overalls had turned up, armed with a mop reeking of that cheap disinfectant. Judging by his equally miserable face, he didn't appear too pleased to be doubling as the designated protector of school property. The ladies didn't argue, not wanting said mop waved in their faces, and had left of their own accord.

"I really mucked things up." Daisy hung her head low as they traipsed back to the car.

"You have nothing to apologise for," Fiona reassured her.

"That harpy was asking for it," Partial Sue added. "And I don't think it would have mattered what we said or how we said it. We weren't getting past her."

"I wish we could've had the nice receptionist," Daisy muttered. "I told you, didn't I? Every school has a nice one and a mean one."

"You weren't wrong," Fiona replied. "Question is, how do we get the information we're after?"

"Excuse me?" came a small voice from behind them.

They turned to see the nice receptionist. Outside of her glass booth, she was petite with small feet and a neat pixie-like head complete with large bright eyes. Her bag was slung across her chest, having finished for the day. "Sorry, I couldn't help overhearing your conversation back in school."

"It was hard to miss," Partial Sue remarked.

She smiled nervously. "Please forgive Theresa. She doesn't mean to be rude."

"Could've fooled me," Daisy said.

The receptionist gazed at her feet. "I know she can be quite abrupt but she's really nice once you get to know her."

Fiona found that rather difficult to believe but wanted to steer the subject back to the investigation. "Did you know Colin Barclay at all?"

"Yes," she nodded. "I did, and I can tell you all about him."

Fiona expected a story of a harsh sports teacher, bordering on sadistic. The kind who would use humiliation as a tool to motivate his pupils, which only resulted in embarrassment for those on the receiving end. Perhaps it had created an indelible bitterness in one particular individual that had grown and festered away for years until, one day, it became unbearable, and ended in murder.

But the answer the receptionist gave did not fit with the narrative currently expanding in Fiona's head.

"The kids really liked him. His lessons were all about having fun."

"Really?" Partial Sue baulked. "That doesn't seem like the Colin we've heard about."

"Oh, yes," she continued. "He wasn't bothered about competing or winning trophies."

"Really?" Fiona found this unbelievable. "And what did the headmaster make of that?"

"He turned a blind eye to it. Like most headmasters, he was more concerned with academic performance. Besides, he knew Colin was winding down to his retirement and then he could get in a young replacement."

"That's so odd." Partial Sue scratched her head. "Everyone we've spoken to said he was a strict disciplinarian. Liked being bossy. What about his relationship with the other teachers?"

"Oh, he kept mostly to himself. I mean, he was polite but never really got involved with them. 'Kept his head down' would be the best way to describe him."

"No disagreements? Bust-ups in the staff room?" Daisy asked. "Telling people to put the lid on the coffee jar. Or to wash up their cup — that always used to bug me when I was a teaching assistant."

The receptionist shook her head. "No, nothing."

"Are you absolutely sure?" Partial Sue asked.

The receptionist grinned impishly. "One of the perks of my job is I hear every bit of gossip. And I can tell you, Colin was never the centre of any of it. Never raised so much as an eyebrow. I suppose he wanted an easy life."

Her rationale made perfect sense. The mellow wind-down before collecting one's carriage clock was a well-trodden path for most people on the sluggish final straight to retirement. However, Colin was not most people. He was an authoritarian and, in Fiona's experience, authoritarians never had days off and certainly never put aside their compulsion to tell people what to do and how they should be doing it. The idea that Colin would let things slide towards the end of his career and allow the kids to "have fun" went against everything they'd learned about him. "This doesn't seem like the same person we've been investigating."

"That's how he was, you can ask anyone." The receptionist chewed the side of her lip as something occurred to her. "Although it might have been a different story at his previous school in London."

"His previous school?" Fiona couldn't hide her shock. "In London?"

"Yes, he'd been there his whole career before he moved down here. I suppose this would be his cushy little number before retiring."

"Do you know what it was called?" Fiona asked.

"No," the receptionist replied. "But I think it was in Islington."

A choking cloud of incompetence swirled around Fiona's head, making her dizzy. They'd been amateurish and had ignored the most basic of questions. They should have carried out a thorough background search, instead of just assuming Colin was local to the area. Fiona wanted to kick herself in several places. But before she berated herself too much, it occurred to her that no one they'd questioned had mentioned anything about Colin being from London, not even his nosy neighbour. Had he been keeping it quiet? And if so, why?

CHAPTER 40

A text popped up on Fiona's phone, littered with exclamation marks and dotted with shocked-face emojis. Beth confirmed that she had no idea Colin had moved down from London either. That same evening, they had heard similar stories from his therapist and his neighbour. It appeared Colin had been keeping his past life in the capital under wraps — a secret that might hold the key to his murder.

Daisy plonked a pot of tea down in the centre of the round table. Although it was after closing time, they'd decided to regroup back at the shop that same evening for want of a better place to meet. This was an emergency, plus they did their best thinking there, despite being interrupted every now and then by passersby out for an evening stroll, who kept ignoring the "Closed" sign and peering in through the window, mouthing the words, "Are you open?" It seemed no one could resist a rummage around a charity shop, whatever the time of day.

Gasping for a cuppa, Partial Sue poured her tea first. "So, Colin kept schtum about his time in London. In my experience, people who've worked in London are a bit partial to spouting off about it and will tell you every opportunity they get. As if that's supposed to impress us simple folk out in the sticks."

"Hey, I worked in London," Fiona protested.

Partial Sue's face reddened then she smiled apologetically. "Present company excepted, of course. But my point is, he's kept it a secret on purpose, which makes me think something has happened that he doesn't want people to know about."

Fiona agreed. "Yes, something's gone on there. Daisy, how's the search going?"

She looked up from her phone and sighed. "There's no record of a Colin Barclay teaching in Islington that I can find online. But I've found a little news story about a teacher in a paper from the early nineties. Just a tiny paragraph, no pictures I'm afraid. But it's not Colin Barclay. It's someone called Colin Bartlett."

Fiona and Partial Sue scooched their chairs closer so they could view Daisy's screen. The brief article tucked away at the bottom of the page concerned an inquiry into a pupil who'd been injured during rugby practice at Islington Secondary Modern. The sports teacher, Colin Bartlett, had joined in the practice, playing on one of the teams to even out the numbers, but had briefly knocked a pupil unconscious while attempting to catch the ball. The unnamed lad had sustained a dislocated shoulder during the clash. The inquiry had reached the conclusion that the incident was accidental and occurred during the "rough and tumble" of the game. It cleared Colin Bartlett of any wrongdoing, stating that he had not breached any safety guidelines and had followed all the correct procedures. The family of the pupil vowed to pursue the matter further.

"What do you make of that?" asked Daisy.

Fiona poured herself some tea. "Sounds like a big enough reason to keep your previous job quiet — knocking a kid out."

"But he was cleared," Daisy replied. "An accident."

"Doesn't matter," Partial Sue replied. "Mud sticks, as they say."

Daisy still wasn't convinced. "But it's not the same person."

"What are the odds of two sports teachers in Islington having such similar names?" Fiona asked. "He might've changed it when he moved down here because he didn't want anyone finding out about the accident. It's not a good look for someone after a new job. And people using a new name often pick something that sounds very similar to their old one. They stick with the same initials because it's easier to remember and to avoid slip-ups."

Daisy sighed. "But even if he changed his name, his new headmaster in Southbourne would've known about his past. He'd want references from his old school, surely?"

"That's a good point," Fiona replied. "The incident would be on his record, regardless of a name change, and they'd do background checks as well."

"So why would a headmaster employ someone like that?" Daisy asked.

"Well, like you said, he was cleared," Fiona replied. "But also, even back then, teaching staff were in short supply. His choice may have been limited. And Colin would've been working out the last few years until retirement. But I suppose it'd be in both their interests if he kept a low profile. They wouldn't want staff or parents to know about his little 'accident' even though it happened a long time ago. So, just to be on the safe side, Colin changed his name before starting the job, in case anyone else checked up on him."

Partial Sue took a slug of tea. "That would certainly explain why Colin went soft on his pupils, letting them have fun in his lessons. He probably didn't want a repeat of what happened in London. Or maybe the headmaster suggested it, especially if he's only worried about academic performance."

"This all makes sense." Fiona helped herself to tea. "But I think we're getting ahead of ourselves. First, we need to establish if Colin Barclay and this Colin Bartlett are the same person."

Partial Sue rubbed her hands gleefully. "Which means a visit to the National Archives. I've always wanted to go. It'll feel like we're in a Bond movie, or *The Bourne Identity*."

"Can't we just check on their website?" Fiona asked.

"No, I tried once before, when I wanted to find out about my neighbour." Partial Sue sounded slightly stalkerish. "I thought she was Dorien from *Birds of a Feather*, living incognito under a different name."

"You mean the actress Lesley Joseph?" Daisy asked.

"That's the one. She didn't live next door for very long. Moved away for some reason."

Fiona thought she had a pretty good idea.

"So I've never used the National Archive," Partial Sue continued. "But I did find out you have to actually go there in person, sift through their records. It's in Kew. Hey, maybe we could combine it with a trip to Kew Gardens." She glanced over at Daisy for her reaction. Normally, she would be bouncing up and down like an excitable child at the mere suggestion of a jolly up to London, and positively exploding at the thought of wandering around Kew's elegant Victorian glasshouses, rich with botanical rarities, leaving the best bit until last — a trip to the café and gift shop, for a generous wedge of cake and to add another tea towel to her collection. But her attention was elsewhere, nose buried deep in her phone screen.

"Did you hear that, Daisy?" Fiona asked.

"I've got something." She spun her phone around to show a grainy image posted on someone's Facebook page, reminiscing about their school days. Taken in 1990, three rows of pupils, who'd mostly outgrown their uniforms, posed stiffly for their final-year class photo at Islington Secondary Modern. They were bookended on either side by two small clusters of teachers, smiling and dressed in shirts and ties or smart blouses — apart from one bulky and awkward-looking fellow in sportswear, his face more of a grimace than a grin.

Partial Sue stabbed at the screen. "That's Colin Barclay!"

Fiona pulled up a more recent photo of the sports teacher they'd seen in a local news story reporting his death. They compared the two, just to be sure. "That's definitely him, isn't it? Just younger. Same hairline, same small eyes . . ."

"Same not-very-convincing smile," Daisy remarked. "That's the smile I give the supermarket assistant when the self-service checkout goes wrong for the umpteenth time."

"Colin Barclay and Colin Bartlett are the same person!" Partial Sue blurted. "And we've got photographic evidence to prove it! Finally, we're getting somewhere."

But Colin's face wasn't the only one Fiona recognised. In the bottom right-hand corner sat a boy a lot smaller than the others. There was something familiar about his thin lips and small features. His arm had been folded into a sling. But she couldn't for the life of her place where she knew him.

Partial Sue jabbed a finger at the seated pupil. "I bet he's the one Colin bashed into, and he doesn't look too happy about it. We should find out who he is."

"I'm sure I know him." Fiona's mind fumbled through the flip book of faces in her memory but came up blank.

"Someone from work perhaps, when you lived in London," Daisy suggested.

"Possibly," Fiona replied but she was sure it was more recent than that.

Daisy had another idea. "It's not that chap from the greengrocer's who thinks daylight savings causes inflation?"

Fiona shook her head.

Partial Sue had a more practical approach. "Well, whoever it is, they'd be a lot older now. Middle-aged. He's fresh-faced there. Maybe add in some wrinkles and bitterness caused by life's inevitable disappointments."

Her cynicism did the trick. Fiona imagined the relentless tug of gravity on the lad's features and life's relentless letdowns slowly diluting his youthfulness. Gradually, the face grew more recognisable until his identity revealed itself, jolting her where she sat.

"I think that's . . . Oh my gosh! It's George from the wild swimming club! It all makes sense now. He's got a London accent. Swims with a bodyboard because of a frozen shoulder."

"From where it was dislocated by an oafish sports teacher," Partial Sue quickly added, her eyes widening with possibility. "It never healed properly, and he's been bitter ever since. Wanted revenge for what Colin did to him at school. So he tracks him down, joins the wild swimming club, then kills him. We've got a motive! We've got a killer!"

"But would you murder someone just because they hurt your shoulder?" asked Daisy.

"Yeah, of course," Partial Sue snorted. "And it sounds like more than a dislocated shoulder. That's a life-changing injury, and he's had plenty of time for the bitterness to fester until his desire for justice became unbearable."

"Okay," Daisy said. "But if that was the case, wouldn't he have just gone to one of those 'Had an accident that wasn't your fault?' places you see on the telly?"

"Maybe he did," Partial Sue replied. "Maybe they wouldn't take it on."

Fiona piled on more scepticism. "Wouldn't Colin have recognised George if he was an ex-pupil? Especially after what happened."

"Mm," Partial Sue muttered. "That is a bit of a pickle. But you didn't recognise him either, Fiona. Not straight away. Remember, this happened over thirty years ago. Plenty of time for his mind to block it out."

Daisy conceded the point. "Actually, that is possible. I still get strangers coming up to me in the street who remember me from when they were little, when I was their teaching assistant, but I have no idea who they are." Daisy turned to Fiona. "Has George ever hinted that he knew Colin?"

Fiona shook her head. "No, but he was quite open about disliking him. Freely admitted it."

Partial Sue clicked her fingers. "There you go! It's got to be him. We should go to DI Fincher with this information. George ticks all the boxes."

Though the evidence was mounting up into a fairly convincing pile, Fiona was a little reluctant to bother the young detective just yet. "Trouble is, she's not looking for a killer. She doesn't think a murder's been committed. We have to be absolutely sure we have all the facts before we make that call.

We've cried wolf too many times with half-baked theories and ended up on the wrong side of her. I'll question George first thing tomorrow. Make sure we're right about his past and see if he denies it."

"Why don't we go and question him now?" Daisy asked.

"We could, but I'd rather do it when we're swimming. It'll catch him off guard."

"Makes sense," said Partial Sue. "But we're going with you."

Daisy tensed up.

"You're coming swimming?" Fiona asked.

Partial Sue grimaced. "Don't be daft! We'll be on the beach as backup, just in case he turns nasty."

Daisy relaxed.

"Don't worry, the other swimmers will be there," Fiona reassured them. "He won't try anything. Too many witnesses. I'll be fine."

Partial Sue folded her arms. "No, we're not taking any chances. We'll be there, keeping an eye on you."

"Wrapped in several warm layers," Daisy hastened to add.

"Thank you," Fiona replied. "It'll be good to have you there." She smiled mischievously. "And maybe you'll be tempted to have a go next time. Once you've seen how much fun it is, being in freezing cold water."

"Along with a murderer," Partial Sue muttered.

"We haven't established that yet." Fiona attempted to be calm, balanced and rational. Not counting her chickens until the contents of all the eggs had been thoroughly verified, weighed and scrutinised to establish their legitimacy. However, she couldn't help the excitement leaking into her bloodstream, turning it fizzy with expectation. Tomorrow morning would be pivotal to this case — there was no doubt in her mind.

CHAPTER 41

Daisy had her hands punched deep into the pockets of a thick duffel coat. A brown scarf swirled around her neck like a walnut whip, her head almost disappearing beneath it, protecting her from an impatient early-morning easterly. The three ladies stood on the gloomy beach as dark waves tumbled towards them and stinging raindrops flicked into their faces.

Daisy's head sank deeper beneath her scarf. "I don't like this weather."

"There's no such thing as inclement weather, just inappropriate clothing," Partial Sue declared smugly. She had sensibly ensconced herself head to foot in proper waterproof hiking gear to protect her against the elements. The drawstrings of the hood had been pulled so tightly around her head that only a small porthole of her face could be seen. At first, Fiona thought her usually pennywise colleague had splashed out and invested in high-quality outdoor gear, judging by the logo, which appeared to be "The North Face". But on closer inspection, she noticed the wording read "The Long Face". Perhaps "The Deep Fake" would have been more appropriate.

"Are you sure you don't want to wait until he comes in?" Daisy asked, not realising that this would undoubtedly prolong their stay on the exposed beach, and therefore her discomfort.

Enveloped by her changing robe, also with her hood up, resembling an aquatic Obi Wan Kenobi, Fiona surveyed the dishevelled water in front of her. It wasn't particularly inviting, but then it never was. She watched George's little legs kicking him out to sea, his bodyboard protruding in front of him. Almost all the club had taken the plunge, including Rani, Ahmed and Will, human-torpedoing his way out to the buoy.

Daisy was right. It would be far easier to wait until George returned, questioning him where they stood, and there would be three of them. A real interrogation. But by that time, the other members of the club would be drifting back to the shore to get warm. They'd be questioning him with an audience. Fine if he was guilty, but if he wasn't, accusing him of Colin's murder in front of bystanders would not be a good look. However, at the moment, George was swimming alone. Fiona could confront him out of the blue, the freezing seawater acting like a truth serum, his mind distracted by the cold, hopefully making it harder for him to lie.

Fiona threw off her robe. "I'm going in."

"Be careful," Daisy said.

"We'll be here," Partial Sue reassured her.

Marching into the waves, Fiona hoped the prospect of sidling up to a potential killer would take the edge off immersing her body in cold water. No such luck. The icy liquid stung her bare flesh and sent tremors all the way up her spine, causing her jaw to clamp shut, presumably a natural reaction to prevent any spare heat from escaping. Fiona didn't waste any time attempting to acclimatise. She kicked forward off the bottom, plunged her shoulders under and swam out to George.

Sculling alongside him, he was his normal chirpy self. "All right, Fiona? Back for more punishment? Proper brass monkeys out 'ere, innit?"

Fiona waded straight in. "Are you from Islington?"

"That's right. What little birdy told you that, then?"

Fiona ignored the question. "Did you go to Islington Secondary Modern?"

George's cheeky smile faltered but quickly recovered. "Er, yeah, I did. Have we got a mutual friend or somethin'?"

"You could say that. Colin Barclay used to teach there, didn't he? But I think you knew him as Mr Bartlett."

George was already white with cold but his complexion somehow drained of more colour, turning his skin almost translucent. He swallowed hard and stopped kicking, hugging his bodyboard tighter to keep himself afloat as he was buffeted by the churning water. It was the first time Fiona had seen him stuck for words.

Fiona trod water beside him. "He's the reason you've got that dicky shoulder, isn't he? Knocked you out during a school rugby practice. He was cleared but you're stuck with the injury. Sounds like a perfect reason to—"

"It ain't what you think," George gasped. "I swear. Okay, I admit, as my shoulder got worse each year, I became more and more bitter about what he did. Till I went looking for him. Wanted to confront him."

"So you tracked him down here?"

"Yeah, then I followed him around, from a distance. Saw that he'd retired and watched him wild swimming with the club. I thought that would be a good place to have it out with him. So they'd all know what he did to me. So I turned up at the beach one day to see the look of shame on his face. But he looked straight through me. Didn't recognise me."

"You didn't reveal who you were?"

"Nah. It threw me, if I'm honest. I'd been building it up in me head for so long, but I had no Plan B if he didn't recognise me. So I just stood there like a lemon. People started staring at me so I asked to join the club. I figured I could keep an eye on him. Bide my time. Thinking my hate for him would push me into action. But something weird happened."

"What?"

"I started feeling sorry for him. After a few weeks of wild swimming, I realised nobody liked him. They tolerated him but tried to avoid him. Apart from maybe Beth, but she's a good sort, you know? Nice and that. But everyone else couldn't stand him. So he was getting his own comeuppance, as it were. Sorta took the wind out of me sails."

Fiona shivered as the cold began to bite. "And if the wind hadn't been taken out of your sails, what had you planned to do to him?"

"Not kill him. I swear I had nothing to do with that. Like I said, I just wanted to see the look on his face. Let him know what he'd done."

"But you didn't confront him?"

George's lower lip trembled, possibly from the wintry sea or, more likely, resurfacing emotions. "You know, I was scared of 'im when I was a nipper. He's a big geezer and I'm not. After I left school and grew up a bit, I got a bit more cocky, or so I thought. I worked out all the things I'd say to him. How I'd give him a mouthful. But, truth be told, when I saw him for the first time after all them years, I was straight back to being a quiet little sparrow of a lad. Lost me bottle."

"When you heard he died, weren't you frightened someone might find out about your past and suspect you? Why didn't you disappear?"

George frowned. "That would've made me look guilty. I didn't kill him, so why run? Besides, I like it here. Love being by the beach. Don't get me wrong, I'm an Islington lad through and through, but it's not a patch on Southbourne. And I like these people. They're my friends."

Fiona's teeth were almost on the point of chattering. "So, who did kill him?"

"Er, I don't know."

His hesitation led Fiona to believe the opposite. "You have an idea, don't you?"

George kicked away from her, further out to sea. Fiona swam after him. With only his legs to propel him, Fiona was faster and rounded on him, blocking his path. "George, is there something you're not telling me?"

"I don't know nothin', I swear."

She was about to push George further, coerce him if she had to. Get a name out of him one way or another. But she was interrupted by splashing behind her.

"Cooee!" The smiley, breathless face of Beth appeared, her strong arms scything a front crawl towards them. "I did it! I'm back!"

"Oh, Beth! Well done!" Fiona had wanted more than anything to see Beth regain her confidence after Colin's demise and make a welcome return to wild swimming. Just not at this precise moment. Not when Fiona had their best suspect on the hook, or perhaps a key witness on the brink of divulging something crucial.

"All right, Beth?" George swiftly reverted back to his usual chipper self. "Good to see you back in the briny again."

Beth trod water while grinning from ear to ear. "Oh my gosh, I've really missed this! If it wasn't for you, Fiona, keeping on at me, I wouldn't have taken the plunge again."

"I'm really pleased for you." Fiona wished she could muster more enthusiasm, but having her line of questioning abruptly curtailed had thrown her.

"You two looked very serious a moment ago." Beth grinned. "What were you talking about?"

After all the times Fiona had attempted to lure Beth back into the water, she had chosen this occasion. Coincidence? Or had her sudden appearance been a cynical attempt to prevent George from revealing something he shouldn't? Which would imply she had something to do with Colin's murder after all. Or perhaps they were both in on it. Fiona shivered, and it wasn't just the cold nipping at her skin.

"We were trading swimming tips," George laughed. "Right, I'm heading back in. Getting a bit chilly now." Like a miniature riverboat, he kicked his legs, frothing the water behind him, and made for the shore.

Beth turned to Fiona. "You look like you're getting a bit cold too. Gotta keep moving." She resumed her powerful front crawl, heading further out to sea, leaving Fiona out of her depth and treading water alone. One suspect heading one way, and perhaps a new one heading the other.

Fiona decided to follow George in and continue her questioning while they got changed. Not ideal but better than nothing.

But before she had a chance to take a single stroke back to land, something clamped itself around her ankle and yanked her down. She wanted to cry out, but the shock sent her breath the wrong way, making her gasp. She managed to thrust a hand in the air before she slipped below the surface and plunged into watery darkness.

CHAPTER 42

The cold air slalomed around Daisy and Partial Sue as they stood on the beach gazing out to sea. They hadn't resorted to huddling together for warmth yet, but give it time. Ignoring the odd sniff and shiver, their watchful eyes never wavered from their friend, currently swimming beside George, two unlikely swimming buddies locked deep in conversation. No words reached their ears, but George's face had lost its cheerful demeanour the moment Fiona had breaststroked beside him.

"Do you think he's confessed?" Daisy asked.

"What killer ever confesses?" Partial Sue snorted. "He'll lie his way out of it. But I'm sure he did it."

"I know he's the best suspect we've got, but what happened to believing Colin was lured over to the Purbecks and killed by a surfer?"

Partial Sue had no such reservations. "George has that bodyboard. Maybe they went bodyboarding over there."

"But his bodyboard's to help him swim with his frozen shoulder. I can't imagine someone with that sort of injury would go to Kimmeridge with all them rocks."

"Could all be a ruse and his shoulder's absolutely fine now."

Daisy shuddered. "Well, I hope he confesses soon. My toes are going numb. Oh, that reminds me. I've been looking into holidays. Somewhere nice and warm."

Partial Sue wasn't fond of holidays. Holidays were expensive and unnecessary. Why endure hours of claustrophobia in a plane, breathing one another's air, paying for food you didn't particularly like and queuing for a glorified prison toilet, to fly to a beach when you had a perfectly serviceable stretch of sand on your doorstep? Okay, not particularly serviceable at the moment, but just wait until the summer and it'd be like southern California, except better because it had fish and chips, and Punch and Judy. "Why do you want to go on holiday?"

Daisy was never cynical, and certainly not the sarcastic type, but this time her response was more acerbic than usual. "Really? You want to know why I want a holiday when we're standing here freezing our behinds off? Plus, all this talk of surfing has got me interested. I thought I could combine the two. A surfing holiday. Somewhere warm and tropical. Where you can do it in a cossie, like Agatha Christie. Ride gentle little waves then unwind beneath swaying palm trees, sipping peanut colanders."

"It's pina coladas. But that does sound nice."

Daisy continued selling the idea. "We should all go. Learn together. It'd be so much fun. The holiday of a lifetime."

Someone hurried across the sand behind them. Flustered and panting hard, they turned to see Beth, who appeared desperate to get in the water and join her fellow wild swimmers. Throwing down her beach bag and casting off her changing robe to reveal a flowery-patterned bathing suit, she barely noticed Daisy and Partial Sue standing nearby.

"Everything all right, Beth?" Partial Sue asked.

Her faced relaxed. "Oh, yes. Hello. Sorry. I'm miles away. I made the decision to go swimming this morning. I haven't been since Colin died and if I think about it too much, I'll change my mind."

"Good for you," Partial Sue encouraged her.

"Don't let us stop you," Daisy added.

"Thank you. Well, here I go." Beth marched forward, wading into the arctic water. Not baulking once at the cold, the rest of her followed until she was deep enough to submerge her shoulders and commence a front crawl out towards the others.

"She didn't waste any time," Daisy commented. "Not bad for someone who hasn't been in for ages."

"That's the attitude you need when facing your fears. Stoic and steadfast. Single-minded."

"Does that mean you're going to give wild swimming a go?"

"Not on your life."

The ladies went quiet observing the strange watery reunion. Smiling swimmers flocked around Beth, presumably to congratulate her return to the cold-water fold. Apart from Will, who was unaware of Beth's appearance due to his head being down in the water, arms and legs pistoning him back from his trip out to the buoy. And, of course, Fiona and George, who were still locked in deep conversation.

Partial Sue grew impatient. "I want to know what the pair of them are saying."

"Me too. I wish I could lip-read. That's another thing I'd like to learn."

"You'd need a pair of binoculars from this distance."

"I wonder if you can book surfing holidays with a lip-reading course," Daisy mused, bending the conversation back to the subject of her dream holiday. "I've been looking into the top destinations. Honolulu is number one. That's where Agatha Christie learned to surf. It looks amazing."

"And expensive, I bet," Partial Sue replied.

"Oh, don't worry. I've been looking into other places that are nearer. There's Biarritz in France, Caleta on Lanzarote, Cádiz . . ."

"Wait, did you say Cádiz?"

Daisy nodded.

"Where do I know that name from?" Partial Sue's eyes narrowed and her brow became wrinkled, the answer not forthcoming.

"It's in Spain."

"Yeah, I know where it is," Partial Sue huffed. "What I mean is, Cádiz has popped up in conversation recently. I'm sure Fiona mentioned it, but I can't remember what she was referring to."

The two ladies gazed around them, desperate for an answer to emerge from the deep recesses of their minds.

Partial Sue had a partial answer to the puzzle. "I remember Fiona said that someone had spent their summers growing up there."

"Well, if they did, they're bound to be a surfer. That place is surrounded by surfing beaches. Tons of them. That's why it's so good for learning."

"Well, if there's a chance this person's a surfer then there's a chance they're a suspect in this."

"But what about George?" Daisy asked. "I thought he was our number-one suspect."

Partial Sue glanced out to sea at Fiona and George, who had been momentarily interrupted by Beth swimming past them. "It doesn't hurt to have another one lined up. In case this one turns out to be a dead end, although I can't see how."

The pair of them fell silent for a minute or two, then Daisy suddenly blurted. "Oh my gosh. I think I remember who Fiona was talking about." She rapidly clicked her fingers as the name eluded her.

"Who? Who is it?" Partial Sue demanded.

Daisy gabbled uncontrollably. "It's whatshisname, thingamajig. You know."

Partial Sue almost exploded with anticipation. "I don't. Tell me!"

"Wait, wait. Hold on a second." Daisy scuttled around on the spot, as if trying to contain a sneeze that had become stuck. “My head’s gone weird, like there’s a different brain inside it. Just give me a moment.” She continued moving erratically on the sand, her face and body contorting in agony. Suddenly she straightened up. “Gosh! I think I know how he did it — well, some of it. Most of it, actually.”

“Who! Who?!” Partial Sue sounded like a frustrated owl.

Daisy fell silent, distracted as her eyes frantically surveyed the sea.

“What is it?”

“I can’t see Fiona.”

The pair of them scanned the water in front of them like a couple of anxious meerkats, desperately hoping to lock onto their friend. They immediately spotted a flustered George kicking his way back towards the beach. But Fiona was not with him. Nor was she with any other members of the club. Fiona had disappeared.

CHAPTER 43

The surface slipped from Fiona's grasp as she was tugged down and down by an unseen entity. Sheer desperation forced her legs into action. She kicked hard, hoping to dislodge whatever held her by the ankle. But her captor would not relinquish its grip, no matter how hard she struggled.

Frantically searching around her feet, she hoped to catch a glimpse of what or who had her in its clutches, but the water was too murky and her vision was obscured by a gush of bubbles rising up from below. The cold, already debilitating, suddenly intensified, rapidly draining the power from her helpless, flailing limbs. But that was the least of her problems. Her body shifted sideways as she was dragged out to sea into deeper water. She screamed, only resulting in a despairing gurgle, sacrificing precious air.

Exhausted from her efforts, her body went limp, a ragdoll jerked through a dark sea, accepting its inevitable fate. In this strange moment of defeated calm, the smug image of Sophie Haverford sashayed into her mind. Dressed in the same teal-coloured swimming costume as Fiona, she tutted and shook her head. *See, I wasn't pretending to be a damsel in distress. Well, maybe I was a bit at the end, but something did pull me under, and it certainly wasn't a seal or a jilted lover.*

Now it all became clear. Fiona had been the target all along, but Sophie had been attacked by mistake, because she had been wearing the same costume.

Oh, please, Sophie sneered. *As if anyone would mistake this svelte body for yours. Probably what saved me.*

Fiona's brain became foggy and oxygen starved, while the cold numbed any desire she had to save herself. Her eyes were about to slide shut until the annoying figment of her imagination pecked at her. *At times like these, one needs to look up.*

In her delirious near-death state, Fiona couldn't believe her nemesis was giving her life-coaching instructions.

As if reading Fiona's mind — though she was, in fact, generated by her mind — Sophie clarified her meaning. *No, silly, I literally mean look up.*

Fiona raised her weary head to witness the odd sight of a hand fishing around above her, as if it had lost a wedding ring. Using her last modicum of strength, she reached up, thrusting her arm towards the probing hand. Only managing to brush the fingertips, she was suddenly pulled down, out of reach, but it was enough. Above her, the water became a maelstrom of thrashing arms, as someone desperately tried to locate her. She was heartened to see the worried and wide-eyed face of Beth frantically swimming down towards her.

A new spurt of hope ignited Fiona's resolve. She outstretched both arms, as did Beth. A second later, they clutched hands like a couple of trapeze artists in slow motion. Immediately reversing engines, Beth attempted to pull Fiona up to the surface. No matter how hard she yanked, Fiona wouldn't move, but at least she wasn't dragged any deeper.

Another body swam down to join Beth. Ahmed immediately hooked both his hands under Fiona's armpits and kicked hard with his legs in a bid to free her. Again and again, their combined efforts failed to liberate her.

Rani appeared, her unmistakable thick dark hair swirling around her like an angry storm. Swimming down past Ahmed and Beth, she headed for the source of the problem, attempting to prise Fiona's ankle free.

The three of them wrenched and hauled in unison. Blessed freedom came almost instantly. Her body shot up to the surface like a popped cork. As she rose, a blur of red Speedos flew past her in the opposite direction. Too late to aid in her rescue, Will joined Rani, wrestling with her captor.

Fiona burst through the water, sucking down a massive gulp of air, supported on either side by Beth and Ahmed. She took several more gluttonous lungfuls. "Th-Thank you."

"Don't speak," Beth said. "Just slow, deep breaths."

"Okay," Fiona was conscious, lucid and breathing, and hadn't taken any water into her lungs. All positives, she told herself. And she was alive, thanks to her wild swimming friends.

"We need to get you warm," Ahmed said.

Numbed with cold and drenched in shock, Fiona's limbs refused to move. Gently, they shifted Fiona onto her back, Beth supporting her head, tilting it backwards to help her breathe, while Ahmed held her shoulders. With sideways, sculling strokes, the pair of them slowly eased Fiona towards the beach. More members of the wild swimming club swam over to lend their assistance, helping to convey Fiona back to shore as safely and as swiftly as possible. All the while Beth reassured her. "Don't worry, you're safe now. Nothing to worry about. Everything's fine."

That promise was shattered when a tumult of thrashing limbs and water exploded behind them.

Grappling with some strange creature, Will had it firmly in a headlock while Rani had both arms clamped around its flippered legs. With its slick, glistening black body writhing around, desperate to free itself, Fiona couldn't tell whether it was a giant fish or an alien. It nearly escaped, but more club members swarmed around it, seizing whatever limbs they could get their hands on, bringing it under control. As it ceased thrashing, she realised it wasn't some creature from the deep or another world, but a man in a diving suit, complete with mask, regulators and air tank — the culprit responsible for her attempted drowning. But Fiona didn't have the inclination or capacity to go into shock, as her investigative brain took charge, all cells deliberating on who could be behind the mask. At least she knew it wasn't George.

The moment she reached the shore, Fiona collapsed on the sand, shivering. Daisy rushed forward and threw a changing robe around her. The fleecy lining had never felt warmer or more welcoming. Someone from the club pulled a second robe over her shoulders. Partial Sue thrust a steamy mug of tea into her hand. Fiona grasped it with both hands, grateful for the warmth that radiated out from her palms.

"Oh my gosh, are you okay?" Partial Sue asked.

"We were terrified," Daisy cried.

"I'm fine." Fiona shuddered, swilling down her tea. "Just a bit cold and exhausted. Thought I was a goner there."

"Has someone called an ambulance?" Beth called out.

"On its way," Daisy replied. "And so are the police."

"Thank you," Fiona said to Beth and Ahmed. "You and Rani saved my life."

Beth waved it away as if it was all in a day's work. "I'm just glad you're okay."

"You can buy us a drink in the pub later." Ahmed smiled.

"What the hell happened out there?" Partial Sue asked.

Fiona gathered her swirling thoughts. "One minute, I was treading water, the next minute someone pulled me under."

"It was just lucky I turned when I did," Beth said. "I saw your hand disappear beneath the waves."

"We think we know who did it," Partial Sue said.

"We made a minor breakthrough while you were swimming," Daisy added.

Before they had a chance to explain, a small band of wild swimmers scrambled onto the shoreline led by Rani, a black wriggling mass in their collective arms. Unceremoniously, they dumped his body on the sand and stood over him, ensuring he didn't make a run for it — although that would have been almost impossible and highly comedic, considering the amount of diving gear amassed on his person.

One by one, everyone grabbed their changing robes for warmth and gathered around him, eager to learn the identity of the underwater assassin, including Fiona, who shakily rose to her feet assisted by Daisy and Partial Sue.

Rani knelt beside his head and pulled the regulator from his mouth and ripped off the diving mask.

Exchanging confused glances, none of the swimmers recognised him. But the three lady detectives did. Partial Sue and Daisy had only seen pictures of him online, but Fiona had met him on a couple of occasions. Sat opposite him in his smart house, exchanged pleasantries and listened to him pledge to help the investigation in any way he could, presumably so he could keep tabs on them.

A wave of nausea passed over her. She'd been in the presence of a calm and collected killer and had never known.

CHAPTER 44

"Just who the hell are you?" Rani demanded.

Possibly realising there was no way out of this, the man in the diving gear lay on his back unresponsive, not catching anyone's eye.

Fiona drew closer, standing directly over him. "That's Ted Maplin. Colin's therapist."

Murmurs and gasps spread through the gathered swimmers, who had crowded around to get a better look at the accused. Confronted by the angry and slightly puzzled mob, Ted Maplin suddenly sat bolt upright.

Fiona flinched and several swimmers took up defensive stances just in case he tried anything.

No longer the suave therapist, Maplin was an odd sight, decked head to foot in neoprene. A tight-fitting wetsuit balaclava squished his features, bulging his cheeks and pouting his lips, as if he were a spoiled, insolent child who refused to accept he'd done anything wrong. He sent a murderous look in Fiona's direction.

"Did you kill Colin?" Beth demanded.

Maplin redirected his homicidal stare towards her but issued no reply.

"Well, answer her." An indignant rage had driven the shock from Fiona's body. "And why did you just try to kill me?"

Maplin stayed mute.

"Because he thought you were on to him," Partial Sue answered. "He didn't realise there were three of us investigating the murder. He thought it was just you and needed to get you out of the way."

"But I wasn't on to him," Fiona replied. "I mean, we weren't on to him. He wasn't even on our radar."

"Don't be so sure," Daisy said. "We figured it out in the last few minutes. But it was too late to warn you."

"But how could he have known that?" Fiona replied.

"For a while, we thought Colin was killed by a surfer," Partial Sue explained. "Trouble was, we couldn't find any link between Colin and surfers or surfing until Daisy stumbled onto something just now."

Everyone turned to listen to Daisy. "I'd been researching surfing holidays, and the name Cádiz came up."

"That's where he spent his summers growing up." Fiona nodded to Maplin.

"That's right," Partial Sue replied. "It's a surfing Mecca, which means there's more than a good chance he'd be a surfer."

Fiona slapped her forehead. "And I phoned him up to ask if Colin had mentioned anything about surfing. No wonder he tried to kill me."

"But lots of people surf around here," Beth said. "What made you think it was him?"

"Throughout this investigation, we've continually hit a stumbling block," Partial Sue said. "How did Colin get to the sea on that fateful day? He always took his car, and never accepted lifts or took taxis, but on this occasion, his Land Rover stayed put and hadn't moved since the last day he was seen alive."

"We spoke to his neighbour," Daisy added. "He's a little slow on his feet but he listens out for engine noises. Always knew when Colin was leaving or coming home because of the sound his Land Rover makes. But on the day Colin disappeared, he never heard him leave, or anyone else picking him up. However, Maplin drives an electric SUV. Hardly makes a sound. He could have picked him up regularly and the neighbour wouldn't have known anything about it."

"Is that true?" Fiona asked.

Maplin clenched his gloved fists, attempting to contain his rage. Lips tightening, again he resisted the urge to answer her.

"But why would he be picking Colin up at all?" Beth asked. "Especially if he didn't accept lifts."

Fiona's body may have been numb with cold but her brain was fired up. "He'd been treating him for depression. He suggested Colin try new things — one of them was wild swimming." She turned to Maplin once more. "Did you suggest surfing as well? Maybe offered to teach him for an additional fee. Make some money on the side."

The therapist didn't reply.

"If he charged him for surfing lessons," said Partial Sue, "then picking him up would be part of the service, and he would have all the equipment for Colin to borrow. Wouldn't count as a lift."

"But why would Colin need to be picked up?" Ahmed asked. "Why wouldn't he just meet him down at the seafront?"

"Because that weekend the sea was flat," Partial Sue replied. "Colin would have noticed something was up if they arranged to meet here, but there were waves over on the Purbecks, and, more importantly, powerful spring tides. There are several secret spots that Colin wouldn't know how to get to without being driven there. Or at least that's how Maplin probably sold it."

"Secret spots sound like a good place to murder someone," George suggested.

Beth shook her head. "Hold on a second. Surely Colin would have told us if he was learning to surf."

"We don't get along with surfers," Rani pointed out.

"That's right," Fiona agreed. "Colin probably hid his surfing because he didn't want to jeopardise his friendship with all of you."

"Oh my gosh! We wouldn't have been bothered about that. If only he'd told us." Beth's eyes alighted on the shamed therapist. "What have you got to say for yourself?"

Maplin's gaze briefly flicked in her direction then he returned to his non-responsive state.

"Hey! I'm talking to you." Beth wouldn't take no response for an answer. "Why did you kill Colin? He was my friend. Would always help anyone."

Finally, Maplin responded. Although it wasn't much of a reaction. A slow hand clap, slightly muffled by his gloves and accompanied by a patronising grin. "Well done, well done on being the biggest bunch of hypocrites ever. Mourning Colin's death. None of you could stand him. Self-righteous twit that he was."

"We might not have liked him," George said. "But we're not the ones who killed him."

"Do you think I'm that petty?" Maplin snapped. "Do you think I'd kill someone just because I didn't like them?"

"So why did you?" Fiona asked.

Maplin clamped his mouth shut, fearing the answer might escape his lips of its own volition.

Fiona decided the only way to get an answer was to needle one out of him. "You know, you really are the world's worst counsellor. Colin came to you for help and wound up dead."

Partial Sue cottoned on to Fiona's strategy. "Is that the solution to all your clients' problems — you get rid of their issues by killing them? Is that the Maplin approach — 'murder therapy'? Because I don't think it's going to catch on."

Maplin glared at them, his eyes cautious, sensing a trap. Thankfully, his professional pride was stronger than his prudence. "I'm an excellent counsellor. The best around here. I helped him beat his depression and what thanks did I get? He betrayed me."

"How did he betray you?" Beth asked. "Colin would never betray anyone."

The last phrase triggered the therapist. He grinned devilishly, as if Beth was the world's most naive person. "He's not the do-gooder you all think he was."

Fiona noticed George shifting uneasily on the sand.

Maplin pointed at Beth. "You didn't know him like I knew him. Hour after hour, he'd sit there . . . Bleating on and on about how he couldn't get a woman to look at him twice. Whining all the time about his life, when he could've done anything with all that money of his—" He paused for breath, spat onto the sand. "I was the best friend he ever had. He said he wanted to help me . . . but he couldn't even manage that. He was a coward who lacked vision and courage, and he got what—" He stopped himself before he went too far.

"Go on," said Partial Sue. "You were about to say he got what he deserved, I believe."

His eyes lost their fire and gazed down at the sand.

"Answer her," Beth demanded.

The therapist returned to his catatonic state, flopping onto his back, unresponsive to outside stimuli, his face blank and unreadable like a passport photo.

Sirens whined in the distance.

"Well," said Partial Sue. "Looks like you're about to get what you deserve. And you're going to have all the time in the world to explain it to the police."

CHAPTER 45

Fiona had stayed away from large bodies of water. Whether it be seasides, swimming pools, rivers or ponds, even her own bathtub had stood neglected, which made her sound as if she had hygiene issues. However, she'd opted for showers instead of long, relaxing soaks, which were no longer relaxing, as she was constantly in fear that something might grab her by the big toe and yank her down the plug hole. Quite understandably, she wanted to avoid sizeable quantities of the medium in which she'd almost lost her life as much as was humanly possible. But perhaps she was being a little unfair on the liquid. The water had nothing to do with it and had been minding its own business. It was what had been lurking in the stuff that had been the cause of her near-death experience, namely a murderous local therapist — not what you expected to find in the English Channel. Although her attempted murderer and Colin's actual murderer was safely behind bars, she still couldn't muster the courage to don a swimming costume and return to swimming, or any sort of bathing, dipping or paddling.

She knew this would be a temporary arrangement and she'd be back in the briny soon. But before that could happen, she needed to give her mind a period of adjustment, to analyse and make sense of what had happened. Process the shock and file it away under things that, yes, had been highly traumatic but were extremely unlikely to ever happen again. Once past this point, she would be back in her cossie again in no time. Although not the teal one, which had gone straight in the bin.

In the meantime, she took solace in the warming embrace of Dogs Need Nice Homes, submerging herself in sorting out donations at the table. A lucky dip of the most dismal kind, the simple repetitive task of delving into one cardboard box and binbag after another did wonders for her mental health. Ably assisted by her two best friends and accompanied by their gentle, pointless banter, it was the best therapy a person could wish for.

Daisy flinched, pulling a couple of small glittery red objects from a bag of clothes. "Oh, someone's donated a pair of nipple tassels."

"Not again," Partial Sue complained. "That's the third time this month. They must think we're into all that."

"How do you know we're not?" Fiona's sense of humour had returned. Always a good sign she was getting over things.

"Urgh. No thank you." Partial Sue winced. "We should put a sign up. No seedy gear. Please donate such items across the road to the Cats Alliance."

"Can you imagine Sophie's face when she's inundated with nipple tassels?" Fiona giggled.

Daisy held them up and jiggled them around. "I think they're quite pretty. I might keep them and make them into tiebacks for my curtains."

"Now that's what I call upcycling!" Fiona smiled.

DI Fincher and DS Thomas wandered into the shop, catching Daisy mid-twirl. Her cheeks went the colour of toffee apples as she snatched the tassels out of sight, below the table.

The young DI was her usual, immaculately dressed self, decked out in an expensive-looking beige raincoat and smart grey slacks, while her muscly, monosyllabic sidekick went for comfort in mismatched, slightly ratty sportswear.

At best, the ladies had an uneasy relationship with these two. One that ranged from mildly irritating them to verging dangerously close to wasting police time. Generally, the two detectives would have preferred it if they had kept their noses out of their investigations. But on several occasions, the ladies had cracked cases that had stumped the two detectives. They never took any credit or sought any media attention, but it must have smarted this pair of professionals that a trio of amateurs, doing it purely for fun, had succeeded where they had failed.

However, on this occasion the ladies had not bothered the detectives once. Mainly because they didn't have anything to bother them with, and the police had been blissfully unaware that a murder had been committed, thanks to the coroner's verdict of accidental death. That is, until Daisy and Partial Sue had called them from the beach to inform them that a) Colin had very much been murdered, and b) by someone they believed was Ted Maplin, who appeared to be currently engaged in a second murder, involving their best friend Fiona, and therefore c) could they please hurry up and get here fast.

So the two detectives hadn't expected to arrest a killer that morning but had turned up at the scene to find one caught wetsuit-handed, as it were, alongside a nice stack of evidence against him for a previous murder, gathered by the ladies. Admittedly, it was a very small stack and not complete by any means. A bit like ordering one of those meals online that you have to make yourself, DI Fincher had to do a bit of work, but the ladies had supplied her with all the main ingredients, and things were simmering away nicely, judging by the contented smirk on her face. She even managed a few pleasantries. "Good morning. How are you all?"

"Mustn't grumble," Partial Sue replied.

"We're all in fine fettle," Daisy added.

"How about you, Fiona?" DI Fincher asked.

"I'm fine, honestly."

"Counselling is available, should you need to talk to someone." DI Thomas's attempt at victim support was admirable, but it did come across as if he were reading off a whiteboard at a training afternoon. "It's free at the point of contact, independent and confidential, and will help you understand what you've been through."

"She understands what she's been through," Partial Sue pointed out. "Ted Maplin tried to kill her, and he was a counsellor, so counselling is the last thing she needs."

"Is he talking?" Fiona asked.

DI Fincher shook her head. "Nope, still refusing to cooperate, but I don't know where he thinks it's going to get him. We've got him for your attempted murder, and Colin's murder."

"You have?"

"As you know, I'm not supposed to reveal any details, but after what you've been through, and the valuable information you've supplied, I think you've earned the right to know. You were correct about him luring Colin over to the Purbecks. Thanks to your tip-off, we secured doorbell cam footage of his SUV over there, early Saturday morning."

"It was caught passing through the village of Worth Matravers," said DS Thomas.

"Oh, I love Worth Matravers," Partial Sue gushed. "There's a pub that's also a fossil museum."

"And do you know what's also there?" DI Fincher asked.

The ladies shook their heads.

"An abandoned quarry with direct access to the sea."

Fiona's stomach lurched.

"We're working on the theory that Maplin took Colin there, making out it was a secret surf spot. Colin wouldn't have known any better. But it's the perfect place to clunk him on the back of the head with a rock. Isolated and very difficult to get to, they'd be undisturbed. Once he'd killed him, Maplin could dump his body in the sea, as you said, then let the spring tide currents drag his body to Hengistbury Head."

"How can you be sure that was the exact place?" Fiona asked. "According to the warden, there are lots of secret spots on the Purbecks."

DI Fincher pulled up a chair. "Because the stone used to build the groynes at Southbourne originally came from that quarry. The coroner did a more thorough examination of tissue samples taken from the injuries on Colin's body. He found fragments of stone in his head wound that matched. Maplin was being extra cautious. Wanted to make it look consistent with a knock on the head at Southbourne."

"But how do you know Colin didn't just slip and bang his head on one of the groynes down here?" Daisy asked.

DS Thomas piped up. "The coroner also found tiny particles of neoprene rubber lodged in the scratch marks on his skin."

DI Fincher continued. "At first, the coroner thought they were travel marks. But he conceded that they could've been made by a knife, but couldn't be absolutely sure, because the body had been in the sea for a week. We're assuming they were, and that Colin had been wearing a wetsuit at the time, then was cut out of it to make it appear as if he'd been wild swimming. Just as you suggested."

"Wow," Fiona gasped, shocked at hearing the last moments of Colin's life coldly played out to Maplin's exact and premeditated plans. But also, that they had occurred almost exactly as the ladies had theorised, while sitting at this very same table. Perhaps they were getting better at this detective lark.

"Now the million-dollar question." Partial Sue cleared her throat. "Why did Maplin kill Colin?"

DI Fincher answered immediately. "Money, plain and simple. We've gone through his business accounts. Colin made a very large payment to Maplin of thirty thousand pounds. We think Colin loaned him the money for his business."

"Ted told me he was expanding," Fiona said. "Planning to move to new premises."

"Yes, we checked that out too. There was no expansion plan. No calls to estate agents or property renters, no enquiries whatsoever. But we did find that he'd run up a ton of debt keeping up appearances, spending money he didn't have. He knew Colin wasn't short of cash and, thanks to you, we also know that Colin had a habit of helping people. Maplin persuaded Colin to lend him money for his imaginary business plan. But it went straight to paying off his debts."

Daisy frowned. "But he said on the beach that Colin betrayed him."

"We think Colin got wise to it," DI Fincher said. "Maybe asked for his money back, or worse, threatened to shop him to the powers that be for unethical behaviour. We found an interesting search term on Colin's computer — reporting a therapist for misconduct. He never followed it up, but if he had, Maplin's career would've been over. Maplin probably used his counselling skills to smooth Colin's fears. Reassured him that they were mates, and that he would get every penny back with interest. Colin trusted him and must have bought his lies, but Ted still had a big problem. He had no way to repay him — and now he was at risk of losing everything. Only way to fix it was to take Colin out of the picture. But he had to make it look like an accident, to avoid us poking our noses into Colin's finances and finding a big hole that led straight to him. Hence the one-way surf trip over to the Purbecks."

Fiona sighed heavily and grimaced. "No good deed goes unpunished."

"I'm afraid it looks that way," DI Fincher said. "Maplin took advantage of Colin's good nature."

"He said Colin lacked vision. What do you think he meant by that?" Daisy asked.

"Maplin's materialistic," DI Fincher replied. "Had a lifestyle he couldn't afford, while Colin was frugal. Sitting on a big pile of disposable cash he wasn't using. Must've infuriated the life out of Maplin, who had plenty of ways to spend it. I reckon bitterness and jealousy also played their parts."

The shop went quiet. A moment of silence perhaps, out of respect for the deceased. A good person, not perfect by any means, but nonetheless losing their life at the hands of a bad one. A tale as old as time. Not likely to change any time soon, and destined to plague the world far into its precarious future.

Partial Sue broke the silence. "You know, we floated that theory around for a while — the local businessman in debt, tapping Colin up for cash."

"Once again we were looking in the wrong place," Fiona added.

"We thought it was Roger at the surf shop," Daisy said. "Didn't even think of Ted Maplin."

DI Fincher smiled sympathetically. "Don't be too hard on yourselves. These things happen in detective work. Take comfort in the fact that your instincts were right. But you've learned something today. If you have a good theory, don't just apply it to one suspect." DI Fincher got to her feet. "Well, we'll be on our way. And thanks again for your help. It is very much appreciated."

The two police officers shuffled out of the shop.

"Hear that?" Daisy grinned. "We just got a 'very much appreciated'. That's a first. It's usually a filthy look or a telling off."

"Well, I'm not surprised," Partial Sue remarked. "If it wasn't for us, they wouldn't have caught Ted Maplin."

"To be fair," Fiona replied. "Beth and the wild swimmers caught Ted Maplin."

"But we did figure out it was him," Partial Sue blurted then adopted a humbler tone. "Well, Daisy did."

"It was a joint effort," Daisy said, magnanimously. "If you hadn't spotted Cádiz, I'd never have made the connection." She glanced at Fiona. "Sorry, it was just a bit too late."

"No apologies necessary. But I suppose without our intel they wouldn't have been able to pull it all together." Fiona felt her face droop and her body sag.

"Are you okay, Fiona?" Daisy asked.

"How about a cup of tea?" Partial Sue offered.

Fiona shook her head. "What I really need is a holiday. Change of scenery."

Daisy got excited. "I know just the place."

Partial Sue headed off her idea. "I don't think Fiona wants to go on a surfing holiday. I doubt she wants to go anywhere near water at the moment. Not after the traumatic experience she's just had."

"It's just a suggestion." Daisy's enthusiasm for her dream holiday hadn't been dampened by the murderous surfing therapist.

Fiona didn't appear to be put off either. "You know what?" She perked up. "I think I do. I'm not going to let Ted Maplin put me off doing something I love. I want to go on holiday, and I want to go swimming. Get back on the horse, as it were."

Daisy's grin grew larger. "You know, this place I've got in mind, you can do both. The horse swims in the sea with you on its back. It looks magical."

"Do they have shire horses?" Partial Sue became interested. "I'd be up for that if they do."

"Oh, I don't know. I can check . . ."

"Just regular swimming will be fine." Emboldened by her decision to go back into the water, Fiona felt her spirits soar. She couldn't face going back to wild swimming at her local beach just yet. But easing herself back into it on a sun-drenched tropical beach would be a most agreeable way to circle back to her love of the sea, and what better way to do it than with her two best friends by her side?

EPILOGUE

In the end, it had taken a great deal of effort to overcome her fears, more than the other two ladies had expected. They had known she'd have some reservations, and they'd have their work cut out for them, breaking down the anxiety she'd built up. However, bit by bit, choosing their words very carefully, they had persuaded her until she finally plucked up the courage and took the plunge. This was not, as you might think, to do with Fiona taking her first tentative steps back into the sea, but Partial Sue's instinctive fear of spending money.

The large sum it cost to fly to and stay in Hawaii had almost given her palpitations. Heated and colourful protestations had followed, the main thrust of which was pointing out just what she could buy with that sort of money. She'd rattled off a list as long as her arm, ranging from a reasonably priced second-hand car, to a high-quality cinematic flat-screen TV. Fiona had countered by asking if she would actually purchase said items if they decided not to go. Horrified at this proposal, her only rebuttal was that she might need to buy them at some point.

Following this logic, Fiona had asked her to do a simple calculation: work out the total cost of every conceivable item she might require in the future, then subtract it from what she had saved in the bank. Logically, whatever she had left over could be spent on nice things like holidays with her friends.

A sheepish Partial Sue, knowing her vast savings far outweighed any conceivable future cost she would incur, unless her house got hit by a meteor, conceded and reluctantly bought a plane ticket. Possibly the first time anyone had been forced to go to Hawaii, coerced by basic accountancy principles.

However, a fortnight later, as they made their final descent into Honolulu, her monetary grumbles fell silent as their first glimpse of the island of Oahu held them enrapt. Rising from an impossibly blue ocean, it was a land dreamed up only in fairytales, with lush rainforests and soaring green mountains that disappeared into the clouds.

But Partial Sue wasn't the only one to have her opinions drastically altered by this wondrous place. After settling into their hotel, they headed straight for Waikiki Beach. Stepping onto the talcum-powder-soft white sand, any trepidations Fiona had after the incident with Ted Maplin completely fled. The iridescent water was mesmerising and irresistible, just begging to be swum in. Utterly transparent all the way to the horizon, any danger she feared had nowhere to hide. The only thing that troubled the ladies as they plunged into the ocean were playful fish of the most joyously bright colours darting around their toes.

"Oh, it's just like *Finding Nemo*," Daisy gushed.

"Let's hope not," Partial Sue grumbled. "We don't want to get lost at sea." But as they floated on their backs, staring into the Pacific sky, any trace of cynicism melted in the warm tropical water. "You know, I could get used to this. I'm glad I came."

"So are we," Fiona said.

"I've always wanted to come here, since watching *Magnum Pie*," Daisy said, dreamily.

"Do you mean *Magnum, P.I.*?" Fiona asked.

"With Tom Selleck?" Partial Sue righted herself at the mention of the iconic crime drama. "Now that's a great bit of eighties TV."

"I never really watched it," Daisy confessed. "I just liked the beginning, where he speeds off in his Ferrari. So glamorous."

"Technically, the 308 wasn't his." Partial Sue split hairs. "It belonged to his benefactor Robin Masters and Magnum would borrow it."

"Speaking of borrowing things," Fiona's tone became serious. "I wonder how the shop's doing without us there."

After Fiona's ordeal, she'd been granted compassionate leave to help her recover from her near-death experience. Although she felt fine, she had persuaded head office that she needed her close friends by her side. Not wanting any negative press, her superiors had agreed, allowing all three of them to take time off at once. However, to keep the shop running while they were absent, they'd pulled in a favour from the Wicker Man after he'd returned from Australia. He was happy to reciprocate and man the charity shop in their absence. However, his presence in the shop didn't exactly reassure Fiona, if his own shop was anything to go by.

"I'm sure it's doing just fine," Partial Sue replied.

Daisy changed the subject. "I saw a food stand selling fish tacos on the beach. I've never had a fish taco before. Who fancies trying one?"

"I do," said Fiona, swivelling upright.

"Do they sell chips?" Partial Sue asked, not doing much for the reputation of Brits abroad.

"Probably," Daisy replied. "But you'll have to ask for French fries or they'll just give you a big bag of crisps."

"Good enough for me."

After lingering in the water far too long, judging by their pruney fingers, the three ladies got out and towel-dried themselves. Not that this was really necessary — the fragrant warm air did a pretty good job of that by itself.

As they got ready to head over to the food stand, a smiley Hawaiian sauntered over to them, his T-shirt emblazoned with the words *Eddie's Surf School.* "Aloha, ladies. My name's Eddie and I run the best surf school in Honolulu. Now, you can't come to Hawaii without having a go at surfing. I have a few vacancies this afternoon and I guarantee to have you on your feet, riding a wave in no time."

Fiona could feel Daisy's eyes on her, like a hopeful child outside a toy shop. She'd been itching for them to have a surfing lesson since they'd first booked the holiday, but had shown great restraint, sensitive that Fiona didn't need unnecessary pressure placed on her where water activities were concerned.

Eddie must have registered the reluctance on Fiona's face. "I'm a qualified lifeguard and we only go out in the gentlest of waves. But you have to know, there's nothing like the feeling of gliding down a wave. It's like pure magic . . ."

"We were just about to get fish tacos," Partial Sue interrupted, leaving out her preference for chips.

"Not from that stand over there?" Eddie nodded behind them.

"What's wrong with it?"

"It's an overpriced tourist trap." Eddie was talking Partial Sue's language. "There's one further up the beach where I give my lessons. It's cheaper and better. I eat there every day."

"Can't beat a recommendation," Partial Sue replied.

"How far is it?" Fiona asked.

"Only a couple of hundred yards. Look, why don't I show you the food stand? You can eat your tacos and watch me give a lesson. Decide if you like what you see."

"That sounds like a good idea." Daisy's eyes glittered with excitement.

Eddie decided to sweeten the deal. "And I can do three lessons for the price of two." He glanced in Partial Sue's direction, clearly an excellent judge of character.

"What do you say, Fiona?" Partial Sue jittered, not wanting to miss out on a bargain.

Fiona didn't like being put on the spot. She'd only just got used to being back in the water, the idyllic Hawaiian ocean soothing away any fears she had. Would this now be a step too far, too soon?

She mulled it over, trying to ignore the debilitating negative voice in her head. She'd been worried the *It* might make a comeback after her near-death experience. Thankfully, it had stayed silent, but she didn't want to tempt fate by giving in to those undesirable thoughts that were often a precursor to the *It*'s appearance. She couldn't risk that happening, and if she didn't seize the moment right now, there was a danger she never would. Eddie was right. This was a once-in-a-lifetime opportunity. She couldn't come to Hawaii without trying surfing. That would be a travesty.

"Okay, let's take a look," she said.

They gathered up their things and followed Eddie up the beach. "You won't regret it," he said, already assuming the lessons were in the bag. "Surfing is a blessing. Will make you feel superhuman." He certainly had his sales patter worked out, but there was authenticity and genuine enthusiasm in his words.

Fiona began to get butterflies and a smidgen of tinnitus as trepidation was replaced with excitement.

"Say, are you from England?" Eddie asked.

"We are," they chorused.

Eddie smiled. "There's a very famous English lady who learned to surf on this very beach. I bet you can't guess who."

"Agatha Christie!" they blurted.

"Oh." Eddie sounded disappointed. "How did you know that? Most people are shocked when I tell them."

"We're big fans," said Partial Sue.

The Hawaiian gave her a warm grin. "Well, you know what she said about surfing — 'It's one of the most perfect physical pleasures that I have known.'"

Fiona smiled to herself. They couldn't have picked a better surfing instructor than one who could quote their favourite crime writer.

Up ahead, the water was peppered with people of all ages, shapes and sizes on large, plank-like surfboards — "logs" as Ralph would say — picking off perfectly formed little waves, gently rolling in. Rising to their feet at a leisurely pace, they'd ride them all the way to the beach, then spin the board around, paddling back out, eager to catch another one.

"Oh, that looks so much fun!" Daisy gasped.

"'Idiotically pleased with yourself,'" Eddie said. "That's another way Agatha Christie described surfing."

Fiona had to agree. Everyone who stood up on a board shared the same immensely contented expression as they slid effortlessly towards the shoreline. She couldn't wait to try it but became suddenly distracted by the waft of fresh cooking carried on the temperate breeze. The food stand Eddie had promised them — little more than a tumbledown shack roofed with palm leaves — was producing the heavenly aroma of sizzling fish, lime and coriander. Her stomach rumbled while her mind busied itself with the excitement of riding on a surfboard, just like her hero Agatha Christie all those years ago. She had the overwhelming feeling that this would turn out to be one of the most beautifully memorable days of her life.

THE END

THE JOFFE BOOKS STORY

We began in 2014 when Jasper agreed to publish his mum's much-rejected romance novel and it became a bestseller.

Since then we've grown into the largest independent publisher in the UK. We're extremely proud to publish some of the very best writers in the world, including Joy Ellis, Faith Martin, Caro Ramsay, Helen Forrester, Simon Brett and Robert Goddard. Everyone at Joffe Books loves reading and we never forget that it all begins with the magic of an author telling a story.

We are proud to publish talented first-time authors, as well as established writers whose books we love introducing to a new generation of readers.

We won Trade Publisher of the Year at the Independent Publishing Awards in 2023 and Best Publisher Award in 2024 at the People's Book Prize. We have been shortlisted for Independent Publisher of the Year at the British Book Awards for the last five years, and were shortlisted for the Diversity and Inclusivity Award at the 2022 Independent Publishing Awards. In 2023 we were shortlisted for Publisher of the Year at the RNA Industry Awards, and in 2024 we were shortlisted at the CWA Daggers for the Best Crime and Mystery Publisher.

We built this company with your help, and we love to hear from you, so please email us about absolutely anything bookish at feedback@joffebooks.com.

If you want to receive free books every Friday and hear about all our new releases, join our mailing list here: www.joffebooks.com/freebooks.

And when you tell your friends about us, just remember: it's pronounced Joffe as in coffee or toffee!

www.ingramcontent.com/pod-product-compliance
Ingram Content Group UK Ltd.
Pitfield, Milton Keynes, MK11 3LW, UK
UKHW020652240325
5121UKWH00031B/271